CLARET
And
PRESENT
DANGER

Books by Sarah Fox

The Literary Pub Mystery Series

Wine and Punishment
An Ale of Two Cities
The Malt in Our Stars
Claret and Present Danger

The Pancake House Mystery Series

The Crêpes of Wrath
For Whom the Bread Rolls
Of Spice and Men
Yeast of Eden
Crêpe Expectations
Much Ado About Nutmeg
A Room with a Roux
A Wrinkle in Thyme

The Music Lover's Mystery Series

Dead Ringer
Death in A Major
Deadly Overtures

CLARET
And
PRESENT
DANGER

SARAH
FOX

KENSINGTON
PUBLISHING CORP.
www.kensingtonbooks.com

KENSINGTON BOOKS are published by

Kensington Publishing Corp.
119 West 40th Street
New York, NY 10018

All Kensington titles, imprints, and distributed lines are available at special quantity discounts for bulk purchases for sales promotion, premiums, fund-raising, educational, or institutional use. Special book excerpts or customized printings can also be created to fit specific needs. For details, write or phone the office of the Kensington Special Sales Manager: Attn. Special Sales Department. Kensington Publishing Corp, 119 West 40th Street, New York, NY 10018. Phone: 1-800-221-2647.

Library of Congress Card Catalogue Number: 2021940071

ISBN: 978-1-4967-3402-0
First Kensington Hardcover Edition: December 2021

ISBN: 978-1-4967-3404-4 (ebook)

10 9 8 7 6 5 4 3 2 1

Printed in the United States of America

Chapter 1

The sword blades glinted in the sunlight. The crowd watched with anticipation as the weapons clanged together again and again. The duelers managed to make it look like their fight wasn't choreographed, and now and then they hurled Renaissance insults at each other. Both men wore a combination of leather and plate armor but still managed to lunge and dodge with relative agility. I wasn't sure how they could stand the heat in their costumes. Summer was in full swing in Shady Creek, Vermont, and the sun was beating down from a gorgeous blue sky.

The taller of the two fighters parried a blow and then moved in for the kill. His opponent gasped as the sword blade slid between his arm and side, appearing from my vantage point as though it had pierced his abdomen. The wounded man staggered before dramatically falling to the ground.

The other man raised his sword in victory.

"Huzzah!" the crowd cheered, and I joined in.

"He killed him!" nine-year-old Kiandra Williams exclaimed as the crowd slowly dispersed, everyone moving on to check out other parts of the Trueheart Renaissance Faire and Circus.

"It was just pretend," my best friend, Shontelle, reminded her daughter.

"I know," Kiandra said. "I like the sound the swords make when they hit each other." She bounced up onto the balls of her feet. "Can we go watch the acrobats now?"

I checked the time on my phone. "It would probably be a good idea to go find seats."

The three of us made our way toward the red-and-white-striped tent that stood near the far end of the park, which had been transformed into a Renaissance village for the duration of the two-week event. This was my first time attending a Renaissance faire, and although I'd been at the park for less than an hour, I was already thoroughly impressed.

There were various stalls and huts where people in period costume demonstrated skills such as glassblowing, metalworking, basket weaving, leatherworking, and candle making. Many of the goods the craftsmen and craftswomen had made were available for sale, and I was considering doing some early Christmas shopping before the faire was over.

Musicians had gathered on a small stage and were playing a variety of instruments, including lutes, violins, and others that I couldn't name. Food vendors sold snacks from huts, and a tavern had been set up in one of the larger structures, where adult fairgoers could sit down for a meal and enjoy a tankard of ale. Here and there, costumed actors interacted with each other and with the spectators. Kiandra, like many other children at the faire, had already had her face painted. She now sported a unicorn on one cheek and a butterfly on the other.

At the entrance to the tent, we handed over our tickets to a woman in a tight-fitting bodice and full skirt, with a crown of flowers in her dark hair. Bleachers provided the unassigned seating in the tent. We'd arrived early, so we had our choice of spots. We decided on the third row back in the middle section.

"Sit next to me, Sadie," Kiandra requested as she plopped herself down on the bench.

I did as asked, and Shontelle sat on Kiandra's other side.

"We've got a good view from here," I said.

Kiandra's gaze traveled up and up. Her eyes widened. "Look how high that is!"

I followed the finger she was pointing up toward the ceiling of the tent. Way up high was a tightrope, as well as two trapezes. I wouldn't have the nerve to climb the ladder to get up that high, let alone swing out on a trapeze or balance along a wire.

I also noticed some silks hanging from the metal framework up near the tent's ceiling. I'd never watched a live performance with aerial silks, but I had seen one on TV and thought we could be in for a spectacular show.

When I'd first heard that the Renaissance faire was coming to my adopted home of Shady Creek, Vermont, the fact that it included circus elements had surprised me. Apparently, the faire had previously been more traditional but had recently added new attractions. Most people I knew were excited to take in both aspects of the faire, and so was I, starting with the acrobats' show that was about to start.

The bleachers quickly filled with spectators, and soon the lights dimmed. As the tent grew darker, I caught sight of a thin girl with wavy blond hair slipping into the tent while the ticket lady had her back turned. The girl appeared to be about eight or nine years old and didn't look familiar, but I didn't have a chance to notice anything more about her. She disappeared behind the bleachers, and music began to play, signaling the start of the show.

For the next hour, we were wowed by the high-flying feats of half a dozen acrobats. They walked the high wire, swung on the trapezes, flew through the air, and performed with the aerial silks. Kiandra was riveted the entire time.

"I want to do that," she whispered as a young woman let go of one trapeze and soared through the air before another acrobat on the second trapeze caught her.

"I don't think so," Shontelle said with alarm.

"Please!" Kiandra turned her beseeching eyes on her mother. Shontelle put a finger to her lips. "We'll talk about it later."

She shot me a look of dismay over Kiandra's head. I didn't blame her for her concern. The thought of Kiandra flying through the air way up high terrified me, and she wasn't even my daughter.

At one point, I caught another glimpse of the blond-haired girl who'd sneaked into the tent. She watched the show from between two sets of bleachers, her eyes as wide as Kiandra's. When the show finished, I looked for her again, but she was nowhere to be seen.

As we headed out of the tent, Kiandra bounced up and down between me and Shontelle, chattering nonstop about the amazing feats of the acrobats. She eventually wound down and asked for a snack. Shontelle and I were hungry too, so we wandered away from the tent, in search of something to eat. Along the way, we paused to study a poster affixed to the wall of one of the thatched huts. The poster advertised the most talked-about and anticipated attraction of the entire faire. Illusionist Ozzie Stone would be performing in the main tent each night.

I'd heard of Ozzie Stone before the faire had arrived in Shady Creek. He'd appeared on a televised nationwide talent show a year or so ago, and his star had been on the rise ever since. I'd hoped to catch one of his shows, but when I'd inquired at the gate that morning, I'd been informed that the tickets for all his performances were already sold out. That had disappointed me, but I was still determined to enjoy the faire as much as possible.

We moved on from the poster and spotted a hut with a sign that read ROSIE'S FARE. Another sign indicated that the vendor sold burgers, fries, cheese melts, and milkshakes. Before we reached Rosie's Fare, we paused to watch a juggler performing for passersby. He looked to be in his midtwenties and had curly brown hair. At the moment he had four beanbags in the air. He wrapped up the juggling act by catching all the beanbags. The crowd applauded, and he bowed.

"Now for some magic," he told everyone who was watching. He had three upside-down cups on a roughly hewn wooden table. He picked up one of the cups and placed a ball beneath it.

As he opened his mouth to speak to the crowd again, another man strutted over to his side, a self-assured smile on his face. I knew who he was right away—illusionist Ozzie Stone. He wore a white shirt beneath a blue velvet cape with a black silk lining, just like in the photo on his poster. He had piercing blue eyes, and his jet-black hair was a little on the long side. Despite the beautiful summer weather we'd been having in Vermont, I suspected his deep tan had been sprayed on.

There was a collective intake of breath from the crowd. I clearly wasn't the only one to recognize the illusionist.

"Lords and ladies," Ozzie said to the crowd, "if it's magic you desire, it's magic you shall get." He whipped a blue mug out from beneath his cape and snapped his fingers. "Water, please, Tobias."

The juggler frowned but handed over a small pitcher of water that had been sitting on the table.

"Observe," Ozzie commanded, "as I instantly turn this water into a block of ice."

A hush fell over the crowd as he poured the water into the blue mug. As soon as the pitcher was empty, he turned the mug upside down. No water flowed out, but a small block of ice fell into Ozzie's waiting hand.

The crowd cheered, me included.

"That's so cool!" Kiandra exclaimed with delight.

It seemed Ozzie had captivated her almost as much as the acrobats had.

Out of the corner of my eye, I noticed the curly-haired juggler slink away, looking disgruntled. I couldn't blame him.

Ozzie really had stolen his thunder, and he wasn't finished yet. For his next trick, Ozzie produced a small piece of paper and had a woman from the audience sign her name on it. He rolled up the paper and held it up for all of us to see. Then, with a flick of his hand, he made it disappear.

He fished a lemon out of his pocket, showed it to us, and then cut around the middle of it with a knife. When he pulled the two pieces of the lemon apart, a rolled-up paper protruded from one half. Ozzie removed the paper, unrolled it, and had the woman from the audience confirm that it was the same paper she'd signed. We all burst into applause as Ozzie bowed.

While the illusionist posed for selfies with fairgoers, we headed over to Rosie's Fare and purchased our snack, which turned out to be more of an early lunch. Shontelle bought some fries and a cheese melt to share with Kiandra, and I bought a cheese melt for myself. All three of us ordered chocolate milk-shakes. We needed something cold to drink to keep us from getting too hot in the summer sunshine.

I gave myself a brain freeze with the first sip, but after that I drank more slowly and was able to enjoy the delicious creaminess of the chocolate shake. The cheese melt was heavenly too, and it calmed the growling of my hungry stomach. We ate at a rustic picnic table, watching the goings-on around us.

At one point a stout, costumed man came stumbling out of the tavern, another actor following on his heels.

"Away, you varlot! You rampallian!" shouted the taller man from the tavern's doorway. "I'll tickle your catastrophe!"

The stout man staggered about as if drunk. "You sodden, contumelious louse!" he yelled before weaving and lurching his way down the grassy walkway that stretched between the two rows of vendors.

I was pretty sure Kiandra had no idea what the insults meant, but she laughed along with me and Shontelle.

As I was finishing up my cheese melt, I caught sight of an attractive dark-haired man dressed in a costume that included black boots, dark trousers, a leather doublet and arm bracers, and a gray cape. He carried a sword at his side, and his hair reached nearly to his shoulders.

"He looks like Aragorn from *The Lord of the Rings*," I said to Shontelle, with a nod in the man's direction.

"He really does," Shontelle agreed. "He's almost Viggo Mortensen's doppelgänger." She watched him walk by. "Very easy on the eyes."

"Don't let him hear you say that," a man's voice cautioned. "It'll go to his head."

I turned to find local man Matt Yanders standing next to our picnic table. Matt owned the Harvest Grill, one of Shady Creek's restaurants. He was also a member of the science fiction and fantasy book club I hosted at my literary pub, the Inkwell.

"You know him?" Shontelle asked Matt, her gaze returning to Aragorn's look-alike.

"As much as it pains me to admit it, he's my brother." Matt's grin softened his words. "Flint, you scobberlotcher, get over here!" he bellowed.

Flint's face broke into a grin when he spotted Matt. "It's my knave of a brother!"

Matt pounded Flint on the back when he reached his side. "Flint, allow me to introduce these three fine ladies, Shontelle and Kiandra Williams, and Sadie Coleman."

Flint bowed. "Ladies, I'm honored to make your acquaintance."

"Is that a real sword?" Kiandra asked him.

"But of course." Flint pulled the blade from its scabbard. "It's a weapon of the finest craftsmanship."

"Cool!" Kiandra said before taking a long sip of her milkshake.

"How are you enjoying your day, ladies?" Flint asked me and Shontelle.

"It's great," I said.

"We're having a blast so far," Shontelle added.

"Excellent! I'm glad to hear it."

A woman wearing several gauzy scarves and many bracelets breezed past him.

"Minerva!" Flint called out.

The woman stopped in her tracks and turned to Flint. She smiled when she saw him.

Flint gestured at her with a flourish. "Have you ladies met our most esteemed soothsayer, Minerva the Mysterious?"

Minerva came closer and addressed us. "If you wish to have your fortune told, I am most happy to oblige."

"For a price." Flint chuckled.

Minerva gave him a sidelong glance. "Worth every penny."

"Undoubtably," Flint said.

"I wouldn't mind having my fortune told," Shontelle said. "It sounds fun," she added to me and Kiandra.

"Then please," Minerva said, "come this way."

"I'll stay with Kiandra," I told Shontelle.

Her daughter waved at her, but most of her focus was on her milkshake.

Shontelle followed Minerva the Mysterious into a small tent across the grassy walkway from our picnic table.

Flint bowed again. "My ladies, I'm afraid I must depart," he said to me and Kiandra. Then he addressed his brother. "You useless knave, we shall meet again."

Flint headed off, with several female fairgoers flitting along behind him, snapping photos with their phones.

Matt laughed before turning his attention to me. "I'll see you at the Inkwell sometime soon, Sadie."

I said goodbye, and he took his leave.

Kiandra finished off her milkshake with a loud slurp.

"All done?" I asked her.

She nodded and jumped up from the table. "Can we go look at the costumes?"

Next door to Minerva the Mysterious's tent was a costume rental shop. While we were eating, I'd seen two women, dressed in regular clothing, go into the store. Now they emerged, fully decked out in Renaissance wear.

"Sure," I said in response to Kiandra's question. "Let's go take a look."

I gathered up all our garbage and tossed it in a nearby bin. Kiandra skipped off ahead of me and disappeared into the shop. I followed after her, then paused one step inside the door so my eyes could adjust to the dim interior.

We browsed the store for a few minutes, until Kiandra lost interest.

"Let's go look at the hats," she said when we emerged from the costume rental shop.

She dashed over to a shop called the Mad Hatter and tried on a pirate's tricorn hat.

"How about this one?" I suggested, holding out a blue velvet hat with a fake peacock sitting on top, the tail feathers cascading down over the back rim.

Kiandra removed the hat she was wearing, and I plunked the peacock one on her head. She checked her reflection in a small mirror set out for that purpose.

She giggled, and I snapped a picture of her with my phone so we could show Shontelle later.

"You try this one," Kiandra said, handing me a gray cavalier hat with a single feather.

As we tried on several other hats, I noticed the curly-haired juggler we'd seen earlier standing nearby, speaking with a raven-haired woman who was texting on her smartphone. The device looked out of place, considering that she was wearing a Renaissance costume.

"I deserve my own show, Rachael," the juggler was saying. "I could draw in as much of a crowd as Ozzie."

Rachael continued to tap away at her phone, not even glanc-

ing up. "It's not happening, Toby. How many times do I have
to tell you? Ozzie is our biggest draw. And your strength is
street busking."

"But—"

Rachael cut him off. "But nothing. That's all I've got to say
on the matter."

Toby looked as though he was about to protest again when
Rachael squirmed in her costume.

"This bodice is too tight," she complained. "You'd think
Patty was trying to suffocate me when she laced me up."

For the second time in the past hour, Ozzie Stone appeared
on the scene.

He dipped down in a theatrical bow. "Allow me to assist
you, milady."

While she'd talked with Toby, Rachael's expression had been
stern, a crease traversing her forehead. Now the crease smoothed
out, and she smiled.

"Thank you, Ozzie." She turned her back to him.

Ozzie loosened the laces on the back of her corset and began
retying them. As he worked, he spoke quietly into Rachael's
ear. She giggled, her dark eyelashes fluttering.

Toby the juggler scowled at them, but they took no notice.
He muttered something under his breath that I couldn't quite
hear. Ozzie rested his hands on Rachael's shoulders, and she
giggled again. Toby's nostrils flared. He stormed away and disappeared into the crowd of fairgoers.

Chapter 2

Ozzie was still whispering in Rachael's ear when Shontelle and Minerva the Mysterious emerged from the fortune-teller's tent. Seeing Minerva up close, I realized she was younger than I'd first thought. She was probably in her mid-thirties, a few years older than me. Somehow her heavy makeup and numerous scarves had given me the impression that she was closer to middle age.

Minerva was smiling as she said goodbye to Shontelle, but then she stopped in her tracks, her gaze riveted on Ozzie and Rachael. A dark shadow passed over her face, and her mouth turned down at the corners. As soon as Ozzie noticed her, he dropped his hands from Rachael's shoulders and strode over to Minerva.

"There you are, my beautiful," he said before kissing her on the lips. "I was hoping you'd join me for lunch."

Minerva's dour expression melted away. She tucked her arm through his. "Of course I will."

The two wandered off together.

"So, how was your fortune?" I asked Shontelle. "Is your future full of riches and romance?"

She laughed. "I don't know about the riches, but she did say that my budding romance has a promising future."

"I could have told you that for free."

"It probably was a waste of money. She claims she can communicate with the dead, but I can't say I'm a believer." Shontelle held up a business card. "I think she's hoping I'll be in touch again, but if she really is psychic, she'll know that's not going to happen."

She tucked the card in her purse. When she looked up again, she raised a hand to shield her eyes from the sun. "Rachael?" she said, sounding surprised.

Rachael glanced over our way, and her face broke out into a smile. "Shontelle!" She hurried over and hugged my friend.

"I can't believe you're here in Shady Creek," Shontelle said. "Are you one of the faire's actors?"

"I'm the manager." Rachael smoothed out the skirt of her costume. "This allows me to blend in as I keep an eye on everything that's going on."

"Mommy, can I have this hat?" Kiandra asked, the peacock once again perched on top of her cloud of curly hair.

Shontelle smiled in Kiandra's direction but didn't reply. Instead, she spoke to Rachael again. "That's my daughter, Kiandra." She placed a hand on my shoulder. "And this is my friend Sadie Coleman. She owns the local pub."

"Nice to meet you," I said to Rachael, and she said the same in return.

"Rachael and I went to college together," Shontelle explained. "We haven't seen each other for more than a decade."

"It's been a long time," Rachael agreed.

"I thought you were working for a theater company in Boston," Shontelle said.

"I was, up until last fall. This is my first year as manager of the faire." Rachael's cell phone buzzed in her hand. She checked her text messages. "I'm so sorry. Duty calls. Maybe we can meet up sometime and catch up?"

"I'd love that," Shontelle said. "How about at Sadie's pub this evening?"

"Can we make it later in the week? I'm tied up for the next few evenings."

"Sure. Let's exchange numbers so we can text each other."

Shontelle handed over her phone, and Rachael used it to send a quick text message to herself.

After sharing a few more words with Shontelle, Rachael hurried off to wherever it was she was needed.

"That's cool that you know the faire's manager," I said as we joined Kiandra by the display of hats outside the Mad Hatter.

"It definitely sounds like an interesting job," Shontelle said. "She must get to travel quite a bit."

The Trueheart Renaissance Faire and Circus spent a couple of weeks in various towns between May and September of each year. This was the first time the faire had come to Shady Creek, but it often made stops in Maine, New Hampshire, Massachusetts, and Connecticut.

"Mommy, can I please have this hat?" Kiandra asked again.

Shontelle raised an eyebrow as she took in the sight of the fake peacock perched on her daughter's head. "Are you planning to wear it to school?"

Kiandra giggled. "Maybe. Or for Halloween."

Shontelle checked the price tag. She took the hat off Kiandra's head and set it back on the display rack. "Sorry, honey. Not at that price."

Kiandra frowned with disappointment, but her eyes lit up as she noticed a vendor selling ice cream across the way.

"Can I have a chocolate ice cream cone? Please?" she asked.

"You just had a chocolate milkshake," Shontelle reminded her.

"So?"

"Not today, sweetheart."

Kiandra frowned again, but the unhappy expression didn't last long. She quickly became distracted by a group of dancers performing to music played by the faire's minstrels.

We watched the dancing for a while and then made our way to the exit at the edge of the park. There was still plenty more to see at the faire, but Shontelle needed to get back to the Treasure Chest, the gift shop she owned. Her mother was watching the store at the moment, but Shontelle had promised to be back in the early afternoon.

It was a busy time of year for the local business owners, including Shontelle and me. The usual summer tourists had come to Shady Creek to enjoy a small-town vacation, and the faire had attracted an extra surge of visitors. That was great news for us store and restaurant proprietors, but it kept us plenty busy. This was the one day of the week when my literary pub wasn't open, so I'd jumped at the chance to check out the faire with Shontelle. Hopefully, I'd manage to squeeze in another visit before the faire moved on to the next town.

We took our time walking back to the center of town, Kiandra skipping along beside us. When Shontelle turned a corner to head south, I stayed with them, planning to stop in at the grocery store to buy a bag of oats so I could have oatmeal for breakfast the next day.

When we were a block and a half away from the village green, I recognized one of my employees, Mel Costas, up ahead. She was easy to spot from a distance, with her tall stature and her short blond and blue hair. She was in the midst of painting a mural on the side of a building that housed a lawyer's office and a dental clinic.

Mel was a talented artist in addition to being one of my valuable employees. She and several other local artists were taking part in the town's mural project. Scenes relating to Shady Creek's past or present would decorate six walls around town. Mel was currently at work on the one she had designed. It depicted the covered bridge over on Woodland Road, surrounded by autumn foliage, the mountains in the distance. The mural was still in the early stages, but I had seen Mel's concept drawings and had a good idea of what the final product would look like.

Although scaffolding had been set up to make the work easier, at the moment Mel had her feet planted firmly on the ground and was talking to Zoe Trimble, the twin sister of another of my employees.

I called out a greeting to Mel and Zoe, and they both waved in response.

Shontelle took a moment to say hello when we reached them, but then she and Kiandra continued on toward the Treasure Chest so she could relieve her mom of shop duty.

"What's going on?" I asked Mel and Zoe.

They seemed to have been in the midst of a serious discussion when I arrived.

"I left my mural to go grab some lunch," Zoe said. "When I got back, some of my paint was gone."

"Somebody stole it?" I asked with surprise.

Zoe shrugged. "I guess so. I've been going around asking the other artists if they borrowed it, but no one knows anything about it."

Mel picked up one of her paint cans and handed it to Zoe. "You can take my blue paint. I don't need it anymore today."

"Thanks, Mel," Zoe said. "I'll be able to pick up new paint tomorrow, but this will keep me going for now."

"Where's your mural?" I asked her.

"Over at the bank on Mulberry Street. I've got the wall that faces the side street."

"I'll have to drop by so I can see it sometime soon," I said.

"Anytime," Zoe said with a smile. "It'll be another couple of weeks before it's finished, though, especially if I run into any more snags. I'd better get going."

I walked with her as far as the village green. She continued along Hillview Road, while I headed south to the grocery store. After purchasing a bag of oats and some eggs, I cut across the village green to the Inkwell. My literary pub was housed in an old stone gristmill with red-trimmed windows and a red water-wheel. I loved the charming building, and the entire town of Shady Creek, which had been my home for a year now.

I took my time crossing the footbridge that led to the Inkwell. The water in the creek below the bridge babbled cheerily, and a pair of mallard ducks paddled lazily through the water. It was a beautiful summer afternoon.

Since this was my only day off, I intended to make the most of what remained of it. I had a good book waiting for me in my apartment above the pub, and my comfy lounge chair was already out on the lawn. I ran up to my apartment to fetch my book, a cold drink, and my sunglasses. Then I was back outside to enjoy the beautiful summer weather and the latest cozy mystery by Jenny Kales.

Chapter 3

The next afternoon I was glad I'd taken time to rest and relax on my day off, because I hardly had a moment to breathe once I opened the Inkwell. This was my first full summer as the owner of the local pub. I'd expected good tourist traffic, but with the faire in town, business was even brisker than I'd anticipated. Not only had the Renaissance faire brought more tourists to Shady Creek, but also many of the people who worked for the faire ventured into the center of town during their free time.

Tourists, performers, and locals kept the pub packed all afternoon, and that didn't change as evening approached. Mel's shift had ended recently, and now Damien Keys was behind the bar, pulling pints and mixing cocktails. I was helping him with that, but I was also delivering meals from the kitchen whenever Zoe's twin sister, Teagan, had them ready.

I was pretty sure that a boisterous group of six at a table in the middle of the pub was made up of actors and other performers from the faire. When I delivered two platters of nachos to their table, I chatted with them for a few moments and found out that I was correct. One man and two of the women were acrobats, and the others in the group were actors and musicians. I would have liked to stay and chat with them longer, to find out more about what it was like to work for a Renaissance faire and circus, but I had plenty of other customers to serve.

Later in the evening, Ozzie Stone walked into the pub, drawing many gazes and spurring a flurry of excited whispers. He had left his costume behind and wore a formfitting black T-shirt with jeans, but he was still easily recognizable. He walked with the same confidence—and hint of arrogance—that I'd noticed at the faire. It took me a moment to realize that the woman with him was Minerva the Mysterious. She looked so different in a short, tight red dress than she had when she wore her Renaissance costume, accessorized with numerous scarves and bangles.

Ozzie said something to Minerva and then headed toward the bar, while she wandered over to a table where three other faire workers were seated.

Ozzie leaned casually against the bar and addressed me. "This is a nice place."

"Thanks," I said before stating the obvious. "You're the illusionist performing at the faire."

He flashed me a smile that showed off perfectly straight, bright white teeth. "Guilty as charged." He glanced around. "What's with all the books?"

Part of my extensive book collection was on display on a shelf that ran along the exposed stone walls of the pub. The mystery genre was my favorite, but I had everything from classics to recently published urban fantasy novels.

"It's a literary pub," I explained. I slid a menu across the bar to Ozzie. "Can I get you anything to eat or drink?"

"What have you got on tap?" he asked without glancing at the menu.

I listed the available choices. At the moment we had five

beers on tap, all brewed by my next-door neighbor and boyfriend, Grayson Blake, who owned the Spirit Hill Brewery.

"The stout for me and the IPA for my girlfriend," Ozzie decided.

"Minerva the Mysterious," I said as I filled a pint glass with Obsidian Skies. The stout beer was smooth, with notes of roasted malt and black barley, chocolate, and coffee, and with a hint of caramel.

"Maybe not quite so mysterious as she thinks," Ozzie said with a brief chuckle.

I wasn't sure what he meant by that, so I didn't comment.

He read the menu while I filled a second glass with IPA for Minerva. When I set the two pints on the bar before him, he slid the menu back my way.

"We'll have the mushroom burgers, both with sides of Lord of the Fries."

I jotted that down on an order slip. "I'll bring the food over to you shortly."

He nodded but made no move to join his girlfriend. "Looks like this place is pretty successful."

There were only a couple of free tables at the moment. Luckily, that had been the case most evenings of late. Business could get slow at certain times of year, when the number of tourists dwindled, but over the months since I'd purchased the business, the locals had become more and more supportive of the Inkwell. It also helped that Shady Creek was a town with many annual events. The biggest draws for tourists were the autumn festival and leaf-peeping season, but people also flocked to town for the winter carnival and summertime events, like the Renaissance faire. A Taste of Shady Creek—a food and drink festival—would take place for the first time in October. I hoped it would attract lots of tourists as well.

"I've been very fortunate," I said in response to Ozzie's comment.

"So you're the owner, not just a bartender?" He sounded a bit surprised.

He wasn't the first person to be taken aback by the fact that I was the proprietor. It irked me that some tended to assume that a man must own the pub, but I didn't let my tiny flicker of irritation show.

"That's right," I said, keeping my tone pleasant. "I bought this place a year ago."

"Huh. Are you from here originally?"

"No, I moved to Shady Creek from Boston, but I grew up in Knoxville and went to UT."

Ozzie's blue eyes lit up with greater interest. "Hey, me too, on both counts."

I smiled, my irritation forgotten. "I didn't know that."

"Yep. Go, Big Orange!" he said with a grin. "Which high school did you go to?"

"Bearden," I replied.

"My cousin went there, but she was probably several years ahead of you. She's nearly forty now. I went to West."

Minerva appeared at his shoulder. "What's taking so long with the drinks, Ozzie?"

"Sorry, babe." He kissed her on the cheek but otherwise barely glanced at her. "I'll bring the beers over in a second."

Minerva sighed, crossed her arms over her chest, and popped out one hip as she waited.

Ozzie returned his full attention to me. "Are you interested in seeing my show?"

"Absolutely," I said with sincerity, "but I was told the tickets were all sold out."

He produced two tickets from the back pocket of his jeans. "I've got a couple right here. They're yours if you want them."

"Really?" I said with a thrill of excitement.

He nudged them across the bar to me. "All yours." He winked at me and then picked up the beers. "Enjoy."

"Thank you!" I called as he and Minerva headed across the room to join their colleagues.

"You look like you won the lottery," Damien observed as he came around behind the bar. He'd just delivered a tray full of cocktails to two tables across the room.

I held up the tickets, a big smile on my face. "Ozzie Stone gave me free tickets to one of his shows!"

Damien grabbed a cocktail shaker and a bottle of Scotch. "The illusionist?"

"He came in with his girlfriend. It turns out he's from Knoxville."

I dashed into the kitchen with the order slip and then tended to a table of three women in their twenties. I returned to the bar to get their drinks. Damien was still there, mixing a cocktail I'd named the Malt in Our Stars. It was made from Scotch whiskey, lemon juice, and ginger ale.

"I don't plan on going to the faire myself," he said as he worked, "but my daughters are excited about it. I got them tickets for tonight's show, which must be over now if Ozzie's here." Damien was a single father of two teenage girls. He pulled his phone out from beneath the bar. "Just checking to make sure they're home now."

They must have been, because he tucked his phone away again without showing any hint of worry or irritation.

"That was lucky about the tickets," I said after he'd delivered the drink and returned to the bar. "I tried to get some this morning, and they were all sold out."

"I ordered them online last week, before the faire arrived in town."

"That was smart."

"But things have worked out for you too."

I studied the tickets more closely. My excitement drained away. "Except the show's in the evening. I'll be busy with work."

Damien collected empty glasses from the other end of the bar. "I'd offer to handle everything myself, but with the way business is these days . . ."

"I know," I said, disappointment weighing on my shoulders. "It's too much for one person."

"Maybe Mel will take on an extra shift."

"Maybe," I said.

I wasn't holding out much hope, though. Between her afternoon shifts here at the Inkwell and all the work she was doing on her mural, I suspected she already had enough on her plate. Still, it wouldn't hurt to ask.

I tucked the tickets into the drawer of the cash register for safekeeping. I'd text Mel later to see what she said. In the meantime, I had drinks to mix and customers to serve.

The kitchen shut down for the night shortly after I delivered Ozzie and Minerva's food order to them. The crowd thinned out slightly after that, but within one hour of closing, the pub was still half full.

Two men at the end of the bar were both on their second pint of beer. I gathered from the snippets of conversation I'd overheard that they were both musicians working at the faire. The shorter of the two men had thinning light brown hair and a rotund build. He didn't seem to be in a bad mood until Ozzie and Minerva got up from their table and headed out of the pub.

The musician watched them go with a scowl on his face. "He's going to ruin the faire for everyone," he grumbled.

"Who?" the second man asked with surprise. "Ozzie?" This man appeared to be several years younger and more physically fit than his companion. "He's bringing in more people. Isn't that a good thing?"

"He steals the show."

The younger man nudged him with his elbow. "Come on, Hamish. I don't think that's true. He's good for the faire."

Hamish glowered at his beer. "All anybody cares about is Ozzie Stone now. People barely listen to my music."

"That's nothing new." The man said it jokingly, but his smile faded when he saw that Hamish wasn't impressed.

"Everything started going downhill when Rachael took over," Hamish groused.

"I disagree, man. She's injected new life into the faire."

"New life? We used to be a traditional Ren faire. Now look at us. A circus? *Mermaids*? Mermaids don't belong at a Renaissance faire."

"Why not?" his friend asked. "People love them."

Hamish muttered something that I couldn't make out.

His friend got up from his stool. "Let's go, Hamish. I think you need to sleep off your bad mood."

I expected Hamish to grumble some more, but instead he drained the last of his beer and followed his companion out of the pub.

Maybe Hamish didn't like the fact that the illusionist was the star of the faire, but I still wished I could use the free tickets Ozzie had given me.

Chapter 4

When I opened the pub at noon the next day, I propped open the front door to allow the gentle summer breeze to waft into the old gristmill. I'd likely have to turn on the air-conditioning before too long, but at the moment the outdoor temperature was still pleasant, and I wanted to make the most of it.

I took a moment to stand in the doorway and enjoy the fresh air. I also took the opportunity to give my white-haired, blue-eyed cat, Wimsey, a pat on the head. He was perched on one of the two whiskey barrels that flanked the front door of the pub. It was one of his favorite places to hang out. Although he mostly preferred to cuddle only on cold winter evenings, he enjoyed watching customers come and go from his kingdom, and he didn't mind having his silky fur stroked occasionally.

I just had to make sure that he didn't venture into the pub while the door was open. I didn't want to get in trouble for any health violations. He didn't look like he planned on going anywhere at the moment, though. He was half asleep, his cute pink tongue sticking out partway.

Before heading inside to await the first customers of the day, I ventured out onto the lawn and snapped a picture of Wimsey on his barrel. With colorful flowers blooming in pots by the whiskey barrels, the photo of the front of the gristmill could have been used on a postcard. At the moment, it was destined for my social media accounts.

I uploaded the picture and was about to head back indoors when my aunt Gilda came across the footbridge toward me. She had her auburn hair tied up in a fancy knot, and she wore a summery outfit of white capris and a flowy blue top. I greeted her with a hug and a kiss on the cheek, always happy to see her. I'd come to visit my favorite aunt the previous summer, after breaking up with my boyfriend and losing my job to a merger. She'd provided me with a place to stay and a shoulder to cry on. I'd never expected to remain in Shady Creek permanently, but I'd fallen in love with the old gristmill, which had happened to be up for sale at the time.

Now I was grateful for the series of events that had led me to this town, as difficult as they might have been at the time. I was happy and at home in Shady Creek, and I'd forged some great friendships here in the past year.

"You're my first customer of the day," I told Aunt Gilda.

"That means I've got you all to myself. For the moment, at least."

"Absolutely," I agreed.

Gilda paused to greet Wimsey but then followed me into the pub. She requested a Red Cabbage of Courage salad and a cup of coffee, so I headed to the kitchen while she took a seat at a table by one of the windows. Former college football player Booker James was working the afternoon shift in the kitchen. When I relayed Aunt Gilda's order to him, he acknowledged it with a playful salute and then went back to singing John Lennon's "Imagine." Booker was a talented musician as well as a great chef, and I didn't think he ever worked a shift at the Inkwell without humming or singing at least one song.

Mel was on shift for the afternoon too, and she'd already poured Aunt Gilda a cup of coffee. I was about to sit down and join my aunt when half a dozen customers wandered into the pub. By the time I took their orders, three more customers had arrived.

"Go ahead and spend some time with Gilda," Mel told me as she poured two glasses of white wine. "I've got things covered for the moment."

"Thanks, Mel," I said with a grateful smile.

I dashed into the kitchen and fetched Aunt Gilda's salad of red cabbage, crispy ramen noodles, almonds, sunflower seeds, and delicious seasoning. I set the plate in front of her and joined her at the table. Outside the window, the sun shone brightly and the green leaves of a maple tree swayed in the breeze.

"How was the faire?" Aunt Gilda asked as she started in on her salad. "Did you have a good time with Shontelle and Kiandra?"

"I had a great time," I said. I proceeded to tell her about the acrobats and other performers we'd seen. "And the next night, illusionist Ozzie Stone came into the Inkwell."

"I've heard he puts on a great show," Gilda said.

"I've heard that too, and I really wanted to catch one of his performances. The tickets are all sold out, but Ozzie gave me a couple of free ones when he was here. It turns out he's from Knoxville."

"I didn't realize he was a Tennessee boy. So you're going to the show?"

My shoulders sagged as I remembered my dilemma. "No, I can't. I have to work. I asked Mel if she could take on an extra shift, but she's got too much on her plate at the moment."

Gilda nodded. "She's working on that beautiful mural."

"And teaching a girls' boxing class at the community center," I added. "Would you like the tickets? You could take Betty or another friend with you."

Betty worked in Aunt Gilda's hair salon and was her closest friend in Shady Creek.

"I have a better idea," Gilda said. "You go to the show, and I'll help out Damien here at the pub."

"I couldn't ask you to do that," I protested.

"You aren't asking. I'm offering. I might not know how to mix all the cocktails on the menu, but Damien can take care of that. I can easily pour wine and beer, take orders, and deliver meals. Don't forget that I used to waitress at Calhoun's back in the day."

Calhoun's was a popular eatery in Knoxville that had been around for decades. Gilda had worked there while she trained to become a hairstylist.

"I know you'd do a good job, but I don't want to impose," I said.

"Honey, it's not an imposition. I think I'd find it quite fun. And I want you to go to the show." She picked up her coffee mug. "Take Grayson with you. The two of you haven't had enough time together recently."

That was certainly true. Grayson and I had started seeing each other two months ago, but since then we hadn't managed to fit in as many dates as either of us would have liked. The Inkwell kept me busy, and Grayson's brewery was also enjoying a steady stream of visitors. His already popular craft brewery had recently enjoyed some great nationwide publicity, in the form of an episode of the television show *Craft Nation*, which featured craft breweries across the country.

The episode had aired a couple of weeks earlier, and already visitors were mentioning to his staff that they'd chosen to come to Shady Creek after seeing the Spirit Hill Brewery on the TV show. The episode had also led to many requests for interviews with Grayson from newspapers and other media outlets. He'd made several recent trips to Boston, New York City, and Toronto, Ontario, for related interviews and meetings. Even when he was at home, he barely had a spare moment.

I understood how time consuming it could be to run a business, but I still wished we could see more of each other. It felt like our relationship had barely had a chance to get off the ground.

"You're right," I said to Aunt Gilda. "Grayson and I haven't been spending enough time together. I'd love to go to Ozzie's show with him."

"Then that's settled. What time do you need me here?"

"Around six, maybe," I said. "But I have to talk to Grayson before we make any concrete plans. He might not even have time to go to the show."

"I'm sure he'll make time if he's able."

"I hope so." I pushed back my chair. "I'll text him right now."

I sent him a quick message, asking if he was free to go to the show with me that evening. It was probably a good thing that I didn't have time to sit around waiting for a response to come in. The pub was getting busier by the minute, keeping me and Mel constantly on the go.

It wasn't until a couple of hours later that I was able to check my phone.

I smiled when I saw Grayson's response.

It looked as though I'd be attending Ozzie Stone's show that night, after all.

Chapter 5

Aunt Gilda insisted on taking over for me at the Inkwell shortly after four o'clock so Grayson and I would have time to take in the sights at the faire before Ozzie's show started at seven. After she arrived and got to work helping Mel, I ran upstairs to my apartment to put out some food for Wimsey, much to his delight, and to change my clothes. I decided to wear a pistachio-green sundress with a pattern of tiny white daisies. Flat sandals completed my outfit. There was no way I wanted to walk around the fairgrounds all evening in heels. Once dressed, I applied sunscreen and grabbed my sunglasses before deciding I was ready to go.

I left the gristmill through the back door, so I wouldn't be tempted to help with taking orders or mixing drinks on my way out. I knew that Aunt Gilda and Mel—and later Damien—could handle everything, but sometimes it was still difficult for me to take time away from the pub when business was hopping. At least I had my phone with me, so they could text me in case of emergency. I hoped that wouldn't be necessary.

As I crossed the footbridge, I greeted a group of four adults who were heading to the Inkwell. I didn't recognize them and figured they were tourists. My suspicion was confirmed when I overheard them exclaiming about the scenic nature of the old gristmill. I couldn't help but smile with pride when they stopped to snap photos of the building.

My smile brightened further when I reached Creekside Road. Grayson was walking toward me, dressed in jeans and a blue T-shirt that matched the color of his eyes. He was clean shaven, and his dark hair was tousled in its usual way. As he drew closer, I realized that the design on the front of his shirt was the logo for the Spirit Hill Brewery.

"You look amazing," Grayson said, reaching for my hands.

I greeted him with a kiss. I'd meant to compliment his appearance as well—he always looked great, in my opinion—but all thoughts of conversation disappeared as our kiss deepened.

When we finally drew apart, Grayson grinned at me, setting off a fluttering of butterfly wings in my chest.

"In case you couldn't tell, I really missed you," he said.

I smiled at that. "I really missed you too. I'm so glad you were free tonight."

He kept hold of one of my hands as we set off along Creekside Road, heading for the park where the Renaissance faire was taking place.

"I was about to call you when I saw your text," he said. "I was hoping to see you tonight, even if it meant sitting at the bar while you worked."

I gave his hand a squeeze. "You're welcome to do that anytime, but I'm glad to be going to the show with you."

We paused for a car to go by and then crossed the street.

"How have you been?" I asked.

We'd exchanged text messages over the past few days, but we hadn't had a real conversation since the previous week.

"Crazy busy, but good. A craft brewing club from Boston called. They wanted to book private tours for later this month. They've got thirty-two members who want to come."

"That's awesome!"

"It is," he agreed. "And with all the tourists already in town, I don't think business is going to slow down anytime soon."

"That's a good thing."

"Definitely. As long as I still get to spend time with you."

My heart danced a happy jig in my chest. I was so glad he wanted to spend time with me as much as I did with him.

We'd reached the park, so we got in line at the gates and waited for our turn to buy tickets to enter the fairgrounds. Some of the people in the line wore Renaissance costumes, but most people were dressed in modern clothes like me and Grayson. When we passed through the gates a few minutes later, my stomach gave a loud rumble. I hoped Grayson hadn't heard it, but his brief chuckle dashed those hopes.

Heat rushed to my cheeks. "I haven't eaten since this morning," I confessed. "I didn't have a chance to take a break after opening the pub."

"I'm hungry too." Grayson took in the sight of the nearest food vendors. "Looks like we've got some good choices for dinner. Why don't we eat early?"

I wasn't going to argue with that suggestion.

Before we could take another step, a curvy woman wearing a Renaissance-style dress with a very revealing neckline threw herself into Grayson's arms, almost knocking him off balance.

"My Lord," she said, clutching at his shirt and gazing up into his eyes, "art thou desiring of some passion this fine night?"

Even though I didn't have any food in my mouth, I almost choked.

"Mayhap," Grayson replied smoothly. "But not with thee."

The woman gasped, as if mortally insulted. She pulled back from Grayson. "Which mistress hath stolen thy affections?" She aimed her sharp gaze at me. I knew my cheeks had already gone bright red, thanks to Grayson's words and their possible meaning.

The woman was about to say something to me when a costumed man rushed over and grabbed her arm.

"Impertinent wench!" The man tugged her away from us. "Get thee to the tavern and fetch yon ale!"

The woman hurled insults at him as he pulled her into the tavern.

Several people had filmed the exchange with their phones, laughing as they watched. I hoped I hadn't been caught on video.

Grayson seemed amused but unruffled by the incident.

"How did she not take you by surprise?" I asked as he took my hand and we continued walking.

"She did a bit," he confessed. "But I know to expect things like that."

I narrowed my eyes at him. "You expect to have women throw themselves at you?"

He laughed. "I meant this isn't my first Renaissance faire, and I know the actors like to interact with the fairgoers."

"You've been to a Renaissance faire before?" I never would have guessed that.

"More than one."

I glanced at him. "Have you ever gone in costume?"

"Costumes aren't really my thing, but I do enjoy the faires."

I would have asked him more questions if my stomach hadn't given another loud rumble. All my attention quickly turned to finding food.

I had such fond memories of the cheese melt and milkshake I'd had earlier in the week that I decided to have the same again. This time I added a side of fries to share with Grayson. He ordered a salmon burger and a beer from a nearby vendor.

"Drinking the competition?" I asked as he joined me at a picnic table.

"Research." He grinned as he popped the top off the bottle. "Besides, a cold beer goes well with a nice summer evening."

So did a chocolate milkshake.

We chatted about life in general as we ate our food. It didn't take me long to devour my cheese melt. I had finished the delicious sandwich and was snagging a fry from the dwindling pile when I caught sight of a familiar figure disappearing between two tents.

"Huh." I munched on the fry.

"What is it?" Grayson asked me.

"I just saw Damien."

"Is he supposed to be at the Inkwell?"

I glanced at the time on my phone. "His shift starts in ten minutes, but that's not why I'm surprised to see him here. He said he had no interest in the faire."

"Maybe he changed his mind."

"Or maybe he's here with his daughters. But he didn't look happy."

I hadn't seen much of his face, but the way he'd been walking had given me that impression. He'd looked as though he was storming off between the tents.

"He was probably worried he'd be late for work," Grayson said.

I figured that was the most likely explanation.

I returned my focus to my food, and soon we'd finished up our delicious dinner. We strolled around the fairgrounds for a while, walking hand in hand. We checked out some of the craft vendors and watched a jousting match. Then we wandered into a small village square, where a minstrel played a wooden flute up on a small stage. In the middle of the square, an actor was locked in a pillory, moaning at his plight, while people snapped photos of him and posed for selfies with the unfortunate soul in the background.

I paused to snap a few photos of the village square myself, and then we moved on to watch some of the artisans' demonstrations. Grayson was particularly interested in watching the swordsmith at work, crafting a new blade. I was enjoying the faire, but mostly I was enjoying Grayson's company.

Eventually, we headed in the direction of the largest tent on the grounds. Ahead of us, two actors had drawn a crowd so thick that the wide grassy walkway was completely blocked. We couldn't see what the actors were doing—something amusing, judging by the laughter from the onlookers—so we didn't hang around. Instead, we took a detour around the back of the huts lining the walkway. We were definitely behind the scenes there. Cables ran along the ground, and several trailers sat in a row.

As we drew closer to the back of the largest tent, I caught sight of Ozzie, dressed in a black suit, talking with a woman with long chestnut-brown hair. Wearing a shimmering and slinky copper-colored dress, she looked ready to perform too. I couldn't hear what they were saying, but the woman didn't look happy. Ozzie's face was angled away from me, so I didn't know if he was as angry as the woman. After a few more steps, I was close enough to recognize the woman. She was one of the acrobats who'd performed in the show I'd watched with Shontelle and Kiandra.

The woman said something, almost spitting the words out, and then spun on her heel and stormed off between two trailers. Ozzie shook his head and disappeared through a narrow opening in the tent.

"Looks like there's some backstage drama," Grayson commented in a low voice.

"It seems there's no shortage of it," I said, remembering the disgruntled juggler and the grumbling I'd heard at the Inkwell.

We'd almost reached the flap at the back of the tent when a slender figure burst through the opening and dashed between two trailers. Although she was running full tilt, I recognized her as the young girl who had sneaked into the acrobats' show.

Ozzie flew out of the tent and skidded to a halt, his nostrils flaring, as he searched for the fleeing girl.

"Little brat!" he growled when he realized she'd disappeared.

"What happened?" I asked.

It took a second for Ozzie to recognize me, but when he did, some of his anger seemed to drain away. "The kid was playing with my props. No one's supposed to touch them but me."

Someone within the tent called Ozzie's name.

"Excuse me." He flashed me a brief smile. "Enjoy the show." Before I could say anything in response, he was gone.

Grayson and I reached the main entrance to the tent without any further dramatics. We gained entrance with the free tickets Ozzie had given me and went in search of seats. Several people had already claimed spots on the bleachers, but we still had plenty of options to choose from. In the end, we sat halfway up the middle section, a few rows behind the bench Shontelle, Kiandra, and I had occupied for the acrobats' show.

I waved to a couple of familiar faces in the growing crowd and then told Grayson about the magic tricks Ozzie had performed the other day, when he'd overshadowed Toby, the busker.

"There was a hole in the lemon," Grayson said after I told him about that trick. "He had a decoy piece of paper, which he showed after he stuffed the signed paper into the hole in the bottom of the lemon. Then he held the lemon in a way to hide the hole as he cut it open. I'm guessing he got the lemon out of sight right after pulling the paper out of it."

I wasn't sure I liked having the magic stripped away. "How do you know how he did the trick?"

"At one time I aspired to be a magician."

"Really?" I narrowed my eyes at him. "You're not going to ruin all the tricks, are you? I want to enjoy the show."

"I won't reveal any more of the great Ozzie Stone's secrets." He mimed zipping his lips shut.

"Good," I said with relief. "I'd like to believe—at least for the duration of the show—that magic is real, even if you don't."

He grinned at me. "I still believe in certain types of magic."

Just then, the lights dimmed and music began playing through the tent's speakers. A middle-aged man dressed all in black appeared on the stage and spoke into the microphone.

"Lords and ladies," the MC said, "we thank you for coming to tonight's show. You're in for a special evening full of dazzling magic and spectacular feats. Please welcome illusionist Ozzie Stone and his assistant, Collette!"

The crowd cheered and applauded as Ozzie strode out onstage. He wore the black suit I'd seen him in earlier, but he'd added a top hat and a red cape. He also carried a wand in one hand. His assistant, Collette, was the woman who'd stormed away from him behind the tent. Either she was no longer upset or she was a good actor, because now she was all smiles.

While music played, Ozzie removed his top hat, bowed to the audience, and then tapped the hat with his wand. The hat burst into flames. With a flick of Ozzie's wrist, the flames were extinguished. Everyone applauded, and he tossed the hat to Collette, followed by his wand. She disappeared offstage with the props, then returned mere seconds later. Meanwhile, Ozzie removed his cape in a fluid movement and swished it about.

Collette struck a pose next to him in her slinky coppery dress. He waved the cape so it fluttered in front of Collette, shielding her from the audience's view for a couple of seconds. As his cape drifted toward the floor, Collette struck a new pose, this time wearing a short purple dress.

Several jaws dropped, including mine.

While moving to the music, Collette stepped inside what looked like a bag made of silk. Ozzie raised the bag up around her and gave it a shake before dropping it. Now Collette was wearing a flowing blue dress.

She danced across the stage, toward another silk bag that was puddled on the floor. Before Collette stepped into it, Ozzie tossed her a short green dress. Collette held it up for everyone to see, and then Ozzie raised the bag around her. He dropped it two seconds later to reveal Collette wearing the dress she'd held moments before.

For the last costume change, Ozzie threw sparkling confetti over his assistant. As the confetti fell to the floor, Collette was revealed in a shimmery silver dress. Ozzie retrieved his cape from the floor and swished it around himself. When he swept it aside with a dramatic swoosh, his black suit had turned into a white one.

I cheered and clapped along with everyone else, thoroughly impressed. I glanced Grayson's way. Maybe he didn't look particularly dazzled by the tricks, but he did seem to be enjoying himself.

As Collette cleared away the silk bags, Ozzie disappeared backstage. He reappeared a brief moment later, maneuvering a sheet of glass on wheels onto the stage. Then he produced a gun from the pocket of his suit. The revolver was reminiscent of the Wild West. A shiver of anticipation and apprehension ran through the crowd.

Grayson leaned closer to me. "They didn't have guns like that during the Renaissance," he whispered. "Or clothes like the ones they're wearing, for that matter."

I elbowed him in the ribs. "Shhh!"

With music still playing, Ozzie handed the gun to his assistant and crossed the stage. He faced Collette from the opposite side of the glass. As the music rose in a crescendo, Collette raised the gun and pointed it right at him.

I drew in a breath and held it.

Collette squeezed the trigger.

Bang!

The glass shattered.

The music stopped for a beat, and silence rang through the

tent. Then the music resumed, and Ozzie turned to the audience with a dramatic flair, his lips pulled back in a wide smile, revealing a bullet between his teeth.

Again, the crowd roared.

Ozzie spat the bullet into his hand and dropped it into the pocket of his suit jacket. He bowed and received another round of applause. While Collette wheeled away the frame that had held the sheet of glass and a stagehand quickly swept up the broken shards, Ozzie kept us entertained with a series of tricks, making objects disappear and reappear. When all the glass was cleared from the stage, the music died down.

"And now," Ozzie said to the audience, "my lovely assistant, Collette, will saw me in half."

Collette wheeled a contraption out from behind the curtains. As she rolled it to center stage, Ozzie staggered forward. His eyes widened with confusion. He tried to stand up straight but stumbled again.

Collette stared at him with alarm. Ozzie clutched at his chest and gasped for breath. He staggered another few feet across the stage and collapsed.

Chapter 6

Collette ran to Ozzie and knelt beside him.

"Help!" she screamed.

The music shut off abruptly, and the MC ran out onstage. Two others followed right behind him. They all crowded around Ozzie.

A hush fell over the audience.

"What do you think is wrong with him?" I asked Grayson in a whisper.

"I don't know. Heart attack, maybe?"

"I hope he'll be okay." I couldn't tear my gaze away from the stage.

The MC said something about an ambulance, and one of the backstage workers ran off.

The MC turned to address the audience with a grim expression on his face. "Ladies and gentlemen, we have a medical emergency. I'm afraid I must ask you to leave the tent in an orderly fashion. If you keep your ticket stubs, you can return to the box office tomorrow to receive a refund. Thank you for your cooperation and understanding."

Several people were on their feet now, and as they made their way toward the exit, they spoke to each other in hushed tones. Others stayed rooted to their seats, staring at the scene onstage.

As far as I could tell, Ozzie hadn't moved since he'd collapsed, but much of him was shielded from view by Collette and the MC.

By wordless agreement, Grayson and I got up and joined the line of people snaking toward the exit. When we got outside, into the golden evening sunshine, the rest of the faire continued around us. Actors interacted with fairgoers, and vendors sold their wares. It seemed like such an odd and stark contrast to what had unfolded in the tent.

Grayson took my hand, and I laced my fingers through his.

"Want to walk around for a bit?" he asked.

I nodded, still shaken from what we'd witnessed. I hoped that Ozzie was still breathing, and that the paramedics would reach him in time to help him.

Ahead of us, a tall and brawny actor dragged a shorter man by his collar. "Thou art a cutpurse! To the pillory with thee!"

A small crowd of fairgoers followed the actors, some of them filming the action.

Grayson and I gave them a wide berth. I couldn't lose myself in the fun of the faire at the moment. It was like a heavy, dark cloud hung over my head. The sight of Ozzie staggering and collapsing kept replaying in my mind. I hoped it wouldn't do that all night long.

Grayson and I came upon a large tank of water, and I realized we'd found the mermaids that Hamish the minstrel had grumbled about at the Inkwell the other night. A woman with a mermaid tail and long, flowing dark hair swam in the tank, striking poses near the glass so onlookers could snap pictures.

Another mermaid joined her, and the first one disappeared through a short tunnel that likely led to a place where they could surface and catch their breath without being seen by the fairgoers.

I had to agree with Hamish in one sense at least. I certainly never would have expected to find mermaids at a Renaissance faire. Then again, I'd never been to one of these events before, so I didn't know what was typical. The other faire attendees seemed to like this attraction. Kids came running over as soon as they spotted the mermaids, and young people and adults alike snapped photos and selfies with the mermaids in the background.

I wished I could get as excited as the people around me, but my spirits remained resolutely down near the ground.

Grayson and I hadn't spoken for several minutes now. I glanced his way and sensed that he felt as gloomy as I did.

He caught me looking at him. "Should we get out of here?"

"Yes," I said with relief. "I can't enjoy the faire right now."

"I'm not in the mood for it either," he said.

We made our way to the gates and out of the park. It was still relatively early in the evening, and I didn't want to part ways with Grayson yet.

"Want to watch a movie or something?" I asked him as we walked along Creekside Road. I hoped a movie might help stop my thoughts of Ozzie.

Grayson agreed, and we headed for his place so he could let his white German shepherd, Bowie, outside.

I told Grayson to choose the movie. I didn't really care what we watched, as long as there was something on the screen to distract me from my thoughts.

I gave Bowie a pat on the head as Grayson fetched us glasses of ice water from his kitchen. When he joined me on the couch, he put his arm around me, and I shifted closer so I could lean into him. The movie started playing on the TV, but I didn't see more than a scene or two before I fell fast asleep, my head resting on Grayson's shoulder.

*   *   *

I woke up to find a pair of brown eyes staring at me. I sat up with a start, a blanket falling away from me. Bowie whined and put his front paws up on the couch so he could lick my face. Dazed and still half asleep, I gave him a pat. I was used to waking up to Wimsey staring in my face, but not Bowie.

My last memory was of my eyes drifting shut early in the movie. Sunlight shone in through the eastern windows, and I realized that I'd spent the whole night on Grayson's couch. I ran my fingers through my hair, hoping it wasn't too messy. A faint scent of coffee floated toward me from the kitchen, so I got up and followed it, Bowie trotting along ahead of me.

I'd hoped to find Grayson in the kitchen, but he was nowhere to be seen. Although the half-full coffeepot tempted me, I wandered back into the living room. I spotted my phone on a side table, where I'd left it the night before. When I checked my text messages, I had a new one from Grayson.

Had to run over to the brewery early, the message said. **Didn't want to wake you. Help yourself to coffee. I hope to see you later.**

I let Bowie outside for a minute, in case Grayson didn't return for a while. I decided to forgo the coffee, so I could get home sooner. I was expecting a delivery of produce for the pub in less than an hour, and I didn't want to be late.

After folding up the blanket I'd slept under, I gave Bowie a kiss on the top of his head and then set off for home. Although a gentle breeze whispered its way through the leafy trees and the sun shone down from a brilliant blue sky, I couldn't enjoy the summer morning as much as I usually would. I was too troubled. I barely knew Ozzie, but I was worried about him. I hoped he was okay.

When I got home, Wimsey greeted me with a loud meow that told me he wasn't impressed that his breakfast was late. I quickly appeased him with a dish of food and then jumped in the shower.

While eating a bowl of oatmeal, I scoured the Internet on my phone, searching for any news of Ozzie. I found only one short mention of him on a news site. Unfortunately, it didn't tell me anything I didn't already know. All it said was that Ozzie had collapsed during his show at the Renaissance faire. Maybe I'd have more luck with the Shady Creek grapevine.

That turned out to be the case. After dealing with the delivery of produce, I made the short trip to the Village Bean, the local coffee shop.

"Did you hear the news?" Nettie Jo Kim, the shop's owner, asked me as she prepared the mocha latte I'd ordered.

"About Ozzie Stone collapsing during his show?" I asked. "I was there when it happened."

Nettie Jo's eyes widened as she popped the lid on my travel mug. "Oh no. That must have been terrible." She slid the mug across the counter to me. "I've never seen someone die, but it must have been upsetting."

My heart dropped like a heavy stone. "He's dead?"

Her eyes widened farther. "You didn't know?"

"I was hoping he'd survived."

"I'm sorry, Sadie. I should have kept my mouth shut."

"No, no," I said quickly. "I wanted the latest news. Thank you for telling me."

A line was growing at the counter now, so I had to let Nettie Jo get back to work. I had one last question for her, though.

"Was it a heart attack?"

"Nobody seems to know," she said.

I soon got confirmation of that fact. After the Inkwell opened at noon, I overheard plenty of conversations about the illusionist and his untimely demise. Many of those conversations involved various theories on how Ozzie had died.

Several people assumed a heart attack had killed him, but one woman was adamant that his assistant had shot him in the heart. Another man was just as certain that Collette had actually sawed Ozzie in half. At that point, I considered setting the man straight, but in the end I kept quiet. If I revealed that I'd been at the show and witnessed Ozzie's death, I'd be peppered with questions for the rest of the day, if not longer. I didn't want to have to repeat the tale of Ozzie's collapse over and over, and I had my hands full with a crowd of customers.

By the time Damien arrived for the evening shift, I'd heard several more theories about how Ozzie had died, most of them from people who'd clearly not been present at the time of the illusionist's collapse. If they had been, they would have known that there was no lion on the stage to eat him, and that he hadn't accidentally set himself on fire.

"I guess you've heard about what happened," I said when Damien joined me behind the bar shortly after his arrival at the pub.

"Hard not to. It's all over town." His mouth was set in a grim line as he headed down the bar to attend to a couple who'd just sat down.

When he was filling pint glasses with beer for the customers, I noticed dark purple bruises on the knuckles of his right hand.

"What happened?" I asked with a nod at the bruises.

Damien glanced down at his hand. "Nothing much." He picked up the glasses of beer. "I dropped a two-by-four on my fingers yesterday."

Damien did carpentry work on the side, and he was also in the midst of renovating part of his house.

He delivered the drinks to the customers at the end of the bar while I mixed up some cocktails for a table of four.

"By the way," Damien said as he passed by me on his way to the kitchen, "your table is almost ready. I'm going to finish it up tomorrow."

I brightened at that news. I'd hired Damien to build me a

coffee table for my apartment. The secondhand one I currently had in my living room had seen better days.

"Can I pick it up Saturday morning?" I asked.

"Sure." He disappeared into the kitchen.

As I carried a tray of cocktails across the room, a group of half a dozen people entered the pub. I recognized Collette, Minerva the Mysterious, and Toby the juggler, but I didn't know the others. They claimed one of the bigger tables in the middle of the room. Once I delivered the cocktails to the customers who'd ordered them, I tucked the empty tray under my arm and approached the newcomers. I didn't find it surprising that they all seemed to be in a somber mood.

"Welcome to the Inkwell," I greeted. "Can I get you anything, or do you need more time?"

A few of them were studying the menu.

"I think we're ready," Collette said. She looked to her colleagues for confirmation.

They all nodded, except for Minerva. She seemed to be off in her own world. I thought I detected a sheen of tears in her red-rimmed eyes, but then she blinked, and it was gone.

Everyone in the group ordered drinks, and I was pleased that half of them chose literary-themed cocktails. Collette and another woman ordered the Secret Life of Daiquiris cocktail, and one of the men decided on a Huckleberry Gin. Minerva, looking more present now, asked for a glass of claret, and two others requested beer.

"I was at Ozzie's show last night," I said once I'd noted down all the orders. "I was so sorry to hear he didn't make it. Did he have a heart attack?"

"We don't know what happened," Collette said. "I still can't believe he's gone."

"It must be difficult for everyone who knew him." I wasn't sure if I should ask another question, but I decided to go ahead. "Will the faire be shutting down?"

"Just because Ozzie's gone?" Toby scoffed at the idea.

This time I knew I hadn't imagined the tears in Minerva's eyes. They welled up without spilling onto her cheeks.

"Shut up, Toby," Collette said, glaring at the juggler from across the table.

He shrugged and let his gaze wander off, as if completely disinterested in the conversation.

One of the men I didn't recognize spoke up. "The show will go on, for now at least."

"Well, not Ozzie's, obviously," Collette said. "But the faire in general."

"I could take over Ozzie's show," Toby declared.

It was his colleagues' turn to scoff.

Toby's face darkened. He pushed back his chair and stood up. "Forget my drink. I'm out of here."

He stormed out of the pub.

"Sorry about that," Collette said to me. "We're all on edge after what happened."

"That's totally understandable," I assured her. "I'm sorry if I upset anyone with my questions."

Collette shook her head. "It's fine."

She asked to add two platters of nachos to the order, and I hurried off to the kitchen. When I emerged a couple of minutes later, I noticed that Collette and Minerva were no longer at the table. I served some other customers and then returned to the kitchen to retrieve the food Teagan had ready.

I picked up a plate of Paradise Lox and two Red Cabbage of Courage salads. Teagan also had the nachos ready for the faire workers, but I'd have to come back for those.

I quickly delivered the meals and then headed back toward the kitchen. As I passed by the short hallway that led to the restrooms, I noticed Collette and Minerva standing outside the women's washroom. I would have thought nothing of it, except for their angry expressions. My footsteps faltered.

Collette said something in a fierce whisper, but I couldn't make out any of her words.

Minerva's response was easier to hear.

"Don't you dare," the fortune-teller practically hissed at Collette. "You'll regret it if you do. You know you will."

She pierced Collette with one last glare before whirling around and disappearing into the restroom.

Chapter 7

By the next morning, I'd pushed Minerva and Collette's argument to the back of my mind. I hadn't forgotten about Ozzie's death—not even close—but I had other things to focus on, so I didn't dwell on it. After eating breakfast, I tried brushing Wimsey. His long white coat tended to get matted if not brushed regularly. The problem was that Wimsey wasn't keen on grooming sessions, not after the first two minutes, anyway.

I ran the brush through his coat while he was lying on my bed. He rolled over and exposed his tummy, so I concentrated on that part of him while I had the chance. I managed three strokes of the brush before he attacked it. I snatched my hand back in the nick of time. From there, things went downhill. When I tried brushing Wimsey again, he hissed and swatted at me. I persevered regardless and finished grooming him with only a couple of small scratches to show for it. We went through this routine several times a week. It wasn't something either of us enjoyed.

I gave him a few treat biscuits to appease him, and he purred happily, all forgiven. Until next time. Now that I'd completed that task, it was time for my own hair to get some attention. After grabbing my phone, I left my apartment above the pub. I crossed the corner of the village green, heading for Aunt Gilda's salon. My gaze strayed to the Village Bean as I crossed Sycamore Street, but I couldn't stop for a latte. It was almost time for my appointment, and I didn't want to be late.

"It's such a shame what happened to the illusionist," Aunt Gilda said once I was seated in the salon chair, my hair wet.

"It was awful," I said. "I can't believe he died. He couldn't have been all that much older than me."

"Far too young to die," Aunt Gilda agreed as she combed out my hair. "And I'm sorry your date with Grayson wasn't what you hoped. I know you were looking forward to spending time with him."

"That seems inconsequential in light of what happened," I said. "I'm sure we'll fit in another date soon."

At least I hoped we would.

Gilda began trimming the ends of my hair. "I talked to your mother last night."

"How's Jennifer doing?" I asked.

Jennifer was my sister-in-law, married to my older brother, Michael. She was three months pregnant with their first child.

"Fairly well. Suffering from some morning sickness, but otherwise she's doing fine."

"That's good. I should call her sometime this week." I was closer to my younger brother, Taylor, than I was to Michael, but my sister-in-law was a sweet woman, and I was very much looking forward to being an auntie for the first time.

"Maybe call your mother too," Aunt Gilda suggested. "She said she hadn't heard from you in a long time."

"I talked to her on the weekend!"

"She made it sound like it had been weeks."

"Not even one," I said with a sigh, "but I'll call her later today."

At least phone calls with my mom had been easier lately. Now that Jennifer was pregnant, my mom liked to talk about all the preparations being made for the baby. I much preferred our conversations to focus on that rather than my chosen career. My mom didn't think much of the fact that I'd bought a pub. I wasn't exactly sure why she disapproved so much, but Aunt Gilda had suggested that it was probably more the fact that I'd decided to move to Shady Creek instead of going back to Knoxville after living in Boston for a few years. Whatever the reason, my mom never seemed to tire of asking me why I hadn't chosen to become a lawyer like Michael. Taylor got the same question on a regular basis. My mom *really* didn't understand why he'd decided to become a tattoo artist.

Betty, Aunt Gilda's friend and coworker, shut off the hair dryer she'd been using to dry her client's hair. Gilda and I fell quiet for a few minutes as she snipped away with the scissors. Soon after, Betty's client paid for her appointment and left the salon.

"Did you hear about the graffiti?" Betty asked as she swept up the hair clippings.

"Graffiti?" I had no idea what she was talking about.

"One of the buildings on Mulberry Street," Gilda said.

"I know Zoe's working on a mural over there, but I haven't heard about any graffiti."

Betty disposed of the hair clippings. "It seems someone decided to paint a mural of their own."

"An unsanctioned one," Aunt Gilda added.

"Kids, by the looks of things." Betty tidied up her station.

"Did they paint anything bad?" I was imagining a wall covered in swear words and rude symbols.

"It was more an attempt at a pretty mural than conventional graffiti." Aunt Gilda set aside the scissors and picked up the hair dryer. "But the building's owner didn't want that wall painted."

"The other murals are looking great, though." Betty smiled as her next client arrived.

"I need to check them out," I said. "I haven't seen Mel's for a couple of days, and I haven't seen Zoe's at all." There were also several others around town that I had yet to visit.

As Aunt Gilda switched on the hair dryer, I decided to make a trip over to Mulberry Street in the near future.

With my hair neatly trimmed, I left Aunt Gilda's salon and allowed myself to stop at the Village Bean. I resisted the temptation to get myself a mocha latte, not wanting to go overboard with my sugar consumption for the week. I had to muster up a lot of willpower, but I managed to order regular coffee instead of what I really wanted.

I strolled across the village green with my coffee in hand. A group of teenagers played with a Frisbee, and a couple of young women wearing shorts and bikini tops had stretched out on beach towels. They chatted and sipped on what looked like Frappuccinos in Village Bean take-out cups. There were also several tourists out and about. Three of them had paused to snap pictures of the bandstand.

I stopped at a bench and sat down, deciding to phone my mom before doing anything else. The longer I left the task, the less pleased she'd be with me.

She picked up on the second ring.

"Sadie, I was beginning to wonder if you'd forgotten about me," she said when she answered the call.

I refrained from rolling my eyes, even though she couldn't see me. "Of course not, Mom." I quickly moved the conversation forward. "How are things?"

"I had dinner with Michael and Jennifer last night."

"That sounds nice," I said. "How is Jennifer?"

Even though I'd already asked that question of Aunt Gilda, I figured it wouldn't hurt to bring it up with my mom too. It was, after all, a safe topic of conversation.

She spent the next several minutes updating me on Jennifer's condition and the preparations being made for the arrival of the newest member of the family.

"Of course," she said once she'd exhausted that topic, "it would be nice to have dinner with you sometime too. You're my only daughter, and I haven't seen you in nearly a year."

"It's been too long," I agreed.

"You should be here when the baby's born."

"I'd like to be," I said. "Or shortly after. I'll make meeting my niece or nephew a priority. I promise. In the meantime, why don't you come to Shady Creek?"

"Oh." She seemed taken aback by the idea. "I don't know. What would I do there?"

"Visit with me and Aunt Gilda, for starters, and there's plenty of other things to do here. I'd love for you to see my new home."

"I'll have to check my calendar and see if there's a time when I can get away," she said, remaining noncommittal.

By the time I hung up, I still wasn't sure if I had convinced her to come for a visit or not, but at least I'd extended the invitation. I hoped she would take me up on it, but I'd try not to be too disappointed if she didn't. My mom wasn't much of a traveler, and she liked sticking to her routine. Hopefully, in time, she'd make an exception for me.

After getting up from the bench, I continued across the village green and followed Hillview Road to Mulberry Street. The bank stood on a corner, leaving one of its side walls visible to passersby. It was that wall that had been designated for Zoe's mural.

I found her hard at work, wearing an oversized, paint-splattered button-up shirt over her T-shirt and shorts. She stood up on the scaffolding, painting a puffy white cloud in the blue sky up near the top of the mural.

Her painting showed people in nineteenth-century clothing waiting on a station platform as a train approached. I'd seen her proposed design sketched out on paper during the selection process, but it was even more impressive to see it taking shape on such a large scale.

"Zoe!" I called out to her. "This looks amazing!"

She shaded her eyes so she could see me through the bright sunlight. "Thanks, Sadie!" She set aside her paintbrush and climbed down the scaffolding. "I'm happy with how it's coming together."

"You should be," I said as she hopped down to the sidewalk.

"Have you checked out the other murals?" she asked.

"I've seen Mel's and a couple of others, but not for a few days now."

"They're all coming along really well," Zoe said. "And even though none of the paintings are finished yet, the tourists are already interested."

"That's great."

I knew there was a plan to create a map for tourists that would show the locations of all the murals. The hope was that the maps would be available at the tourist center and from local merchants by the end of the month.

"I hear someone decided to add an extra mural, one that wasn't authorized," I said before taking a sip of my coffee.

"You heard right. It's across the street. Do you want to see it?"

"Sure."

I followed her across Mulberry Street and around a brick building that housed a physical therapist's clinic on the ground floor and an apartment above. There was a tiny parking lot at the back, with room for four cars. Two of the spots were currently occupied. We made our way around the vehicles and stopped to study the back wall, which had been covered with a coat of white paint at some point, unlike the rest of the building.

On top of the white coat, someone had painted a dolphin, as well as a stingray and a starfish. The creatures were cute, but not professionally done. One color had been used for everything.

"Blue paint," I noted.

"Yep. My missing can of paint was found here when the building's owner discovered the new art on his wall."

"Any idea who's responsible?" I asked.

Zoe shrugged. "I figure it was a kid or kids, judging by the look of it, but other than that . . . no idea."

By unspoken agreement, we started heading back toward Zoe's mural.

"It got me thinking, though," she said as we crossed the street. "Maybe it would be fun to give the local kids a chance to paint their own murals."

"Do you think property owners will want kids' murals on their walls?"

"I don't know, but I was thinking of putting them somewhere else. You know the green space behind the community center?"

I nodded. Sometimes the center held activities, like tie-dyeing classes, out on the fenced-in lawn behind the building.

"I thought maybe the murals could go on the fence panels."

"That's a good idea," I said. "What do the people who run the center think?"

"I haven't brought it up yet. The thought occurred to me only yesterday. Do you think I should mention it?"

"Definitely. I bet a lot of kids would enjoy that."

"I'll do that, then," Zoe decided.

We'd reached her mural, and a group of three tourists was in the midst of studying it.

"Are you the artist?" one of them asked Zoe, likely because of her paint-splattered shirt.

She confirmed that she was, and the tourists peppered her with praise and questions.

I sent Zoe a smile and a wave and then headed for the Inkwell.

I finished off my coffee as I reached the pub. The lights were on inside, but I couldn't see or hear Mel. Maybe she hadn't arrived yet. I also couldn't hear Booker. That struck me as odd. He usually sang at full volume while working, up until the pub opened. After that, he kept it to humming or quieter singing.

Wondering what was up, I poked my head into the kitchen. Booker was making a large vat of A Time to Chill, a cold soup featuring avocado and grapefruit. He had his braids tied back and wore an Inkwell apron over his clothes.

"Hey, Sadie," he greeted when he saw me, but he lacked his usual smile.

I stepped farther into the kitchen, letting the door shut behind me. "You okay?"

"Sure. I'm not the one you need to worry about."

That statement set off alarm bells in my head. "Who is it that I do need to worry about?"

"You'd better talk to Mel," he said, his expression somber.

Now he had me downright scared. "Where is she?"

He hooked his thumb over his shoulder. "In the back."

Anxiety humming through me, I passed through the back hallway to the storage room where we kept the extra kegs and other miscellaneous items. When I stepped into the room, I nearly collided with a keg on a dolly.

I jumped out of the way as Mel steered it out into the hallway. She stopped short.

"Sorry about that, Sadie."

"No worries," I said. "Although, actually, I *am* worried. Booker said I should talk to you about something?"

Mel grimaced, scaring me even more. "I was working on my mural this morning when Damien stopped by."

"And?" I prompted, knowing there must be more.

She ran a hand through her short blue and blond hair. "While we were talking, Detective Marquez showed up. She asked Damien to go with her to the police station so she could ask him some questions."

"Questions about what?" I asked, puzzled.

Mel blew out a breath and rested her hands on her hips.

"About Ozzie Stone's murder."

Chapter 8

I put a hand to the wall for support.

"Murder?" I echoed, the word sending a chill along the back of my neck. "Ozzie was *murdered*?" Before Mel had a chance to speak, I added, "And Detective Marquez wanted to question *Damien* about it? Why would Damien know anything about Ozzie's murder?"

"Your guess is as good as mine." Mel got back to wheeling the dolly along the hall, so I stepped out of the way and pressed my back up against the wall as she passed by.

I followed her out to the bar. "Did Damien say anything?"

"Other than to agree to meet the detective at the station? No."

I helped as Mel shifted the keg from the dolly to the under-bar unit.

"Was he shocked?" I asked. "Confused?"

"Nope." Mel straightened up once we had the keg in place. "I'd say he seemed . . . resigned."

"But how could that be? Damien didn't even know Ozzie. Did he?"

"Those are questions you'll have to ask Damien. Once Detective Marquez is done with him."

A terrible thought struck me. "What if she doesn't let him leave the station? What if she arrests him?"

"Let's not get ahead of ourselves," Mel said. "Most likely, Detective Marquez thinks he might have some relevant information."

"But he wasn't at the show that night. He was here at the Inkwell."

"True. Even though he was an hour late, he probably got here before Ozzie died."

"Wait. He was an hour late?" Apprehension overshadowed my surprise.

"I thought you knew."

"No." I hadn't checked when he'd clocked in. "Did he say why he was late?"

"All he said was that something came up at home. He texted me to let me know a few minutes before he was supposed to arrive."

"That must have been right around when I saw him at the faire, which means he wasn't at home."

"Maybe he had to go home from there because of whatever came up," Mel said. "But I thought he had no intention of going to the faire."

"That's what I thought too. But I saw him there before Ozzie's show, and he didn't look happy." My apprehension intensified.

"Maybe he was there to see Ozzie, and that's why the police wanted to talk to him," Mel suggested.

"But why would he go see Ozzie?"

"Again, you'll have to ask Damien that." She glanced at the clock on the wall. "It's two minutes after noon."

"Right." I tried to rein in my swirling thoughts. "I'll talk to Damien tonight."

As long as he was allowed to leave the police station.

*   *   *

Many times over the next few hours, I was tempted to text Damien to see if he still had his freedom. A couple of times I even went as far as picking up my phone. I never actually went through with sending a message, though. I wasn't sure if Damien would want me checking up on him, and I was scared that I might receive no response or a response I didn't want. So I spent the entire afternoon worrying. At least the pub was busy enough to keep me occupied. That didn't make my concerns disappear, but I had to shove them off to the side as I made sure to keep all my customers happy.

To my relief, none of the patrons were gossiping about Damien's trip to the police station. Hopefully, that meant that Mel, Booker, and I were the only ones who knew about it. It probably wouldn't stay that way for long. News, gossip, and rumors could spread with astonishing speed in this town. It was hard to keep anything a secret for long in Shady Creek.

As far as I could tell from the tidbits I overheard while serving customers, the locals were talking mostly about Ozzie's death. It didn't yet seem to be public knowledge that he was murdered, but I doubted that would remain true much longer. For the time being, however, people were still theorizing about how Ozzie might have met his untimely demise. The theories weren't quite as wild as they had been previously. I didn't hear any mention of lions or other wild animals this time. The consensus seemed to be that Ozzie had succumbed either to a heart attack or a deadly allergy of some sort.

When Damien arrived for his shift, I nearly collapsed from relief. At least Detective Marquez hadn't placed him under arrest. I wanted to corner Damien and interrogate him myself, but I was in the middle of taking a long order for a group of half a dozen hungry tourists who were on a vacation from Pennsylvania.

As much as I wanted to talk to Damien right away, all I could do was raise a hand in acknowledgment as he crossed the room and disappeared into the back. I had to force myself to focus on what my customers were ordering. As soon as I'd noted down the last item, I made a dash for the back hallway. Mel and Damien stood in the doorway to the small cloakroom where my employees left their jackets and other belongings while they worked.

Mel said something to Damien in a low voice, glancing my way. He moved past her into the cloakroom and out of my line of sight.

Mel tucked her phone into the pocket of her jeans as she passed me to get to the back door. "Bye, Sadie. See you tomorrow."

"Tomorrow," I echoed as she disappeared out the door.

When I peeked into the cloakroom, I nearly collided with Damien. He had stashed his motorcycle helmet on a shelf and was on his way out of the room. I stepped back.

"Sorry!" I noted Damien's stony expression. It was as good as a flashing warning sign, but I ignored it. "What happened at the police station?"

He moved past me, his jaw tense. "Nothing much."

I scurried after him as he passed through the door that led to the main part of the pub. "Are you in any trouble?" I whispered as he took up his post behind the bar.

He shot me a cold look.

"Not that I think you've actually done anything," I rushed to say. "But do the police think you have anything to do with Ozzie's death?" I said the last two words so quietly that they were barely audible. I didn't want anyone overhearing me.

Damien grabbed a cloth and wiped at a spot on the bar. "I'd rather not talk about it."

"Fair enough," I said, backing off literally and figuratively.

I was disappointed he didn't want to share, and I was concerned about why he didn't want to talk about it, but he clearly wasn't going to give me any details. I didn't want to make his mood any worse, so I left him to his work and got back to serving customers.

Soon after, members of the Inkwell's science fiction and fantasy book club began arriving for their monthly meeting. Sofie Talbot, who owned the local bakery, arrived first. Her friend Gina, who worked as a pastry chef at a hotel, followed close on her heels. They waved at me on their way to the Christie room, where all the book clubs had their meetings. I'd named the room after one of my favorite authors, Agatha Christie. It was a cozy place in the winter, with its own woodstove, and now, in the summertime, I left the windows open wide to let in the evening breeze.

After I'd delivered meals to a table of four, I popped into the Christie room to see if Gina and Sofie wanted anything to eat or drink. They weren't hungry at the moment, but they both decided on the Secret Life of Daiquiris for their beverage. I was on my way out to the bar to mix the drinks when Matt Yanders arrived. To my surprise, he'd brought his brother, Flint, along. Flint attracted many stares and whispers, especially from the women, on his way across the pub. He wore his full costume from the faire, from his boots to his leather arm bracers. The only thing missing was his sword.

"Sitting in on the book club tonight?" I asked Flint once I'd greeted both men.

"I thought it would be fun," he said. "I haven't read the book, but my brother and I share a love of science fiction and urban fantasy, so I'm looking forward to hearing about it."

The club would be discussing *Storm Front* by Jim Butcher. I hadn't read it either, but I'd peeked at the blurb on the back cover of Gina's copy, and it sounded intriguing.

I slipped behind the bar. "Can I get you guys anything to eat or drink?"

They both ordered beers, although they chose different kinds, as well as a platter of nachos to share. I told them I'd have their drinks ready in a moment.

Flint disappeared into the Christie room, but Matt lingered and leaned against the bar. "I tried to get him to leave the costume behind, but he loves all the attention he gets from women when he wears it. They all seem to think he looks like Viggo Mortensen's Aragorn."

"He really does," I said.

Matt rolled his eyes, but he had a good-natured grin on his face. He followed his brother into the other room.

I made a quick trip into the kitchen to ask Teagan to make up a platter of nachos, and then I returned to the bar and got busy mixing drinks. The Secret Life of Daiquiris was a recent addition to the list of available cocktails. Made with coconut rum, cream of coconut, mango, and lime juice, the cocktail had a refreshing, summery taste that I loved. Fortunately, the customers who'd tried it so far also seemed to love it.

I mixed up two of those cocktails for Gina and Sofie and filled pint glasses for Matt and Flint. When I carried the tray of drinks into the Christie room, the group was still awaiting the arrival of the three other members of their club.

As I handed out the drinks, I realized the group was discussing Ozzie's death, everyone's attention focused on Flint.

"The faire was shut down this morning," he was saying. "The police needed to do some investigating, but we're hoping they'll let us reopen tomorrow."

"I can't believe Ozzie was murdered." Sofie's brown eyes were wide.

"It's scary," Gina said as she accepted the drink I passed her. "Thanks, Sadie."

"What are the police looking for?" I asked. "Do they know how Ozzie was killed?"

"Now that they've got the toxicology results back, they do," Flint said. "It turns out Ozzie was poisoned."

Chapter 9

It took a moment for Flint's news to sink in.

"What kind of poison?" Gina asked, voicing the very question that had just popped into my head.

"I'm not sure." Flint settled into an armchair and took a drink of his beer.

"I wonder how it was administered," I said, more to myself than anyone else.

"Maybe in something he ate." Sofie glanced at her daiquiri. "Or in a drink."

"If that's the case," I said, "then it must not have been a poison that acts instantaneously. He performed onstage for about fifteen minutes before he showed any signs of distress."

"I heard he was foaming at the mouth." Gina looked to Flint. "Is that true?"

"I have no idea," Flint replied. "I'm taking everything I hear with a grain of salt, because some of the rumors have been pretty wild."

"I'll say," I agreed. "I was at Ozzie's show that night, and I didn't see him foaming at the mouth. Not before he collapsed, anyway. After that, I couldn't see much, because of all the people gathered around him."

"You were there?" Sofie shuddered. "That must have been awful to see."

"It's definitely not a good memory," I said.

Gina focused on Flint again. "Are you sure the poison part isn't just a rumor?"

Flint sat back in his armchair, resting his pint glass on his knee. "That part I'm sure of. The day after Ozzie died, the police asked all of us if we knew if he had any food allergies or anything like that. I didn't know him well enough to say, but Minerva and Rachael both said he'd never mentioned any allergies or health issues of any kind. Then, late this morning, I saw the police seize Minerva's supply of herbs."

"They're looking for the poison," Sofie reasoned.

Flint nodded at her. "That's what I figure."

"Could Minerva be the poisoner?" I asked. "Does she have a lot of herbs?"

"All kinds of them. She's into herbal medicines and all that." Flint frowned. "I don't know if she killed Ozzie, though, unless she did it accidentally. She seems pretty broken up about his death."

I wanted to keep questioning Flint, but the remaining members of the book club arrived together, and the conversation shifted away from Ozzie. I returned to my duties and soon had every member of the club supplied with a drink, and a few with food as well. They began discussing *Storm Front*, and I left them to it.

Everything I'd learned from Flint about Ozzie's death whirled around in my mind. Someone had poisoned the illusionist, but why would the police think Damien would know anything about that? I felt certain the reason had to do with Damien's mysterious visit to the faire. I desperately wanted to know why he'd been there and what exactly the police had questioned him about. His stony expression hadn't softened at all since his arrival at the Inkwell, so I knew not to broach the subject with him again.

Almost an hour had passed since the start of the book club meeting when Grayson showed up at the Inkwell. A smile lit up my face as soon as I saw him. We'd texted back and forth a few times since the morning I'd woken up on his couch, but this was the first time we'd seen each other face-to-face.

As he headed my way, I glanced around the pub. Although the place was busy, I thought I could manage to sneak away for a few minutes.

I slipped out from behind the bar and took his hand, then led him through the door to the back hallway.

The door had barely shut behind us when he slid his arms around me and kissed me. When he eventually pulled back, just a few inches, I could barely feel the floor beneath my feet.

"Sweet Sherlock," I whispered.

I felt as well as heard Grayson's low rumble of laughter.

Heat rushed to my cheeks. "Did I say that out loud?"

He kissed me again, and I forgot to be embarrassed.

When the second kiss ended, Grayson rested his forehead against mine. "I missed you."

The heat in his blue eyes sent my stomach tumbling.

"Same." I ran my hand over the rasp of stubble on his jaw. "I'm sorry I fell asleep during the movie."

"Don't worry about it." He grinned. "You're cute when you snore."

I pulled back and glared at him. "I don't snore."

He laughed. "Okay, true. There wasn't any snoring. But you do talk in your sleep."

Oh, for the love of Frodo! I did have a history of talking in my sleep.

My cheeks grew warm again. "What did I say?" I asked with trepidation.

"Just a couple of things."

I could tell he was being intentionally vague. "About what?"

Amusement made his eyes bright. "Possibly about me."

"Possibly?" The word came out as little more than a squeak. Had my sleeping self betrayed me by revealing the depth of my feelings for Grayson?

"Possibly," he repeated, fighting a grin.

I poked him in the chest. "You're enjoying this far too much."

He lost the fight against his grin. "That's probably true."

I gripped his arms. "Please put me out of my misery."

He laughed and gave me a quick kiss. "To be honest, I have no idea what you said."

I narrowed my eyes with suspicion. "Really?"

"Really. You were mumbling incoherently. I think I might have heard the word 'chocolate,' but other than that, I have no idea."

I relaxed with relief. "Oh, thank goodness."

Grayson pulled me closer to him. "Why? What did you think you might have said?"

I tried not to get distracted by the fact that his lips were mere inches from mine. "That's top-secret information."

He moved even closer. "I don't have high enough security clearance?" His lips brushed mine.

"You're getting there," I said, sounding as breathless as I felt.

"It'll be worth the wait."

The intensity of his gaze nearly undid me, but I managed to gather myself together. It was too soon for all that I was feeling for him, and I certainly didn't need to be saying any of it out loud. Yet.

"Did you hear the news?" I blurted out, desperate to change the subject in case I spilled the secrets of my heart.

"About Ozzie? You told me he didn't make it."

I'd shared that terrible news during one of our text exchanges.

"He was murdered," I said in a hushed voice. *"Poisoned."*

That information caught him by surprise. "That's not just another one of the rumors flying around town?"

"I'm pretty sure it's accurate. I got the information from Matt Yanders's brother, Flint. He's one of the actors at the faire."

A swell in the rumble of conversation on the other side of the door caught my attention. I really needed to get back to work.

"Let me guess," Grayson said, "you're already working on solving the crime."

"Not exactly," I said. "I heard the news earlier this evening, and I've been too busy for sleuthing."

Grayson was fighting a grin again.

"What?" I asked.

"I don't think it's possible for you to be too busy for sleuthing."

"I definitely am right now." I tipped my head toward the door. "I've got to get back out there before Damien gets too swamped."

That reminded me that I wanted to tell Grayson about Damien getting questioned by the police, but I'd already opened the door to the pub, and I wasn't going to talk about that within earshot of anyone else. It would have to wait.

Grayson hung around for a while longer, enjoying a drink at the bar while I worked, but then he headed home so he could take Bowie for one last walk before going to bed.

Despite Grayson's teasing, I really did feel too busy to launch my own investigation into Ozzie's murder. Tonight, anyway. Maybe the next day would be a different story.

Chapter 10

The siren call of a mocha latte from the Village Bean was too tempting to resist the next morning. I dressed in shorts and a T-shirt, planning to head over to Damien's place after a trip to the coffee shop. As soon as I stepped out into the fresh air, I could tell we were in for another beautiful day. Only a few puffy white clouds interrupted the expanse of beautiful blue sky overhead, and the sun warmed my skin, even though it wasn't yet nine o'clock in the morning. It was a good thing I'd remembered to apply sunscreen before leaving my apartment. I loved soaking in the sunshine, but like most redheads, I had a tendency to burn easily.

As I crossed the footbridge out in front of the pub, I caught sight of someone down in the creek. I paused in the middle of the bridge, realizing that it was the young girl I'd seen twice at the faire who was stepping from stone to stone, the water dancing and flowing over her bare feet.

"Morning!" I called out.

Startled, the girl nearly lost her balance but quickly recovered. She gave me a tentative smile and wave.

I noticed splatters of blue on her pale pink T-shirt.

A lightbulb clicked on inside my head. "Have you been painting?" I asked. "I saw the cute sea creatures on the wall."

The girl's eyes widened. She froze for a split second and then clambered up the bank.

"Hold on," I called out. "I'm not trying to get you in trouble."

I didn't know if she even heard me. She was already running full tilt on the grass at the side of Creekside Road. She headed west and was soon blocked from sight by the Queen Anne houses that lined the road.

I hadn't meant to scare the girl, but I was pretty sure I knew who'd stolen Zoe's blue paint to create the unsanctioned mural.

As I continued on my way across the footbridge, I spotted a pair of shoes on the bank of the creek. The girl had fled in bare feet, forgetting her sneakers. I decided to leave them where they were for the time being. Hopefully, she'd return for them soon. I worried that she might hurt her feet by running without her shoes, but there wasn't much I could do about it now. Even when I walked out into the middle of Creekside Road, I couldn't see the girl. She was long gone.

I resumed my trip to the Village Bean. I had to wait in line, and while I did, I decided to order drinks for Aunt Gilda and Betty as well. When my turn came, I purchased a hazelnut latte for Gilda, a vanilla one for Betty and, of course, a mocha one for myself. With all three drinks in hand, I headed four doors down to the salon.

I found Aunt Gilda and Betty in the midst of getting ready for their first clients of the day, who hadn't yet arrived.

"You're a sweetheart," Betty said when I announced that I'd brought drinks for them. "Thank you."

Aunt Gilda gave me a kiss on the cheek as she accepted her hazelnut latte. "A delicious drink is a great way to start the day, but a visit from you is even better."

"It's a great way to start my own day too," I said. "I'm about to go pick up my coffee table from Damien's place."

"Be sure to send us a photo," Betty requested. "I can't wait to see how it turned out."

"Better yet," I said, "both of you should come over and see it sometime soon."

Aunt Gilda straightened a stack of magazines on the coffee table in the waiting area. "We'd love that."

"You two know most of the people in this town," I said, thinking of the girl I'd scared off. "I'm trying to figure out who someone is."

I told them about the girl, describing her as best I could.

"Nina Wellington's got three blond daughters." Betty thought for a moment. "The youngest would be about the right age, but her hair's very curly, and Nina always has her kids signed up for so many activities in the summer. I don't know how any of them would have time for running around and visiting the faire."

"What about Missy and Adam's daughter?" Aunt Gilda suggested.

Betty shook her head. "I cut her hair short a couple of months ago. It wouldn't even reach her shoulders yet."

That definitely didn't fit. The mystery girl's hair reached halfway down her back.

"I can't think who else it might be," Aunt Gilda said.

"Neither can I." Betty flipped the sign on the door.

Maybe I'd have to ask the girl her name. If I ever saw her again. And if she wasn't too scared to talk to me.

Betty's first client of the day arrived, so I said my goodbyes and crossed the corner of the village green. With my mocha latte already half gone, I hopped in my car and set out for Damien's house. He lived with his two teenage daughters at the edge of town, on nearly two acres of land with an old farmhouse he'd restored himself. I'd been to his place once before, when he hosted a barbecue in June, so I knew exactly where I was going.

I drove with the window down, the wind fluttering through my hair. I was enjoying the recent stretch of beautiful summer weather. Lots of sun, without being too hot or humid. Perfect, in my opinion.

I soon arrived at Damien's place and turned into the long driveway. I parked at the front of the house and shut off the engine. Fifteen-year-old Bryony, Damien's youngest daughter, was stretched out on the porch swing, reading a book.

"Dad!" she hollered as I climbed out of the car. "Sadie's here!"

"What are you reading?" I asked Bryony as I approached the front porch.

She showed me the book's cover. *"Akata Witch."*

"I've heard good things about it." I knew the author, Nnedi Okorafor, had won the World Fantasy Award. "Are you enjoying it?"

She nodded "It's really good."

Damien appeared from around the side of the house. "Morning, Sadie. Come on over to the workshop."

I followed him around the house to one of two outbuildings. The double doors stood open, and when we stepped inside, it took a moment for my eyes to adjust to the dimmer light. Once I could see properly, my gaze immediately landed on a beautiful coffee table. The sight of it took my breath away.

"Is this it?" I ran a finger along the top edge.

"That's it," Damien confirmed.

I walked a slow circle around the table, admiring it from every angle. Damien had used an old wooden trunk that I'd found at an antique sale and had transformed it into a table. He had kept the metal hasp and brackets on the body of the trunk and had replaced the damaged top with reclaimed wood that matched the rest of it.

"It's beautiful," I said, blown away by how well it had turned out. "Thank you so much."

The table had a hidden storage compartment beneath the hinged lid, which raised up to provide a higher work surface. It would be like having a combination coffee table and desk in my living room. The rustic look of it would fit perfectly in my cozy apartment on the upper floor of the restored gristmill.

Damien opened the top to show me how it worked. The transformation from coffee table to workstation took only a couple of seconds, and there was plenty of storage room in the hidden compartment. I already knew I'd use that mainly for books.

"Let's get it to your car." Damien lifted up one end of the table.

I grabbed the other end, and we carefully made our way out of the workshop and across the lawn.

"I can help you get it from your car to your apartment later," Damien offered as we rounded the house.

"Thank you. I'll probably need to take you up on that." I knew I wouldn't be able to carry it up the stairs by myself.

Maybe that would also give me a chance to talk to Damien out of earshot of his daughter or any customers. I didn't know if he'd be any more willing to talk about his police interview than before, but I at least wanted to try to get some information out of him.

Once we reached my car, we maneuvered the coffee table into the trunk. It was a tight fit, but we got it in there, although I couldn't shut the trunk all the way. Damien helped me secure it with bungee cords so I could drive home safely. Once the table was stowed away, I pulled out my checkbook and paid Damien what I owed him.

As I handed over the check, the sound of an approaching vehicle drew our attention to the driveway.

I did a double take when I saw that it was a police car heading our way. An unmarked vehicle turned into the driveway behind it.

Bryony sat up on the porch swing. "Why are the police here?"

We both looked to Damien for an answer, but he stayed quiet, watching the cars approach with a grim expression.

The two vehicles parked behind mine, blocking the driveway. Two uniformed officers climbed out of the cruiser. I'd met both of them before. One was Officer Pamela Rogers, and the other was Officer Eldon Howes, who'd been dating Shontelle since May. They both had their impassive cop expressions firmly in place.

I also recognized the woman who got out of the unmarked vehicle. Detective Marquez wore a tailored gray pantsuit and had her curly dark hair tied back. She removed her sunglasses and left them on the dashboard before approaching us with her fellow officers.

Damien watched with an expression as stoic as the ones on the officers' faces. He didn't seem confused or curious about why the police were at his house. I, however, was both of those things. Bryony seemed to be too. She left her book on the porch swing and stood on the steps in her bare feet.

"Mr. Keys." Detective Marquez handed a piece of paper over to Damien. "We have a warrant to search the property."

"What? Why?" Bryony sounded scared now.

Damien took a cursory look at the warrant, his expression giving nothing away. "Are we allowed to be here while you search?"

"You can stay on the porch," Marquez said. She glanced back as a second police cruiser turned into the driveway.

My sense of dread grew stronger.

Damien climbed the front steps, his face still revealing nothing about what he was thinking or feeling.

Bryony grabbed his hand. "What's going on, Dad?"

"Nothing to worry about." He put an arm around her and opened the screen door. "Charlotte!" he called.

From somewhere deep in the house, a girl's voice replied, "Coming!"

"We'll start outdoors," Detective Marquez said to her uniformed officers. There were four of them, now that two more had climbed out of the second cruiser.

I stood next to my car, my feet rooted to the ground, as I watched the scene play out in front of me.

Marquez said something to Officer Rogers in a low voice. Rogers nodded and remained in place while the others headed around the side of the house.

If I'd really wanted to, I could have maneuvered my car onto the grass and around the police vehicles, but unless Damien asked me to leave, I wasn't going anywhere. My curiosity was running wild, and I was also deeply worried.

Footsteps pounded from within the house, and seventeen-year-old Charlotte burst out through the screen door. Her hair was a darker shade of brown than her sister's, but their eyes were the same deep blue.

"What's up?" she asked her dad, the words dying away on her tongue, as she noticed the police vehicles and Officer Rogers. "Dad?"

"Everything's going to be fine," Damien said to his daughters.

Bryony leaned into him. "But why are the police here?"

Charlotte's eyes held no curiosity or confusion, only fear.

"Is this about . . . ?" Her unfinished question came out in such a soft whisper that I barely heard it.

"Let's stay quiet," Damien said, his voice firm.

He nudged his daughters toward the porch swing. They both sat down, and Bryony tucked her legs up beneath her. Her book lay forgotten beside her.

I climbed the porch steps. "What's going on?" I whispered.

Damien gave a curt shake of his head, indicating that he didn't want to talk. He folded his arms across his chest, his expression stony.

I sank down into a porch chair, my heart beating much faster than it should have been.

I couldn't bring myself to believe that Damien was involved in anything criminal, and yet he didn't appear surprised by the fact that the police wanted to search his property. What did that mean?

I looked his way, but I could tell I wasn't going to get any information out of him. After casting a glance at Officer Rogers, I checked the time on my phone. I couldn't stay much longer, because I needed to get back to the Inkwell before noon. I didn't want to leave, though. Not until I knew what the heck was going on.

The minutes ticked by slowly, a tense silence hanging over all of us. A light breeze carried birdsong toward us from the wooded area at the edge of Damien's property. The cheery sound seemed far removed from where I sat.

Eventually, I had to accept the fact that I needed to leave. I was about to get up when Officer Rogers's gaze shifted slightly to one side. Detective Marquez and Officer Howes appeared from around the side of the house a second later. Both wore grim expressions. Detective Marquez held a plastic bag with some sort of plant inside it.

"Mr. Keys," Marquez said, "could you please join us down here?"

Damien unfolded his arms and descended the steps.

My heart nearly stuttered to a stop when Officer Howes unclipped his handcuffs from his belt.

"Perhaps your daughters should go inside for a minute," Marquez suggested.

Damien glanced over his shoulder. "Girls. Inside."

The tone of his voice left no room for argument. With wide eyes, the girls scurried into the house. They didn't go far, hovering in the shadows inside the door.

One of them gasped with the detective's next words.

"Damien Keys, you're under arrest for the murder of Ozzie Stone."

Chapter 11

My brain got stuck on the detective's last words, replaying them over and over like a broken record.

Damien under arrest? I couldn't process that.

I stood frozen on the porch until one of the girls let out a desperate wail.

Damien looked back as Eldon led him toward the nearest police cruiser. "Char, call your aunt Tracey."

That was all he had a chance to say before he ducked into the backseat of the cruiser. Eldon shut the door and climbed into the driver's seat. He drove off with Damien, while Marquez and the other officers still present continued with their search.

Either Charlotte or Bryony was sobbing now. I turned and saw that it was Charlotte. She and her sister stood on the other side of the screen door. Bryony had her arms around her older sister, her eyes wide with shock. Charlotte's body shook as she cried, one hand pressed to her mouth and her other arm holding tightly to Bryony.

My mind was spinning wildly, but I knew what I needed to do. I opened the screen door and ushered the girls out onto the porch.

"Sit down," I said gently.

They collapsed onto the porch swing, still holding onto each other.

"Where does your aunt Tracey live?" I asked as I sat on a white wicker chair.

Charlotte sniffled but reined in her sobs. "Rutland."

I figured Tracey must be Damien's sister-in-law. His family lived in England, where he was from, but his late wife had grown up in Vermont.

"Do you want me to phone her?" I asked.

Charlotte shook her head. "I can do it." She fished her phone out of the pocket of her denim shorts. Her hands trembling, she scrolled through her list of contacts.

When she selected a number, I hoped desperately that her aunt would answer. Fortunately, she did. It took a few tries for Charlotte to convey what had happened, because she couldn't stop crying as she relayed the story, but eventually, she got the message across. When she hung up, she wiped the tears from her cheeks.

"Is she coming?" Bryony asked, tears on her cheeks as well.

Charlotte nodded. "She needs to pack a few things, but she thinks she'll be here in an hour or so."

"I can stay until she arrives," I offered.

"Don't you have to open the Inkwell?" Charlotte asked, although there was a hint of hope in her eyes.

"I can ask Mel to do that." I started texting her right away.

Marquez and another officer passed us to enter the house. Charlotte glared at them until they disappeared inside. Then she sank deeper into her seat, as if deflating.

"How can they do this?" she asked with despair. "Dad didn't kill anyone."

Bryony burst into tears. "Will we ever see him again?"

Charlotte put an arm around her sister. "Of course we will. The police have made a mistake. They'll have to let him go soon." She looked to me. "Right, Sadie?"

"Sure," I said, desperately hoping that was the truth.

I tried to put my thoughts in order. The police obviously had evidence pointing at Damien. Eldon had taken the plant away with him, so I figured that was likely what the killer had used to poison Ozzie. Then there was Damien's mysterious trip to the faire. I probably wasn't the only person who'd seen him there.

I remembered something else, my stomach sinking as the memory resurfaced. Damien's bruised knuckles. I suddenly wasn't so sure he'd told me the truth about how he'd sustained the injury.

"Charlotte," I said carefully, not wanting to upset the girls any further, "when the police showed up, you seemed to have an idea why they might be here."

Charlotte fixed her gaze on her hands, which she clasped tightly in her lap.

Bryony had stopped crying now. "Is that true?" she asked her sister.

Charlotte squished her lips to one side, hesitating, before saying quietly, "Dad punched Ozzie Stone."

My eyebrows shot up, and Bryony's breath hitched with surprise.

"Why?" we asked at the same time.

Charlotte hesitated again, but not for long. "Bryony and I went to the faire on Tuesday."

"We saw Ozzie Stone's show," Bryony added.

Charlotte nodded. "But before the show, we were wandering around. Bryony was talking with some friends, and I went off looking for something to drink."

Bryony looked at her sister. "You weren't gone very long."

"No." She paused. "But I took a shortcut between two tents and ran into Ozzie." She still had her gaze fixed on her hands in her lap. "He seemed really nice at first. Charming."

I had a bad feeling that I knew where her story was going. I got up from my seat and quietly closed the front door, not wanting the police to overhear our conversation.

"He was good looking too," Charlotte continued, her voice barely above a whisper. "And I guess I felt . . . flattered that this famous guy was interested in me."

"How interested?" I asked, not sure I wanted to know the answer.

"He said he thought I was pretty. He asked me to meet up with him after his show. He said he'd give me a private tour backstage."

I didn't doubt for a second that a tour wasn't what he really had in mind. I suspected Charlotte knew too, and she soon confirmed that.

"I knew what he really meant. By that point, I was kind of uncomfortable. I told him I couldn't."

"Did he let you go?" I asked, on the verge of being angry with Ozzie, even though he was dead now.

Charlotte squished her lips to the side again. "He put his hands on my shoulders and said, 'Why not spend some time together right now?' I didn't want to, but then he kissed me." Tears welled in her eyes, but she blinked them away. "He had a tight grip on my arms, but I managed to twist away from him. I ran off and found Bryony and her friends."

"You didn't say anything," her sister said, her cheeks still damp from her earlier tears.

Charlotte shrugged. "I didn't want to talk about it in front of your friends. But the next day, I told dad what happened. He got really mad. Not at me. At Ozzie."

"So he went to the faire to confront him," I said, pieces of the picture clicking into place. "And that's how his knuckles got bruised."

Charlotte nodded, her face glum. "So it's my fault he got arrested."

"Of course it's not," I told her.

"If I hadn't told Dad what happened, he wouldn't have punched Ozzie, and the police wouldn't suspect him."

"You did the right thing by telling your dad," I assured her.

"But now he'll go to jail, probably for the rest of his life," she said, her earlier optimism gone.

Both girls started crying again.

I scooted over to the porch swing and sat down next to Bryony, then pulled the girls into a hug. "That's not going to happen," I said, determination building inside me.

Charlotte hiccupped. "How do you know?"

"Because there's no way your dad killed Ozzie Stone," I said. "And I intend to prove it."

Once Charlotte and Bryony's latest round of tears had died down, I wasted no time putting my plan into motion.

"Did you see the plant the police took away in the evidence bag?" I asked the girls. "Do you know what it is?"

Charlotte shook her head, wiping away the last of her tears.

"I don't know what it's called," Bryony said. "But I know where it grows."

"She likes to wander around in the woods." Charlotte made a face. "I'm scared of snakes and spiders, so I stick to the yard."

Bryony rolled her eyes. "It's not like the woods are crawling with hordes of spiders and snakes."

Charlotte shuddered. "Just the thought freaks me out."

"This plant's not even in the woods," Bryony said. "It's in that old garden that Dad keeps meaning to clear out."

My phone chimed, distracting me. Mel had replied to my text, assuring me that she had everything under control at the Inkwell. I sent her another message, telling her I'd get back to the pub as soon as possible. I hadn't given her the reason for my absence. I figured it would be better to break that news to her in person. She'd known Damien longer than I had. Damien wasn't the easiest person to get to know—and neither was

Mel—but they had a solid friendship and a deep respect for one another. The news of Damien's arrest would shock Mel, even if she didn't let it show.

"Do you think you could show me the plant?" I asked Bryony as I set my phone aside.

She nodded and stood up.

"Hold on," I said. "Let's wait until the police are gone."

She dropped back down onto the porch swing.

The three of us sat quietly for the next while, listening to the sounds of the police moving about inside the house.

After what felt like an eternity, the officers traipsed out the front door.

Detective Marquez appeared last and paused on the porch. "We're all done here." She addressed Charlotte. "Is your aunt coming?"

Charlotte nodded, defiance in her eyes as she glared at Marquez.

"One of my officers can stay until she arrives," the detective said.

I saw the alarm that passed over both girls' faces.

"No need," I said quickly. "I'm staying with them."

For a second, it looked as though Detective Marquez wanted to say something more to Damien's daughters, but then she simply nodded and strode over to her unmarked vehicle. I was relieved that the police didn't appear to be taking away any further evidence. Still, the plant might be damaging enough all on its own.

We remained in place until the last car had turned out of the driveway and disappeared.

Bryony jumped to her feet. "Come on. I'll show you now."

She slid her feet into a pair of flip-flops and clattered down the porch steps. Charlotte and I quickly followed after her. She led us all the way to the back of the property, where an overgrown patch of flowers sat between the neatly trimmed lawn and the tree line. She pushed some of the tall flowers aside and stepped in among them, with me right behind her. I glanced back in time to see Charlotte make a face. She hesitated but then joined us in the wild garden.

I saw bee balm and Russian sage growing in the tangle of untamed flowers, but I couldn't identify any of the other plants. I tried not to crush any flowers, and I kept a wary eye out for creepy-crawlies, for my sake as well as Charlotte's. Fortunately, all I spotted were a couple of bumblebees.

We didn't have to go far into the overgrown garden. Within a few feet of the tree line at the back of the property, Bryony stopped and pointed to a green plant with purple flowers in the early stage of blooming. "I'm pretty sure that's what the police had."

I peered at the plant without touching it. "How poisonous is it?"

Bryony shrugged. "I didn't even know it *was* poisonous."

I decided not to touch it. The last thing I wanted to do was accidentally make myself ill, or worse. Instead, I snapped some photos of it with my phone.

"Now what?" Charlotte asked as we made our way back toward the house.

"I'm going to try to identify the plant," I said. "Once I know what it is, I can try to figure out who else might have had access to it, especially among those who didn't like Ozzie. Not all his colleagues were fans of his."

"No wonder," Bryony said with a frown. "What a creep."

"Maybe his girlfriend killed him," Charlotte said as we returned to the front porch.

"You know about his girlfriend?" I asked.

"I only know he had one, because of what his assistant said to Dad."

"Collette, you mean?"

Charlotte shrugged and sat down on the porch swing. "I

don't know her name, but she saw Dad punch Ozzie and tried to calm him down after. She didn't blame him for slugging Ozzie. She said that Ozzie hit on women and girls all the time and wasn't faithful to his girlfriend."

I wondered if Minerva the Mysterious knew that Ozzie wasn't faithful. She'd witnessed him flirting with Rachael after Shontelle had her fortune told, but did she know that was just the tip of the iceberg?

Minerva was familiar with plants and herbs. Flint didn't think she would have killed Ozzie on purpose, but I wasn't ready to take his word for it. In my view, Minerva the Mysterious deserved the number one spot on my list of murder suspects.

Chapter 12

I stayed with Charlotte and Bryony until their aunt Tracey arrived. I gave both girls a hug and asked Charlotte to keep me in the loop about her dad. I hoped his situation would improve soon, but I didn't know how that would happen, unless I could build a strong case against someone else.

After I made the short trip back to the Inkwell, I parked in the small lot at the edge of the pub's property and climbed out of my car, Damien's arrest still consuming my thoughts. The events of the morning had me so distracted that I didn't notice Grayson and his dog, Bowie, walking along Creekside Road until Grayson called my name.

Bowie bounded toward me, and I crouched down and gave him a hug as he wagged his tail. I straightened up in time for Grayson to greet me with a kiss. I was tempted to wrap my arms around him and keep the kiss going, but I was mindful of the fact that Mel had been taking care of the pub on her own for an hour already.

Grayson caught sight of the coffee table as I undid the bungee cords and opened the trunk of my car.

"The table looks fantastic," he said. "And here I thought you'd been off sleuthing."

I leaned against the side of the car and locked my knees to make sure I didn't slide down into a puddle. The events of the morning had suddenly caught up with me, leaving me momentarily overwhelmed.

"Only a bit of sleuthing," I said after taking a second to recover. "And only out of necessity."

"Do you want me to give you a hand getting the table upstairs while you tell me about it?" Grayson asked.

I glanced at my phone. Hopefully, five more minutes away from the pub wouldn't hurt.

"I'll take you up on that offer," I said.

After all, Damien wouldn't be able to help me later in the day, as originally planned.

Together, we maneuvered the coffee table out of the trunk of my car. As we carried it toward the Inkwell, I told Grayson what had transpired at Damien's place.

"Arrested?" Grayson echoed as we set the table down outside the back door of the old gristmill. "*Damien*? Did he even know Ozzie Stone?"

"Their paths crossed."

I opened the door, and we started the slow trek up the stairs to my apartment while I filled Grayson in on what Charlotte had told me about Damien's confrontation with the illusionist.

Bowie remained out on the lawn at first, but when we reached my apartment door, he came trotting up the steps. He squeezed past me and into the apartment.

"Be careful, Bowie," I cautioned the dog. "I'm not sure Wimsey will appreciate a canine intrusion into his domain."

Sure enough, I heard a loud hiss.

I backed into my apartment, holding one end of the table. Wimsey stood on the back of the couch, his hackles up as he stared at Bowie with his blue eyes. Bowie didn't seem the least bit concerned about the cat's less than warm welcome. He was too busy thoroughly investigating every corner of my apartment with his nose.

I sighed with relief when Grayson and I set the heavy table down in front of the couch. I'd already moved the old coffee table into my storage room in anticipation of bringing home the new one.

"Wow," I said as I stepped back. "It looks even better now that it's in place."

"Damien did an amazing job."

The rustic charm of the antique trunk turned coffee table fit perfectly with the overall look of my cozy living space.

Wimsey hopped down to the arm of the couch, taking him closer to Bowie, who was now giving the new coffee table a good sniff. Finally, Bowie took more notice of Wimsey.

I winced as the dog touched his nose to the cat's. To my surprise, Wimsey didn't swat him on the snout. The cat's muscles were tense, but as Bowie gave him a curious sniff and then turned his attention elsewhere, Wimsey slowly relaxed, settling down to lie on the arm of the couch. He still kept his blue gaze fixed on Bowie, but otherwise he no longer seemed bothered by the dog's presence.

At least one thing had gone well today.

I tugged my phone out of the pocket of my shorts and got back to telling Grayson about what had happened to Damien. After relating the story about the plant, I showed him the photos I'd taken.

"Do you know what it is?" I asked, hopeful.

Grayson studied the pictures, swiping from one to the next. "No, but my knowledge of plants is pretty much limited to hops and the herbs I've got growing in pots."

He handed me my phone and called to Bowie. I accompanied them down the stairs and out the back door.

"I'm guessing you don't believe Damien's the killer," Grayson said once outside.

"Of course not."

"So who's your prime suspect?" He grinned. "I know you've got one."

"I do," I admitted. I told him about Minerva the Mysterious, her relationship with Ozzie, and her knowledge of plants and herbs. As I finished relaying all that information, I checked the time on my phone again. I really needed to get to work.

"We can talk about it later," Grayson said before giving me a quick kiss. "Try to stay out of trouble until then."

"I always stay out of trouble."

He nearly choked on his laugh.

I sent him a mock glare. "Don't you need to get back to the brewery?"

He backed away and raised a hand. "Later."

I couldn't keep up the glare any longer, so I ducked inside the door and ran upstairs to change my clothes before getting to work.

I told Mel the news about Damien in whispered snippets when our paths crossed in the kitchen or behind the bar. I filled in Booker as well. Both of them were as convinced as I was of Damien's innocence.

"I hope he's got a good lawyer," Booker said as he slid a tray of bruschetta into the oven.

Mel paused on her way out of the kitchen. "I can put him in touch with one if he doesn't."

Mel had found herself in similar trouble back in the winter. In the end, the police had found the real killer and Mel's name had been cleared. I hoped the same would happen for Damien, and I wanted to do whatever I could to make sure it did. To start, I needed to identify the plant the police had taken away from Damien's property. Unfortunately, Booker didn't recognize it from the photos I'd taken, and neither did Mel.

I spent the rest of the afternoon doing my best to stave off my anxiety about Damien's situation and my own as well. Weekend evenings at the pub tended to be some of our busiest times, and I was now short a bartender. Mel offered to work a double shift, and I really couldn't turn down her offer, but I convinced her to take an hour off before the dinner rush hit.

"Zoe has worked as a bartender and server before," Teagan told me after she'd arrived for her shift and I'd brought her up to date on everything that had transpired. "I bet she wouldn't mind working here in the evenings, at least until Damien gets back."

"That would be amazing," I said with relief.

I'd already started worrying about what I was going to do for the coming week. Mel couldn't work double shifts long term. She was a tough woman, but even she would burn out, especially considering that she had her mural to work on and the girls' boxing class to teach.

Teagan plated two burgers. "Do you want me to ask her?"

"Please do."

I took the plates from her, and she washed her hands so she could text her twin sister. The next time I returned to the kitchen, Teagan had good news for me. Zoe could start work the following evening.

As expected, the pub filled to capacity over the next hour or so. I barely had a chance to worry about anything as I rushed to and fro, making sure all my customers had everything they needed. Business had slowed slightly when my friend Cordelia King arrived, her head of crinkly red hair catching my attention as she entered the pub.

"I came over as soon as I heard," she said as she slipped onto one of only two vacant barstools.

"About Damien?" I asked in a whisper.

In the past half hour I'd noticed a couple of hushed conversations cut off as I passed by groups of locals, and I'd guessed that the news was already out about Damien's arrest.

Cordelia nodded and lowered her voice. "There's no way it was him, right?"

"It definitely wasn't him." I realized I should probably offer to take her order. "Can I get you anything to eat or drink?"

"A Poirot, please."

I grabbed cassis and gin so I could mix her drink.

"I guess you're too busy to chat right now," Cordelia said as I placed her drink on a coaster and slid it across the bar to her.

I ran my gaze over the room. "I might get a spare moment here and there."

A bell dinged in the kitchen.

"Sorry. I'll be right back." I dashed into the kitchen to fetch the meals Teagan had ready.

On my way back from delivering the food to a group of four customers, I took down three drink orders for another table.

The bell dinged in the kitchen again, but this time Mel responded to it, so I focused on mixing drinks.

"Do you know anything about plants?" I asked Cordelia as I worked.

"Sure. I went through a plant-crazy phase in my teens."

"Really?" I wasn't sure if she was joking or not, although she seemed serious.

She nodded and took a sip of her drink. "I wanted to be a botanist when I was fourteen. I still think plants are cool, but I guess I'm just not as passionate about them as I was back then."

I grabbed my cell phone. "Any chance you can identify this?" I showed her the photos I'd taken that morning.

"That's an easy one," she said right away. "Monkshood. Also known as wolfsbane or aconite."

"You're a genius, Cordelia." If not for the bar between us, I would have hugged her.

"Not really. Just a former plant geek."

"It's poisonous, right?" I asked to make sure.

"Definitely." Her blue eyes widened. "Does this have anything to do with . . ." She lowered her voice, so I could barely hear her. "The murder?"

"Yes," I said as I tucked my phone away on a shelf below the bar.

Cordelia's face lit up. "You're on the case. You're going to prove that Damien's innocent."

"That's my hope," I said. "And you've just helped me on my way."

Chapter 13

Cordelia hadn't yet been to the Renaissance faire and didn't want to miss out, so we made arrangements to go together on Monday, my day off. I thought I could wait that long to start looking for clues at the fairgrounds, but by the next morning, I knew that wasn't the case. All I could think about was Damien languishing in jail and his daughters at home without him. It wasn't right, especially since the real killer was still enjoying his or her freedom. That thought sent a shiver down my spine.

I ate a quick breakfast and drank a cup of home-brewed coffee before setting off to the park. I planned to focus my investigation on Minerva the Mysterious, but beyond that, I'd have to play it by ear. Instead of buying a single-day ticket when I reached the gates, I handed over enough money for a pass that would allow me to come and go until the end of the faire. Although I had to hold back a wince as I paid the price, I knew it would likely save me money in the long run, unless I somehow found vital evidence that would lead to the real killer's arrest in short order. If that happened, I'd be so relieved that I wouldn't worry about what I'd paid for the pass.

The faire had opened only a few minutes before I arrived at

the gates, so it wasn't yet crowded. I knew that would likely change before long, since it was a Sunday. Both tourists and locals would probably pour through the gates. Although, maybe interest in the faire had dwindled since it became public knowledge that Ozzie had been murdered. It wouldn't have surprised me if the crime made some people hesitant to attend. Of course, Damien's arrest was also public knowledge now. That might have alleviated such concerns, even though I knew the real culprit was still at large.

I wandered along the grassy walkway, my destination the fortune-teller's tent, where I hoped to find Minerva. On my way there, I noticed Hamish, the musician who'd complained about Ozzie at the pub. He stood near the Mad Hatter hat shop, getting ready to play some music. Toby the juggler strode past me, moving quickly and with purpose. I almost called out a good morning to him, but he didn't so much as glance my way.

A little farther along, I spotted Rachael standing in the narrow alley between two small tents, her cell phone to her ear. Unlike the last time I'd seen her, she wore jeans and a T-shirt rather than a Renaissance costume. She paced up and down the narrow space, running a hand through her hair now and then. I drew to a stop as she jabbed a finger at her phone, ending the call. She let out a sound of exasperation and shoved the device into her pocket.

"I'm guessing it's been a rough few days," I said as she emerged from between the two tents.

It took a second for recognition to show in her eyes. "Sadie, right?" When I nodded, she continued. "You could say that. The faire's owners and sponsors are breathing down my neck. First, they wanted Ozzie's killer caught as soon as possible, and they kept hounding me about it, as if it was *my* job to track down the murderer. Now that the police have caught the guy, everyone keeps pestering me about damage control and the faire's reputation." Her voice rose in pitch with her last words.

"I'm sorry to hear that," I said.

She blew out a breath, and some of her ire seemed to drain away. "Sorry. It's just that I keep getting bombarded with phone calls, from the media too, and I've hardly had any sleep for days." She put a hand to her forehead. "I've got a literal headache from all this."

A woman spoke up from behind me. "I can help you with that."

Minerva joined us, dressed in a full skirt and revealing peasant blouse, accessorized as before with many scarves and bangles. I noticed dark rings beneath her eyes, which hadn't been there before Ozzie's death.

She dabbed at her red eyes with a handkerchief and addressed Rachael. "It's such a difficult time. My poor, dear Ozzie..." She choked back a sob. "I've needed the help of some natural supplements to get to sleep the past few nights myself. I can help you with that, and your headache."

"Didn't the police take all your herbs?" Rachael asked.

Minerva let out a huff of annoyance. "And *still* haven't returned them, even though they've caught the killer now."

I desperately wanted to say that the police didn't have the right man, but I bit my tongue. If Minerva was the murderer, I wanted her to feel safe. I thought I had a better chance of solving the case if the killer wasn't so concerned about getting caught.

Minerva's annoyance disappeared, leaving her looking tired and deflated. "But they didn't take everything. I have another, smaller stash that they know nothing about." She tucked her arm through Rachael's and led her away.

I followed at a distance, not wanting them to notice me. They turned down the narrow space between the two tents and headed away from the main part of the faire and toward the line of trailers at the edge of the park. I hung back and noted that they entered the third trailer from the far end of the line.

Since the police had arrested Damien and not Minerva, maybe they hadn't found monkshood among the herbs they'd seized from her. It was also possible that the police had eliminated her as a suspect because she had an alibi for the time when the killer administered the poison. I'd have to find out if that was the case.

I made a mental note to try to find out how and when the poison was given to Ozzie. That would help me determine who had an opportunity to commit the crime.

For the moment, however, I stayed focused on the fortune-teller and her secret stash. She and Rachael exited the trailer within minutes and paused to chat outside the door. I darted back between the tents and peeked out, watching as they parted ways. Once they had both disappeared from sight, I glanced around. I couldn't see anyone near the trailers, so I decided to take my chance.

It wasn't easy to walk rather than run toward the trailer. I wanted to be as quick as possible, but I figured I was more likely to go unnoticed if I walked casually instead of sprinting. Even though I couldn't see anyone in the vicinity, that didn't mean someone couldn't show up at any second.

When I reached the trailer Minerva and Rachael had entered, I glanced around again. I was still alone. My heart pattered out a nervous beat in my chest, and a small voice in the back of my head told me I should turn around and go home. I ignored it.

I wondered if the door would be locked, but I quickly found out that it wasn't. With one last glance over my shoulder, I slipped inside the trailer and shut the door. I saw immediately that I'd entered somebody's living quarters. More than one person's, judging by the rumpled blankets on the two beds. That made sense. Everyone working for the faire needed somewhere to stay as they traveled from place to place, and I hadn't heard about any of the performers staying at the local hotels or inns. Cordelia certainly would have mentioned it if anyone from the faire had been staying at her grandmother's inn. No doubt the trailers saved significantly on accommodation costs.

It wasn't immediately obvious to me who shared the trailer

with Minerva, but I didn't waste time wondering about that. I needed to conduct my search as quickly as possible. The last thing I wanted was to get caught snooping. I'd probably end up banned from the faire for life, or the police would get called, and Detective Marquez would toss me in jail.

Pushing aside that uneasy thought, I ran my gaze over the trailer's interior, wondering where to start. Someone had left a tote bag on the bench seat by the small table in the kitchen area. I opened it and rummaged around, careful not to disturb the contents more than necessary. I didn't find anything other than items typically found in a woman's purse.

Moving on, I quietly opened and checked all the cupboards, searching for anything that could hold herbs or other natural remedies. One canister appeared promising at first, but when I pried off the lid, I found it contained individually wrapped tea bags.

I turned my attention to the sleeping quarters. Three gauzy scarves lay on top of one of the beds. I dropped down on my hands and knees and peered under the bed. There were two suitcases and a wooden box stuffed into the small space. I knew it wouldn't be easy to maneuver the suitcases out into the open. I barely had room to kneel down in the narrow gap between the two beds. Besides, both suitcases were locked shut, and I hadn't come across a key in my search.

I slid the wooden box out into the open and set it on Minerva's bed. The lid was engraved with a tree, the roots extending down onto the front of the box. Fortunately, the box wasn't locked. I opened the lid and studied the contents. The interior was divided into two sections. Bracelets and bangles of varying colors and designs filled one section, while the other held more than a dozen rings.

Disappointed, I nearly shut the box and put it away, but then I took another look at it. The interior of the box didn't appear to be as deep as it should have been. I grabbed the wooden divider between the bangles and the rings and gave it a wiggle. The bottom lifted up to reveal another compartment below.

"Jackpot," I whispered.

I found several small plastic baggies filled with dried leaves and seeds. Each bag bore a handwritten label. I didn't want to leave any fingerprints on the plastic, in case the leaves and seeds were incriminating evidence, so I fetched a pen I'd noticed on the dining table and used it to nudge the baggies around so I could check each label.

My rising hopes sank back down. I didn't find *monkshood*, *wolfsbane*, or *aconite* written on any of the labels.

I replaced the false bottom and shut the lid. I wiped the box with one of Minerva's scarves, hoping to get rid of my fingerprints, and slid it back under the bed. My search had left me with an aching knee and a growing sense of frustration, but nothing else. I got to my feet and studied the trailer from where I stood, wondering if I should keep searching or give up and head home.

I didn't have a chance to make a decision before someone flung open the trailer door.

Chapter 14

"What are you doing?" The blond-haired girl I'd last seen at the creek stood holding the door open. A split second later, her eyes widened as she recognized me.

"Hey!" I called as she dashed away from the trailer.

I bolted for the door. It slammed shut in my face, narrowly missing my nose. I wrenched it open and burst out into the open. I remembered belatedly that I didn't want to be seen leaving the trailer. Fortunately, there was no one in sight. Not so fortunately, that included the girl, and I had no idea which way she'd gone. If she was the child of one or more of the faire workers, I hoped she wouldn't tell anyone about finding me in the trailer. At least she'd retrieved her shoes from the bank of the creek. I'd seen them on her feet in the split second before she'd dashed away from the door.

Voices drifted toward me, growing louder. Giving myself a mental kick, I hurried away from the trailer and down the narrow space between the two tents. I didn't feel like I was any further ahead with my investigation than when I'd arrived at the faire. Although Minerva's secret stash of natural remedies didn't contain any monkshood, I didn't think she deserved to be struck from my suspect list yet. After all, she could have used up her supply of monkshood when she poisoned Ozzie, or she could have disposed of any leftover parts of the plant so she wouldn't get caught with it.

There was also the possibility that she had procured the monkshood from another source aside from her stash. If the plant grew near Damien's house, maybe it also grew in other parts of Shady Creek. Minerva could have found the plant growing locally and taken only what she needed to carry out her nefarious plan to kill Ozzie. She most likely had the know-how to poison someone with a plant, and she had the strongest motive that I knew of so far.

She had seemed deeply saddened by Ozzie's death, but that could have been an act, and maybe the lack of sleep that had caused the dark circles under her eyes had resulted from stress about possibly getting caught by the police rather than from grief. The problem was that I still had no proof that she was the killer, and without proof, I couldn't clear Damien's name.

When I reached the faire's main walkway, I paused to consider my next move. I'd almost decided to give up on sleuthing for the day when I spotted Rachael again. She was taking small sips of something from an earthenware mug as she stood talking to Hamish, the musician. As I watched, she said a final few words to Hamish and turned my way. I decided to intercept her.

Before I had a chance to say anything, Rachael made a face at the mug in her hand and spoke to me. "I'm really a coffee person, not a tea person."

"But you decided to try something different?" I said.

"It's feverfew tea. Minerva said it would help with my headache. I hope she's right." She began walking slowly, and I fell into step with her.

"I'm sorry things have been so difficult."

She took another sip of tea. "Thanks. I really shouldn't complain. After all, I'm better off than poor Ozzie." She heaved out a deep sigh. "It's still so hard to believe he's gone."

"Were you close to him?" I asked.

"No, not really. Ours was a purely business relationship, and we met only a few months ago. But he was such a large personality, such a major part of my new vision for the faire. And poor Minerva's crushed."

"Even though Ozzie wasn't faithful to her?"

Rachael looked surprised, but only for a moment. "I guess I shouldn't be shocked that his womanizing ways are public knowledge."

"Minerva knows too, right?"

"She does," Rachael said, "but she still loved him, anyway. Passionately, I'd say."

Sometimes passion had a way of erupting into violence.

I didn't say that out loud.

"Do you have any idea who might have killed Ozzie?" I asked instead.

Rachael shot a puzzled glance my way. "The police arrested the man responsible." She stopped in her tracks. "Doesn't he work for you? I was told he was a bartender at the local pub."

"He's one of my employees," I confirmed. "But I don't believe he's the real killer."

"I can understand how it would be hard to believe that of someone you know."

I didn't have any trouble reading between the lines of what she'd said. She believed Damien was guilty and I was in denial. Although that irked me, I couldn't blame her for thinking that way.

I decided to change the subject.

"I keep running into a young girl," I said. "Here at the faire and around town. No one seems to know who she is. I wondered if maybe she's the child of someone who works at the faire? She's about eight or nine, with long, wavy blond hair."

"I think I know who you mean. I've seen a girl matching that description a few times since we arrived in town. She's not connected to the faire in any way. No one here brought their kids along."

It seemed I wasn't destined to make any progress with that mystery today either.

Rachael's cell phone rang, and she excused herself so she could take the call. I wandered around the faire for a while longer, but I didn't see anyone I recognized, and I couldn't think of a way to move my investigation forward.

Leaving the park behind, I decided to use what little free time I had left to drop in at the Spirit Hill Brewery. Hopefully, Grayson wouldn't be too busy for a short visit.

The long driveway leading to the brewery was bordered on both sides by woodland, and birds sang cheery songs from their perches in the trees. I enjoyed the walk up the hill, until a tour bus rumbled up behind me and I had to jump into a thimbleberry bush to get out of the way.

The bus left behind a cloud of exhaust fumes, which sent me into a coughing fit. When I had recovered and had disentangled myself from the undergrowth at the edge of the tree line, I continued on my way. I bypassed the branch of the driveway that led to Grayson's house, and continued on to the brewery buildings. By the time I reached the nearly packed parking lot, the tourists had already disembarked from the bus. The group of at least two dozen people swarmed toward the tasting room. If Grayson was working in there, I'd be lucky to say two words to him.

Hoping I'd find him elsewhere, I decided to check his office, located in a separate building from the tasting room. A couple of tourists stood by a rack of brochures inside the main office, and the brewery's receptionist, Annalisa, was on the phone.

She sent a smile my way as she continued speaking into the phone.

I mouthed Grayson's name, and she pointed toward his office. I sidestepped around the tourists and made my way through the reception area.

Grayson's door stood ajar, so I peeked into the office, only to find it empty.

Something brushed against my shoulder. I almost shrieked with surprise. I whirled around to find Grayson standing right behind me.

"Sorry," he said with a grin. "I didn't mean to startle you."

"Really?" I asked, doubting the truth of that statement.

His grin widened. "Okay, so maybe I did."

"I'm so glad I amuse you," I said with a huff as I walked into his office.

"Don't be mad." He followed me into the room and shut the door before setting his cell phone on his desk. "I saw you sneaking into my office and couldn't resist."

"I wasn't sneaking!"

He pulled me into his arms. "I'm teasing. Let me make it up to you."

I wasn't really annoyed with him, but I let him make it up to me, anyway.

"I'm glad you stopped by," he whispered into my ear a couple of minutes later.

Or maybe it was five minutes later. I'd completely lost track of time.

He ran a hand through my hair and held up a twig. "Were you out for a nature walk?"

"I may have tangled with some plants when a tour bus passed me on the driveway," I said.

Grayson dropped the twig in the wastepaper basket next to his desk. "And the dust bunny?" He plucked one from my hair.

I ran a hand over my head, wondering if I'd picked up anything else since I'd left home that morning. "That came from . . . elsewhere."

"Elsewhere, as in somewhere you shouldn't have been?"

"Why would you say that?" I asked, only the tiniest bit indignant. I would have been more indignant if I didn't strongly suspect I'd picked up the dust bunny while snooping under Minerva's bed.

"Because you're Sadie Coleman, on occasion also known as—"

"Don't say it," I warned, knowing he was going to call me a Nosey Parker.

"A supersleuth."

"Nice save," I said, sliding my arms around him.

Grayson's grin faded. "Any news about Damien?"

"Not yet." I sighed and leaned against him. "And my search for clues has come up empty so far."

"So you *were* searching for clues," he said. "I hope you didn't get caught snooping."

"I'm too good to get caught."

Grayson laughed.

"Hey!" I pulled back from him.

"Do I need to remind you about that time you were snooping around my house?" Grayson asked, on the verge of laughter again. "Or how about that time—"

"Okay, okay," I interrupted, hoping to stop him.

The truth was I didn't have a great track record when it came to snooping without getting caught, but I didn't need him to list every occasion he knew about. I also didn't need to tell him about the mystery girl catching me in Minerva's trailer.

"If you want me to get better at snooping, you should share a few trade secrets," I said.

Before becoming a craft brewer, Grayson had worked as a private detective.

"You still haven't shown me how to pick a lock," I reminded him.

"And I'm not going to. That would just open the door to a whole lot more trouble for you." He tugged me closer and looked right into my eyes. "But I'm happy to share secrets of a different sort with you."

My heart set off at a gallop. I held my breath, waiting to hear what he'd say next.

Someone knocked on the office door.

I sprang back from Grayson as he called, "Come in."

Annalisa poked her head into the room. "Mr. Decker is here."

"Thank you," Grayson said. "I'll be two minutes."

Annalisa retreated, closing the door behind her.

My cheeks were hot and most likely bright red. I hoped Annalisa hadn't noticed. Otherwise, she might have wondered what she'd interrupted.

I wished *I* knew what she'd interrupted, but the moment had passed. Whatever Grayson had been about to say, it would likely remain a secret. For now, at least.

"I'd better go," I said, already heading for the door.

"Hey." Grayson caught hold of my hand, stopping me. "I looked into your prime suspect."

"Minerva the Mysterious?"

"Turns out her real name is Mina Young. She's a successful medium. In fact, she makes quite a bit of money that way, so I'm not sure why she's working at a Renaissance faire."

I considered that. "I wonder if she followed Ozzie to the faire."

"Could be. It's her first year with the fortune-telling gig."

"Did you find out anything else?" I'd always been impressed with the information Grayson could come up with.

"Not much. She has a lot of fans who swear she can contact the dead, but she also has her critics. She's been called a fraud and a con artist by more than one person."

"Hmm. If someone thinks Minerva conned them out of money, that would give them a motive to kill her, not Ozzie."

"Speaking of Ozzie," Grayson said. "He used a stage name too."

"Really?"

"Oscar Stein is his real name. He received some hate mail recently, when the faire was in New Hampshire. The manager reported it to the police."

"Any idea who sent the hate mail?" I asked. "Or the contents of it?"

"It was anonymous, but there's someone else who might be able to answer your other question."

"The faire's manager," I said. "Rachael."

I knew our two minutes had passed. "I'd better get going." I tried not to let my reluctance show.

"How about a barbecue tomorrow evening?" Grayson asked.

I smiled and kissed him, happy to know I'd see him again soon. "It's a date."

Chapter 15

An opportunity to speak with Rachael again arose sooner than I expected. I thought I'd have to wait until I returned to the faire with Cordelia on Monday, but the faire's manager showed up at the Inkwell with Shontelle on Sunday evening.

Shontelle waved at me as the two of them claimed a table on the far side of the room. I waved back but couldn't approach them right away, since I was in the middle of mixing two Secret Life of Daiquiris cocktails.

Mel had worked an extra hour after the end of her shift, helping Zoe get settled into her new job. Fortunately, Teagan's twin sister hadn't required much training. With her past experience, all she really needed to learn now was how to make some of the Inkwell's signature cocktails. Until she had them memorized, I'd given her the recipes to consult. She'd already proved to be a great help, and that eased some of my anxiety about Damien's absence.

I'd contacted Charlotte earlier in the day, and she had told me that Damien was still in police custody but would be having a bail hearing on Monday. She'd promised to update me after it was over. I hoped fiercely that Damien would be released on bail, especially for the sake of his daughters. It didn't look as though I'd be able to clear his name as soon as I'd hoped, but even getting released on bail would be better than languishing in a prison cell while I continued to hunt for the killer.

I wouldn't have felt quite as bad about the slow progress of my investigation if I'd known the police were still working to solve the crime too, but with Damien locked up, the police thought the case was closed. That meant I was on my own. Well, not completely, I remembered. I had Grayson helping me out.

After I'd delivered the daiquiris to the women who'd ordered them, I headed for Shontelle and Rachael's table.

"Evening, ladies," I greeted. "I'm glad you came by."

"Rachael needed a break from the faire," Shontelle said, sending a sympathetic glance at her friend across the table.

"And we have years to catch up on," Rachael added.

"Do you need more time, or are you ready to order?" I asked.

"There are so many good things on the menu," Rachael said, setting down her copy. "But after consulting with Shontelle, I've decided to have the Happily Ever After cocktail and the cold soup. It sounds delicious."

"It is," Shontelle assured her.

The cold soup was a recent addition to the menu, and it had proven popular with the Inkwell's customers since the arrival of the hot summer weather.

"And I'll have the Red Cabbage of Courage salad and the same cocktail as Rachael," Shontelle said.

"The food won't be long," I told them. "And I'll be right back with your drinks."

I relayed their orders to the kitchen and then got their drinks ready. I dropped the cocktails off at their table before veering off to take an order from a group of four. By the time I'd mixed more drinks, Teagan had Shontelle and Rachael's food ready.

"Sadie, why don't you join us for a few minutes?" Shontelle suggested as I set their plates on the table. "We were just talking about Ozzie."

I could have hugged her. I'd kept her up to date on Damien's plight via text messages, and I'd also mentioned that I hoped to clear his name. That hadn't come as a surprise to her, considering my history, and now she was helping me without even being asked. She knew I'd want to see if Rachael had any valuable information that would help my investigation, and she'd opened that door for me.

The Inkwell was busy, but not overwhelmingly so. I figured I could spare some time, especially if it could help me with clearing Damien's name.

I pulled out one of the free chairs at the table. "What are you going to do now that one of the faire's main attractions is gone?"

Rachael sighed and took a long sip of her cocktail, which was already more than half gone. "That's the same question my bosses and the faire's sponsors have been asking every day since Ozzie died."

"Sorry," I said quickly, hoping I hadn't already made a misstep.

Rachael waved off my apology. "It's fine. I just don't have a concrete answer yet. We've got another magician, Toby, who's been working as a juggler. If he ups his game, I might give him his own show on a trial basis, but he doesn't have Ozzie's star power."

"I'm guessing not many people do," Shontelle said.

"That's the truth." Rachael took another sip of her drink and then dipped her spoon into her soup.

I tried to steer the conversation in a more beneficial direction. "I know Ozzie had a lot of fans, but I've heard that some people who knew him weren't nearly as enthralled."

"Also true." Rachael pointed at her soup with her spoon.

"This is fantastic, by the way. So's the drink." She eyed her nearly empty glass.

"I can get you another when you're done with that one," I said.

She smiled. "That would be great. Anyway, there's bound to be some petty jealousy when a charming, attractive man is also highly successful."

"Who was jealous of him?" Shontelle asked.

I shot her a grateful glance, and she sent me a knowing smile in response.

"Toby, for starters. The other magician I mentioned. He hasn't got Ozzie's looks, talent, or flair, and he knows it. There's no way he can fill Ozzie's shoes, but I might have to give him a chance to try. I don't have any other options at the moment." Rachael drained the last of her drink. "And, of course, there's Hamish. He's one of our minstrels."

"Why would a minstrel be jealous of an illusionist?" I asked.

"Hamish used to date Minerva before she worked at the faire, but then she met Ozzie . . ."

"And dumped Hamish," I guessed.

Rachael nodded. "Ozzie sure did have a way with the ladies."

Judging by the way I'd seen Rachael respond to attention from Ozzie, she hadn't been immune to the illusionist's charms.

"Is that why Minerva joined the faire?" I asked. "Because of Ozzie? I heard she has a successful career as a medium outside of the faire."

"I'm pretty sure that's why she snapped up the job when I offered it to her," Rachael said.

"You got along well with Ozzie, didn't you?" Shontelle asked Rachael as she dug her fork into her salad.

"Sure. He was easy enough to work with, most of the time. And he was fun to have around. Now that he's gone . . ." Her expression darkened. "I really think my job could be in jeopardy."

"But it's not your fault someone killed him." Shontelle sounded indignant on her friend's behalf. "Why would your bosses blame you?"

"It's all about damage control," Rachael said. "And making sure the faire doesn't lose money without Ozzie to draw in the crowds. I'm not sure I can do that, but I'll give it my best shot."

"Maybe you can find another high-profile performer to bring in," Shontelle said. "Any chance of that?"

"I'm trying, but at this point it's looking like Toby might be my only option." That thought seemed to depress Rachael.

I decided I needed to get the conversation back on course. "I heard Ozzie received hate mail recently."

"Seriously?" Shontelle looked to Rachael for confirmation.

"How did you hear about that?" Rachael asked me.

"Oh . . ." I faltered, not wanting to reveal that Grayson had done some digging into Ozzie's background. "I think I read it online somewhere."

She seemed to accept that response. "Anyway, it's true." She eyed her empty glass, but I pretended not to notice. "That's not so strange, though. Ozzie was a rising star. Lots of people in the public eye get hate mail. You wouldn't believe how many crazies are out there."

"So he'd received hate mail before New Hampshire?" I asked.

Rachael shrugged. "Once or twice, I think. He didn't seem worried about it. I reported it the last time, but I don't think the police ever figured out who was behind it."

"Did the hate mail contain threats?" Shontelle asked.

"I guess you could say that." Rachael paused to eat a spoonful of soup. "The notes I saw basically said that Ozzie was a terrible person and would get what he deserved."

I'd hoped the contents were more specific, perhaps containing a clue to the identity of the author. "Were they hand-delivered notes or sent by mail?"

"Hand delivered. Ozzie found them stashed in among his stuff. Once in his trailer and once backstage."

"That doesn't sound like hate mail from some crazy stranger," I said. "That sounds like it came from someone close by. Maybe someone working at the faire."

Rachael's gaze held a mixture of annoyance and pity when she fixed it on me. "I get that you don't want to believe your employee is a murderer, but the case is closed. I don't think the hate mail is connected to Ozzie's death."

I didn't think I'd gain anything by arguing with her. I pushed back my chair. "I'll refill your drink."

Rachael perked up at that and nudged her empty glass toward me.

"I'm glad it wasn't Flint's brother who killed Ozzie," she said as I left the table.

I swung back around. "Matt? Why would Matt want to kill Ozzie?"

"They got into a fistfight a few weeks ago, when Matt was visiting Flint." Rachael turned her attention back to Shontelle. "Have you stayed in touch with Kelly?"

Shontelle sent me a glance that told me she was as surprised by the information about Matt as I was. She nevertheless managed to refocus on the conversation and answer Rachael's question. I left them to their chat, my thoughts spinning like some crazy carnival ride.

I hadn't even known that Matt knew Ozzie. Of course, there wasn't any real reason why I should have known that. Matt had been attending the science fiction and fantasy book club meetings for months now and had always struck me as a nice guy. I had trouble picturing him as a killer, but clearly something had angered him enough to engage in a fight with Ozzie.

Although that news had knocked me off-kilter, I forced myself to focus while mixing drinks for Rachael and a couple of other customers. When I returned to Shontelle and Rachael's table with another glass of Happily Ever After, they'd shifted the conversation to Minerva.

"She claimed she could communicate with the dead," Shontelle was saying. "She gave me a business card in case I wanted to get in touch with anyone on the other side. Then she said a dead relative of mine had a message for me. I wasn't sure if I should take her seriously, especially after she made it clear that receiving the message through her would cost more than I'd already paid to have my fortune read."

Rachael flashed me a smile of thanks as I set her new drink in front of her. "You were right to be skeptical," she told Shontelle. "Minerva can't really communicate with the dead. She's just very good at convincing people that she can."

"How does she do it?" I asked, lingering by their table.

"She's incredibly perceptive, I'll give her that," Rachael said. "She can read anyone like an open book. Plus, for her regular work as a medium, she requires clients to make appointments. That way she has a chance to research them beforehand."

That sounded sneaky to me. "She's admitted to that?"

"No, but I'm pretty sure that's how she works."

"And yet you hired her, anyway."

"She's very good at what she does."

"You mean conning people?" I asked.

Rachael's eyes darkened. "Some people might see it that way. Others would say it's entertainment."

Shontelle hadn't missed the change in Rachael's mood and quickly moved on to a new subject. "How's your mother doing these days?"

Sadness replaced the irritation on Rachael's face. "She passed away last year."

"Oh no." Shontelle reached across the table and squeezed Rachael's hand. "I'm so sorry."

I decided it would be best for me to leave them alone. I edged away from their table and turned my attention to the pub's other customers.

Whenever I had a moment to think, I pondered my conversation with Rachael and Shontelle. I still had Minerva placed firmly in the number one spot on my suspect list, but now I had three more names to add beneath hers: Hamish, Toby, and—unfortunately—Matt.

Chapter 16

When I stepped outside the next morning, I immediately felt underdressed in my denim shorts and T-shirt. Cordelia was crossing the footbridge, coming my way and looking like she'd stepped out of another time period. She wore a full-length dress made from emerald-green velvet, with brocade ribbon trim and inset brocade panels in the front of the skirt. The dress had trumpet sleeves and gold ribbon crisscrossed down the front of the bodice. A matching gold headband was nestled in her crinkly red hair. With the morning sun shining down on her, an almost ethereal glow enveloped her.

"You look gorgeous!" I called out as I locked the Inkwell's door behind me.

Cordelia's cheeks turned pink. "Do you really think so?"

"Absolutely! That dress suits you perfectly."

She beamed, clearly pleased. "Gran thought I was wasting my money when I ordered it online, but I couldn't resist. I figure I can use it for Halloween as well."

"Definitely."

"Maybe for the Shakespeare trivia night too."

"That would be perfect," I said.

The Inkwell would be hosting the Shakespeare trivia night at the end of the week. There would be prizes for the trivia contest as well as for the best Shakespeare-inspired costume. I hoped the event would be a success.

I hooked my arm through Cordelia's, and we headed for the road.

"I feel like a scantily clad peasant next to you."

"You don't need to worry," she assured me. "You always look great."

"I don't know about that, but thank you."

Cordelia's skirt swished around her legs as we walked toward the park. "Is Damien still in jail?"

"Unfortunately." I checked my phone, but I didn't have any new messages. "The bail hearing is today. His daughter Charlotte said she'd let me know what happens."

We waited for a car to pass before we crossed the road.

"Are you close to fingering the real culprit?" Cordelia asked.

"It sure doesn't feel like it." I told her what I knew about Minerva, and the fact that I couldn't prove she'd killed Ozzie. Then I filled her in on my other suspects.

"Matt Yanders?" she echoed with surprise when I mentioned his name.

"I was as shocked as you are when Rachael mentioned that Matt had fought with Ozzie a few weeks ago. I have a hard time picturing Matt killing anyone, but I at least want to find out what the fight was about."

Cordelia nodded with approval. "You can't leave any stone unturned."

We cut off our conversation when we reached the faire gates. I used the pass I'd purchased before to gain entry and waited while Cordelia bought a ticket for the day.

"This is so cool!" Cordelia enthused as we made our way along the faire's main walkway, her wide eyes taking in everything around us.

"Hey, look who's here," I said, spotting a familiar face.

Joey Fontana stood near the tavern, talking with Rachael, who was back in her Renaissance costume. Joey co-owned the local newspaper, the *Shady Creek Tribune*, with his father, and he wrote most of the content for the paper. He stopped by the Inkwell now and then, and we'd become friends over the past year.

"Joey!" I hailed him once he'd turned away from Rachael.

He grinned when he saw us and headed our way.

"Hey, Sadie." His gaze shifted to Cordelia, and his dark eyes widened. "Cordelia? Whoa. You look amazing."

This time Cordelia's cheeks turned bright red. "Thank you."

"Since you were chatting with the faire's manager, I'm guessing you're here in an official capacity, right?" I said to Joey.

He raked a hand through his dark hair. "I'm working on a follow-up story to the one I printed last week about Ozzie's death. A lot has happened since then."

"Because now it's known he was murdered," Cordelia said.

Joey rubbed the back of his neck. "And the police have arrested someone." He wouldn't meet my eyes.

"Do you have to mention Damien's name?" I asked.

"You know I do." Joey flicked his gaze my way for a split second. "Besides, everyone in town already knows about his arrest."

That was most likely true. Even so, seeing the news about Damien's arrest in black and white wouldn't be pleasant, especially for his daughters.

"Damien's innocent." I couldn't keep myself from pointing that out.

Joey raised his hands as if in surrender. "I'm not going to say he's guilty, just that he was arrested for the crime. I'm also trying to get some background information on Ozzie. I looked him up online, of course, but now I'm talking to people who knew him personally."

"Then maybe you know by now that plenty of people didn't like him and had a motive to kill him," I said.

Joey finally stopped avoiding my gaze. "I know he had a way with the ladies. Do you think one of them killed him after he broke their heart?"

"It's possible," I said.

I almost asked if he knew about the incident with Charlotte, the one that had led Damien to confront Ozzie, but I stopped myself. If Joey didn't know those details, I didn't want to give them to him. Charlotte already had enough to deal with without her unpleasant experience getting documented in the newspaper for all to see.

I also considered sharing my list of suspects with Joey but then decided not to. At least, not yet. I didn't want my thoughts made public until I'd had more of a chance to dig up the proof I needed to clear Damien's name and finger the real culprit. I especially didn't want to throw Matt under the bus. Since he was a local, that might cause serious damage to his business and reputation.

Joey checked his phone. "I've got to run." He addressed Cordelia. "Do you mind if I get your picture? I'm also writing a piece about the faire."

Cordelia's cheeks brightened yet again. "Maybe if Sadie's in the picture with me . . ."

"I'm not in costume." I grabbed her hand and steered her a few feet to the left so she was standing with one of the thatched huts in the background. "Stay right here."

Cordelia did as I told her, but she didn't seem too certain. "I don't know. I'm not very photogenic."

"Are you kidding?" Joey raised his phone. "Smile."

Cordelia flashed a smile, even though her eyes still held uncertainty.

"Perfect," Joey said as he studied the picture he'd snapped.

"See? Painless," I told Cordelia.

"Are you really going to print that in the paper?" she asked Joey with trepidation.

"Not if you don't want me to, but it's an awesome picture."
He showed her the photo.

"You really do look great, Cordelia," I said.

"Well . . ." She wavered. "All right."

Joey grinned and tucked his phone away. "Great! See you later!"

He jogged off toward the gates.

"Hail and well met, fair maidens!" a man said from behind us.
We turned to find Flint grinning at us, wearing his full costume, as usual.

He took my hand and kissed it. "My lady, 'tis most splendid to cross paths with thee again."

"Hi, Flint," I said, smiling.

He turned his attention to Cordelia. "Fair lady, mine eyes doth taketh interest in thee. What be thy tide?"

"This is my friend Cordelia," I said, hoping I was right in guessing that he'd asked her name.

He kissed Cordelia's hand, causing her to blush yet again. "Thou art most beauteous fair."

"Gramercy," she said, dipping into a curtsey.

"Flint, can we talk in modern English for a minute?" I asked. "It's about your brother."

Flint moved a few steps off to the side, away from the other fairgoers. Cordelia and I followed him.

"What about Matt?" His face had gone serious.

"I heard he got into a fight with Ozzie when he was visiting you a few weeks ago," I said.

Flint untied the laces on his left arm bracer and proceeded to tighten them. "They threw one punch each before I dragged Matt away. Why are you asking about it?" He didn't seem angry about my question, but maybe he was a bit perplexed.

"I'm worried that Matt could have been angry enough with Ozzie to have a motive to kill him," I said.

Now Flint looked even more puzzled. "The police already arrested the killer. And Matt wouldn't kill anyone, anyway."

"The man who was arrested is one of my employees and a friend," I said. "I know he's innocent, and I'm hoping to prove it. But I don't want Matt to end up in trouble if I do manage to clear Damien's name."

Flint considered what I'd said. "The night of the fight, a bunch of us went out for drinks. Matt asked one of the mermaids to go with him. She said yes, but then after an hour at the bar, she left with another man. Ozzie rubbed it in Matt's face and wouldn't let it drop. After a while, Matt had had enough. So had I, to be honest. If Matt hadn't decked the guy, I might have. I bet Matt has an alibi, though. He was probably at his restaurant when Ozzie was killed."

"I hope you're right."

I didn't think it would be too hard to confirm that. It would be a relief if I could scratch Matt's name from my suspect list.

A group of four women with their phones out had spotted Flint and hurried over our way.

He gave them his most charming smile before saying to us, "Fare thee well. I must away."

He met up with the women and posed for pictures.

"I really hope it wasn't Matt who killed Ozzie," Cordelia said in a low voice as we walked away.

"Me too."

We spent the next hour or so simply enjoying the faire. We watched a glassblowing demonstration and a jousting match. We also browsed the vendors' wares and made a few purchases. I bought some handmade soap for my mom and Aunt Gilda and a pretty bracelet that I planned to give to Shontelle for Christmas.

After having something to eat, we attended the acrobats' show, since Cordelia hadn't seen it yet. As the show drew to a close, I noticed the blond-haired girl lurking behind the bleachers again.

"I'll meet you out in front of the tent in a few minutes," I whispered to Cordelia.

I dashed down from my seat and behind the bleachers as the rest of the audience got to their feet, ready to make their way out of the tent. I jogged around the perimeter of the tent, past two sets of bleachers. Up ahead of me, I spotted the girl crawling beneath a loose part of the tent wall. I hesitated for a split second before dropping to my knees and following her. It was a tight squeeze, but I made it out into the open.

Fortunately, I was near the back of the tent, away from the crowds, with no one watching me. The only person in sight on the other side was my quarry.

"Hey," I called to her as I got to my feet.

She swung around, and her eyes widened.

"Wait!" I said, knowing she was about to bolt. "You're not in trouble. I just want to talk to you."

The girl eyed me warily, still on the verge of making a run for it, but she stayed put.

"I'm Sadie. Do you live in Shady Creek?"

It took a moment, but the girl eventually nodded.

"I'm guessing you like to paint, right?"

The fear in her eyes intensified, so I quickly tried to put her at ease.

"I don't want to get you in trouble," I assured her. "A friend of mine might start a program at the community center, where kids can paint murals on the back fence. I thought maybe you'd like to be involved."

She bit down on her lower lip and thought for a second or two. "Really?"

Cautious hope and interest had replaced the fear in her eyes.

"I don't know if it will happen for sure, but it might. If I could tell my friend where to contact you, she could let you know if and when it happens."

The tension disappeared from the girl's stance. "Okay." She perked up. "I'm Tilly."

I smiled. "Nice to meet you, Tilly. Are you new to town?" I

figured there was a good chance of that, since Betty and Gilda didn't know who she was, and they'd both lived in Shady Creek far longer than I had.

Tilly nodded. "Me and my mom moved here at the beginning of the summer. My mom makes stuff."

"What kind of stuff?" I asked.

"Pottery. Plates, mugs, vases, lots of stuff."

"What's her name?"

"Tamara," Tilly said. "Tamara Wilburn. My last name's Wilburn too. My daddy died when I was three. My mom had a boyfriend, but he was a cheating jerk, so we moved here for a new start. We live on Larkspur Lane."

She'd gone from wary to chatty in the space of a few seconds.

"I hope I'll get to meet your mom sometime soon," I said before changing the subject. "Last week, the illusionist chased you out of the big tent where he had his shows. What were you doing in there?"

Tilly cast her gaze down toward her feet. "I just wanted to look at the costumes." She raised her eyes. "Have you seen the way his assistant can change from dress to dress? It's magic!"

"I did see that," I said, "and it really is impressive."

Her enthusiasm faded away. "I didn't get to see the costumes." She perked up again. "I tried on Ozzie's hat, though. He was too busy arguing to notice me at first, but then he caught me trying to open the trunk where he kept all his magic stuff."

"Who was he arguing with?" I thought I already knew.

"His assistant."

Then I was right in guessing that the argument was the same one Grayson and I had witnessed the tail end of.

"She's an acrobat too," Tilly added. "That's so cool."

I agreed with her assessment. "Do you know what they were arguing about?" I hadn't heard any of the exchange on the day of the argument, but since it had taken place shortly before Ozzie's death, I wondered if it could be relevant to his murder.

"The fortune-teller."

"Minerva the Mysterious?"

Tilly nodded and lowered her voice. "Did you know she was Ozzie's girlfriend?"

"I'd heard that," I said. "But why were they arguing about Minerva?"

Tilly shrugged. "Ozzie's assistant called Minerva a fraud. She was really mad. Ozzie joked about it, and that made her angrier. I don't really remember what else they said."

No doubt she'd been far more interested in Ozzie's props than the adults' argument.

"Ozzie was a cheating jerk, though," Tilly said. "Just like my mom's ex-boyfriend."

"How do you know that?" I hoped she hadn't witnessed more than a child her age should.

"I saw him kissing one of the mermaids! Except, she's not *really* a mermaid. It's just a costume. She wasn't wearing her tail when she was kissing Ozzie. She's my favorite mermaid. Her name's Jasmine. She's really pretty." Tilly shifted from one foot to the other, as if she couldn't bear standing still any longer. "I really want to go see the mermaids now."

"Okay," I said, still processing everything she'd just told me.

"Bye!" Tilly dashed away and was gone from sight in an instant.

I remained in place for several seconds, my thoughts swirling like leaves caught in a whirlwind. Then I forced myself to move, remembering that Cordelia would be waiting for me.

Chapter 17

I brought Cordelia up to speed on why I'd dashed off after the show without her and what Tilly had told me about Ozzie, Collette, Minerva, and the mermaid named Jasmine. As I shared the information, we slowly made our way in the direction of the mermaid tank.

"If Collette was mad at Minerva, then why kill Ozzie?" Cordelia asked once I'd told her everything. "Even if Ozzie made her angrier by making light of Collette's complaint, or whatever he did, it still seems like Collette would have been more likely to kill Minerva, not Ozzie. Unless she struck out at him in the heat of the moment."

"Exactly." I'd had those same thoughts. "Collette and Ozzie's argument took place shortly before the show started."

Cordelia picked up where I'd left off. "And the poison could have been administered before the show."

"I wish I knew precisely when and how he'd been poisoned," I said. "But since I don't, I'm adding Collette to my suspect list. Maybe she poisoned Ozzie before the show started, while she was still fuming, and it took a while to take effect." Something else occurred to me. "Maybe she even hoped to frame Minerva for the crime."

"Kill two birds with one stone?"

"It's possible." I turned that over in my mind. "Collette probably knew that Minerva has a stash of natural remedies."

"Was that common knowledge among the people who work for the faire?" Cordelia asked.

"I think so, and I can probably find out for sure." That would likely take only a question or two directed at the right person. Flint perhaps. Or Rachael. They were both aware of Minerva's herb collection and might know if it was common knowledge.

We arrived at the big tank of water, where about a dozen people stood admiring the two swimming mermaids. One wore an iridescent purple tail, and the other mermaid's tail shimmered with shades of green and pink. I wondered which one was Jasmine. Maybe neither, if there were more than two mermaids working different swimming shifts. Tilly could have told me, but she must have already moved on to another part of the faire. She wasn't anywhere in sight.

I hadn't asked her if she had a pass to get into the faire legitimately. It wouldn't have surprised me if she didn't, since she seemed to have a habit of sneaking into the various shows without a ticket. I wondered if her mom knew what she was up to. Tilly seemed to roam freely, and I'd never seen her in the company of an adult, or anyone for that matter. I filed those thoughts away for another time.

"Wow." Cordelia moved closer to the tank for a better view. "They really do look like mermaids."

I had to agree that the fake tails were quite convincing. The only crack in the illusion was caused by the fact that the women had to swim frequently through the tunnel and out of sight, no doubt to breathe in some oxygen.

Some of the other onlookers were posing for photos with the mermaids in the background, so Cordelia and I did the same.

"I'm really regretting wearing this costume now," Cordelia said once we'd taken each other's photos. "I'm sweltering."

"Do you want to get a cold drink?" I asked. "Or would you rather head home?"

"I guess I should go home and change into something cooler before I faint, but maybe we can grab drinks to take with us?"

"That sounds like a good idea." Although I was feeling only slightly hotter than pleasantly warm, I was getting thirsty. I didn't envy Cordelia in her long-sleeved dress. She looked amazing, but her face was flushed, and she reminded me of a wilting flower.

We purchased frozen lemonades from a vendor near the gates and then left the park, walking in the shade whenever possible.

"Will you be at the writers' group meeting tomorrow night?" I asked Cordelia as we reached Creekside Road.

I'd started out hosting book clubs at the Inkwell, but after I'd realized that we had some aspiring writers in town, I'd helped create a writers' group that could meet at the pub too. Cordelia had been working on her first novel for the past few months, a gothic mystery. As curious as I was to know more about her book, she hadn't shared many details with me yet.

"I'll definitely be there," she said. "I'm hoping to finish up another chapter tonight. Then I have only a few left to go."

"I'm so impressed that you've nearly written an entire book," I told her. "What's the reception been like with the group?"

Cordelia stared down at the cold drink in her hands. "I haven't actually shared any of it with the other group members yet."

"None of it?"

She shook her head and took a long drink of her lemonade. "I'm too nervous. What if they hate it?"

"I'm sure they wouldn't hate it. Everyone in the group seems supportive of each other, don't they?" That was what I'd heard from the other members.

"They're all great," Cordelia confirmed. "But up until a couple of months ago, I'd never even told anyone I was writing a book. The thought of actually sharing my words is terrifying."

"If you want to share with just one person to start, I'd love to read it."

"Thanks, Sadie. I'm not sure I'm brave enough yet, but if I get there, you'll be the first to know."

"With you being a mystery writer, you might have a better chance of figuring out who killed Ozzie than I do."

Cordelia's blue eyes widened. "No way! I'm not brave enough to go around digging up clues like you do."

"You mean you're not nosey enough to snoop into things that aren't any of your business," I said.

"I didn't mean that!" She looked horrified by the thought of me thinking she had.

I put an arm around her and gave her a squeeze. "Relax. I know you didn't. But I really am nosey. I can't deny it."

"Well, it served you, and others, well in the past," she said. "I'm sure it will do the same for Damien."

"I hope you're right about that."

Chapter 18

That afternoon I was relaxing in my lounge chair out on the lawn, reading a cozy mystery by Christin Brecher and sipping an Evil Stepmother mocktail, when I heard Shontelle call out, "Hey, Sadie!"

I looked up from my book to see her coming across the footbridge, Kiandra running ahead of her.

"This is a nice surprise." I set my book aside and pushed my sunglasses up on my head.

"I was hoping you might be free for a chat," Shontelle said.

"You have good timing. I was at the faire with Cordelia this morning, and I'm heading over to Grayson's later, but my afternoon is all free."

"Sadie, watch this!" Kiandra called out. She executed a perfect one-handed cartwheel on the grass.

"Nice!"

Kiandra did another cartwheel and then spotted Wimsey on one of the barrels by the front door to the pub. She cartwheeled her way over to see him.

"Can I get you something to drink?" I asked Shontelle.

She eyed my glass. "Sure. I'll have what you're having. Evil Stepmother, right?"

"Yes, the mocktail version. What about you, Kiandra? Would you like something to drink?"

She glanced up from petting Wimsey. "Yes, please! Could I have A Midsummer Night's Cream?"

"That's basically dessert in a glass," Shontelle said.

Kiandra's smile was almost as bright as the sun. "Exactly."

"Sadie might not have all the ingredients ready for that one."

"I do," I assured Shontelle. "I'm happy to make one if it's okay with you."

"Please, Mom," Kiandra pleaded.

"All right," Shontelle said, relenting. "But don't be asking me for ice cream on the way home, then."

"I won't." Kiandra's smile turned cheeky. "I'll wait until we're *at* home."

I laughed as Shontelle rolled her eyes. I grabbed my half-full glass, and the three of us headed inside. Wimsey stayed put on his barrel. It took only a minute to mix up Shontelle's mocktail with sour mix, white grape juice, and ginger ale. Then I moved on to Kiandra's drink, A Midsummer Night's Cream. It was one of my most recent creations. Made with crushed strawberries, cream of coconut, lime juice, and whipped cream, the alcohol-free drink had white and red layers and tasted divine.

Once we all had drinks in hand, we returned to the sunshine. Kiandra plopped herself down on the grass with her drink, and Wimsey wandered over to join her. I pulled up another chair for Shontelle, and we sat down far enough away from Kiandra that we could chat privately while still keeping an eye on her.

"Is there anything in particular you want to chat about?" I asked Shontelle, suspecting that the answer was yes.

She took a sip of her drink before responding. "You and Grayson."

"What about me and Grayson?"

She arched an eyebrow at me. "I've heard rumors."

"Oh no." I rolled my eyes heavenward. "What are people saying about us now? Or do I really want to know?" This wasn't the first time Grayson and I had been the subject of rumors in Shady Creek.

"I won't tell you exactly what was said, because I don't want to be responsible for you murdering Vera Anderson."

I groaned. "If it's Vera Anderson spreading the rumors, there's no way she's saying good things."

Vera was one of my least favorite people in Shady Creek. She seemed to delight in giving me bad news and in judging anyone who wasn't a friend of hers.

"She saw you walking home from Grayson's place one morning last week."

"Of course she did," I said with a sigh. It was just my luck that Vera Anderson had seen me.

"She assumed you'd spent the night there." Shontelle watched me over the rim of her glass as she took a sip of her cocktail.

"I did. On the couch."

Shontelle tried to suppress a smile. "Cozy."

"By myself," I rushed to clarify. "I fell asleep while we were watching a movie, and Grayson didn't have the heart to wake me. That's all there was to it."

"In that case, I don't have to be mad at you for leaving me to hear about it through the grapevine," Shontelle said. "I knew there was a chance that Vera had things wrong."

"What else did she say about me?" I asked, against my better judgment.

"I don't want you getting arrested for murder, remember?"

"It was really that bad?" I wondered if I'd need to get myself a stronger drink after hearing the answer.

"Let's just say she used the word 'scandalous.'"

"Seriously? We're not living in Victorian times. What does it matter if I do or don't spend the night at my boyfriend's place?"

"It doesn't. And don't worry about it," Shontelle said. "It's Vera, after all."

"Does she spread rumors about you and Eldon, or are you spared because Eldon's her nephew?"

"Eldon might be spared, but I'm not. Last week I heard she'd called me a gold digger."

I nearly spit out the sip I'd taken from my drink. "What? Eldon's not exactly rich." I realized I didn't know that for sure. "Is he?"

"No. He lives off his salary as a police officer. But I doubt Vera would think any woman was good enough for her nephew, even though she doesn't get along with her sister, Eldon's mother."

"That woman," I said with a shake of my head. "How is Eldon these days? Anything I should know about the two of you before I hear it through the grapevine?"

"He's good, but he's been busy lately."

"Right," I said. "Of course he has, with the murder investigation."

"And to answer your other question, no. We're still taking things slow." Shontelle's gaze drifted over to Kiandra, who was now hunting through the grass, possibly for a four-leaf clover.

I knew Shontelle worried about letting a man too far into her life too soon because she had Kiandra to consider. I had the same worries, but for different reasons. After getting hurt by my last boyfriend, I wanted to tread carefully when it came to giving away a piece of my heart. The problem was that my heart wasn't always on the same page as my head.

"Has Eldon said anything to you about the case against Damien?" I asked.

"No. He doesn't talk much about work. I told him that you and I believe Damien is innocent."

"I'm glad you believe that too. What did Eldon have to say about that?"

"Not much." She eyed me suspiciously. "Are you hoping for a chance to grill him?"

"Would that be a waste of time?"

"I'm pretty sure it would be."

"I figured as much." I finished off my drink and leaned back in my chair. "Did you have a good time catching up with Rachael?"

"We had a good chat. I hope she doesn't lose her job. She loves working at the faire, and she's been through so much already."

"I overheard her say her mom passed away."

Shontelle swirled the remains of her drink in her glass. "And her mom was the only family she had left. She lost her dad and sister in a car accident when she was still in high school."

"That's awful."

"She told me the people who work at the faire have become like a family to her," Shontelle said. "Now Ozzie's murder could cause her to lose them as well."

My heart ached for Rachael. "Hopefully, it won't come to that."

"She did mention that her bosses are a little happier now that the police have arrested someone for the murder."

I frowned at that. "The *wrong* person."

"Unfortunately. Do you have any idea who the real killer is yet?"

"I'm still thinking Minerva, but I've got other suspects." I filled her in on everything I'd found out since I'd last talked with her.

"You'll figure it out," Shontelle said with confidence once I'd finished.

"I wish I could believe that as strongly as you do, but I'm going to keep trying. Maybe Grayson and I can put our heads together tonight and see if we can figure things out."

Shontelle smiled. "If the two of you have your heads together, I doubt you'll be doing much talking. Or thinking."

"Hey!"

"Am I wrong?" she asked, still smiling.

"Maybe not," I conceded, my cheeks getting warm.

My phone buzzed. I snatched it up, hoping I'd received a text message from Charlotte, updating me on Damien's situation.

When I accessed my messages, I saw that I had a new one from Damien himself. I smiled when I read it.

"Good news?" Shontelle asked.

"Not the best news, but yes, it's good," I said with a hint of relief. "Damien's out on bail."

Chapter 19

I couldn't help myself. I asked Damien if it would be all right for me to stop by his place for a short while. He said yes, so after Shontelle and Kiandra left to go home, I hopped in my car. I didn't have a whole lot of time to spare before I was supposed to go over to Grayson's house, but I figured I could squeeze in a quick trip across town.

When I pulled into Damien's driveway, he stepped out the front door onto the porch. At first, I thought he didn't appear any the worse for wear after his time locked up, but when I climbed the porch steps and got closer to him, I realized he looked exhausted. There were dark rings beneath his eyes and more lines on his face than I remembered. I second-guessed my decision to come by and disturb him, but I was there now, so I simply resolved not to take up much of his time.

"It's good to see you," I said when I joined him on the porch. "How are you doing?"

"I'm fine. Glad to be back home with my daughters." He held the front door open for me. "Come on in."

As I followed him into the house, I wondered how fine he

could really be, considering his situation. Damien wasn't one to complain or share much in the way of feelings, though, so I wasn't going to press for a different answer.

"Can I get you anything?" Damien asked when I reached the living room.

"No, thank you," I said. "I won't stay long."

I could hear voices coming from the kitchen at the back of the house.

"My sister-in-law has been a godsend." Damien took a seat in an armchair and gestured for me to sit down too. "She's baking with the girls at the moment."

I settled on one end of the couch. "I'm glad you had a family member nearby who was able to come help out." I decided to get straight to the point of the reason for my visit. "I'm trying to figure out who killed Ozzie, because I know it wasn't you. Is there anything you can think of that might help me?"

"Sadie, I don't want you getting into any kind of trouble for my sake."

"I don't plan to get into trouble." I knew full well that most of the trouble I did get into wasn't planned, but I wasn't going to bring that up. "I'm going to keep trying to solve the case until your name is cleared, so there's no point arguing with me about it."

The barest hint of a smile tugged at one corner of Damien's mouth. "I guess I shouldn't have expected anything different. Thank you, Sadie. But you need to promise me that you'll be careful."

"I promise."

He seemed satisfied. "I don't think there's anything I can tell you that will help my case. I met Ozzie only once, briefly. I don't know anything about him or why anyone would want to kill him, unless it was because he was a sleaze and a lowlife."

"That could have been the reason." I didn't know why I'd hoped that Damien would have information that would help me clear him. I tried not to let my disappointment show. "How strong is the case against you?"

Damien ran a hand down his face. "They've got the plant, and they know about my confrontation with Ozzie. Plus, they've got witnesses who not only saw me punch him but also heard me threaten him."

"You threatened him?" That definitely wasn't good. "What did you say, exactly?" I wasn't sure I wanted to know.

"I told him that if he ever went near my daughter again, I'd kill him."

My heart sank.

"I know," he said, reading my expression. "That might have been the nail in my coffin."

"Don't say that." I couldn't bear to think it could be true. "Why would the police think you acted on that threat later? Ozzie never did go near Charlotte again, did he?"

Damien didn't answer.

It wasn't hard to interpret his silence. "He did?"

"Charlotte went back to the faire. It turns out she was there when I had my confrontation with Ozzie. I didn't know that at the time. Ozzie saw her with her friends. He whistled at them and made some comments. It must have happened right after I left the fairgrounds."

"And shortly before his final show started."

Damien nodded.

"But you didn't know about the second encounter?"

"Not until after my arrest. The police brought it up. Someone who witnessed Ozzie hitting on Charlotte, and me punching him, also saw him with her and her friends later."

"So the police think you found out about the second incident, went out and picked some monkshood, did whatever was needed to make it into a substance that could be administered to Ozzie, and then poisoned him before his show started?"

"That's about the size of it. If I hadn't been late for work that evening, the case against me wouldn't be as strong, but since I can't account for my movements for a while after my fight with Ozzie, I'm in trouble."

"Where were you after the fight?" I asked.

"I took a long walk until I'd calmed down. Unfortunately, no one can confirm that."

I got to my feet, not wanting to impose on him any longer. "We'll find a way to prove your innocence."

He walked to the front door with me. "Remember your promise."

"I'll do my best to be careful and stay out of trouble," I assured him.

I said goodbye and then hurried over to my car, not wanting to give him a chance to ask me to make any further promises.

Hanging out at Grayson's place that evening turned out to be exactly what I needed. Although we chatted about the murder and Damien's temporary release when I first arrived, we talked about far less serious things while we ate the burgers Grayson grilled for us out on his patio. His back lawn was bordered by the forest, and it would have been harder to find a more private location so close to the center of town. The peace and quiet, interrupted only by our voices and the twittering of birds in the trees, helped me to relax and let go of some of the stress that had haunted me since Damien's arrest.

By the time we'd finished eating, I could almost believe that nothing was amiss in the world. Not quite, but almost.

"Thank you for dinner," I said as I relaxed on the outdoor couch. "It was delicious."

Grayson sat down next to me and put an arm around my shoulders. "I'm glad we had this chance to spend time together."

I rested my head on his shoulder. "Me too."

Bowie trotted over and lay down at our feet.

"I'm working on adding a couple more people to my staff,"

Grayson said. "I've interviewed two candidates already, and I've got a few more lined up. Once I decide who to hire and get them trained, I'm hoping I'll have a little more time available to spend away from the brewery."

"Trying for a better work-life balance?" I asked.

"Trying to make sure I have more time to spend with you."

My heart melted. I couldn't find my voice, so I kissed him. It was a while before either of us spoke again.

"I've been thinking about adding to my staff too," I said eventually. "Teagan's sister, Zoe, is going to fill in for Damien while he's under house arrest, but I think I'm at a point now where I can afford to hire an extra person long term, on a part-time basis, anyway. That would give me a little more freedom."

"I'm glad the pub is doing well." The warmth in his voice told me how sincerely he meant that statement.

"I've been very fortunate."

"You've put in a lot of hard work," Grayson countered.

"That too, but the support from the locals has been invaluable. If I get Damien's name cleared, everything will be as right as rain."

Just like that, my mind was back to obsessing over Ozzie's murder.

"What are you planning?" Grayson asked.

His question surprised me. "What makes you think I'm planning something?"

"I can tell."

"How?"

"There's this look you get in your eyes." He touched a finger to my forehead. "And you get this little furrow right here."

I rubbed a hand across my forehead, hoping to smooth out any creases. Although I couldn't help but feel pleased that Grayson could read me that well already, it also scared me a bit, because it made me fall a little farther. And I'd already fallen a long way. I wasn't quite ready to tell him that, though.

Instead, I answered his initial question.

"I'm thinking I'd like to know more about my suspects, especially the ones who work at the faire. And I was wondering if maybe there was a way to observe them when they've got their guards down."

"You mean when they're not performing for an audience."

"Exactly."

"I think I know where this is going," Grayson said with a half grin.

"You think you've got me all figured out, don't you?"

He laughed. "Not yet, but I plan to get there in time."

My heart did a backflip in my chest. The way his eyes locked with mine stole all the air out of my lungs. I either had to say something or kiss him senseless. I went with the second option.

"So, when are you planning to go?" Grayson murmured the question into my ear several minutes later.

"Go where?" It was hard for me to think straight when he was trailing kisses down my neck.

He stopped the kisses—to my disappointment—and tucked my hair behind my ear. "To the fairgrounds."

He really did know me well.

"Maybe once it's nearly dark," I said.

"All the better for sneaking around."

"You could put it like that."

"How about we take Bowie for a short walk before we go?" Grayson suggested.

"We?"

"Maybe I want in on the trouble."

"Who says there's going to be trouble?"

"You'll be snooping," he pointed out. "Trouble is pretty much guaranteed."

I elbowed him in the ribs. "Very funny."

He stood up and pulled me to my feet. "Come on, Bowie," he said to his dog. "Trouble is calling."

Chapter 20

We ended up taking Bowie with us to the park. We figured he'd help us appear more innocent. If anyone found us on the fairgrounds, we could simply say we were out walking our dog and hadn't realized we weren't supposed to be there. Temporary fencing had been set up around the perimeter of the park, except on the side where it was bordered by a patch of woodland. Grayson knew of a trail that led through the woods and had walked Bowie on it before. He assured me that it wouldn't be too hard to leave the path and cut through the trees to the park. I hoped he was right. I hadn't exactly dressed for an excursion through the underbrush. My shorts, T-shirt, and flip-flops had seemed like a good wardrobe choice earlier in the day, but now I wished I'd worn jeans and sneakers like Grayson.

With Bowie on the leash, we entered the woods and followed the trail Grayson had told me about. Although it wasn't quite dark out yet, not much of the remaining daylight filtered in through the forest canopy. It wasn't so dark that we couldn't see where we were going, but I was glad Grayson had brought a powerful flashlight along in case we needed it later.

The deeper we got into the woods, the more I wondered if we'd need the flashlight sooner than I'd thought. I couldn't make out much in the way of details anymore, and I could feel myself growing jumpier. When something rustled through the underbrush, I clutched Grayson's arm.

"Is that a bear?" I noticed a dark shape in among the trees to our left. "It is a bear!"

Grayson laughed. "It's a stump."

"But . . ." I stared harder at the shape.

Grayson flicked on the flashlight and aimed the beam through the trees.

Sure enough, what I'd thought was a bear was indeed a large tree stump, standing about four feet high.

The tension whooshed out of my body. "I heard *something*."

"I did too, but it wasn't nearly big enough to be a bear. Maybe a raccoon."

I dropped my hand from Grayson's arm, feeling silly now.

"Don't worry," he said. "We walk this way all the time, and we've never run into a bear. Have we, Bowie?"

Bowie glanced up at him, but only for a split second. Then he focused straight ahead again, leading us along the path.

Something else rustled in the bushes. I nearly jumped and grabbed Grayson's arm again, but I managed not to. I didn't want him to know how freaked out I was by walking through the woods in the growing darkness. I would have been fine in the daylight, but everything looked and sounded more ominous at night.

Maybe Grayson had an idea of how I was feeling, anyway. He took my hand and gave it a reassuring squeeze.

He's a keeper, a voice said in my head, scaring me almost as much as the non-bear.

"Let's not go there."

"Go where?" Grayson asked. "The fairgrounds?"

Now I was grateful for the darkness, so Grayson couldn't see my flaming red cheeks. I hadn't meant to talk to myself out loud.

"Um. No. Never mind. We're still going to the fairgrounds."

I hoped he wouldn't ask me more questions about what I'd meant.

To my relief, he stopped on the path and shone his flashlight into the trees to our right. "If we cut through here, we'll reach the park." He aimed the flashlight at my feet. "Maybe we should have stopped by your place so you could get better shoes."

"Too late now," I said. "Just don't go too fast. And don't leave me behind."

I thought I heard a quiet chuckle coming from his direction. "Don't worry," he said. "I won't leave you for the bears. Or the wolves."

"Wolves?" The word came out as a squeak.

This time I definitely heard Grayson laugh.

"Argh." I gave him a shove. "No teasing."

"No promises," Grayson said.

Even without looking at him, I knew he was grinning.

Still holding my hand, he led me off the path, his other hand gripping Bowie's leash. The dog's tail wagged happily. He was excited to stray from the path and explore the woods. I wasn't quite as enthusiastic. I was determined not to complain, though, even when a sharp twig poked at my foot, nearly causing me to swear from the sudden pain.

After we'd crashed through the undergrowth for a minute or so, Grayson drew to a stop. "This is the tricky part."

I moved up next to him so I could follow the beam of his flashlight. Ahead of us, the ground dropped away, sloping steeply downward.

"A ravine?" I said. "You didn't mention a ravine."

"Didn't I?" He tightened his hold on my hand. "I'll help you down."

"I'll be fine." I slipped my hand out of his. I'd managed to sound more confident than I felt.

Bowie was ready to bound down into the ravine, but Grayson kept a firm grip on his leash as we slowly began our descent. I nearly lost my right flip-flop at one point, but I stopped and slipped my foot back into it before it could tumble out of reach.

We'd almost reached the bottom, and I was beginning to feel relieved about how much easier the descent had been than I'd expected. Then the dirt crumbled away beneath my feet, and both my legs went out from under me. I crashed to the ground and rolled and bounced the rest of the way down the embankment.

"Sadie!" Grayson yelled.

I came to a stop on my back at the bottom of the ravine. Bowie's cold, wet nose nudged the side of my face. Grayson reached my side a second later.

"Sadie, are you okay?" He sounded worried.

I tried moving my limbs. "Nothing's broken." I sat up. "In fact, I don't think I'm hurt at all." If I didn't count my bruised pride.

Grayson helped me to my feet and gave me a kiss before running the beam of his flashlight over me from head to toe. "It doesn't look like you've got any cuts."

"I'm fine. Really." I brushed some dirt from my clothes. I hadn't even lost a flip-flop. "Let's keep going."

We crossed the bottom of the narrow ravine and began our climb upward. This time I let Grayson help me. I really didn't want to take another tumble.

When we reached the top of the ravine wall, we stopped for a moment to catch our breath. To my relief, I realized we were standing a mere stone's throw from the edge of the woods. With Bowie in the lead, we made our way through the trees and out into the park.

We stopped again to get our bearings. Grayson and Bowie hadn't led us astray. We were indeed within the area fenced off for the faire. I could see the tents and huts looming out of the darkness. The place had clearly shut down for the night, but I could see a faint glow of light beyond the faire's temporary structures. I thought it was coming from the area where all the trailers were parked.

"Where to first?" Grayson asked, switching off his flashlight. Now that we were out of the woods, the moon provided us with enough illumination to see by.

"Let's head toward the trailers," I said. "Maybe we'll find some of the faire workers over there."

We made our way down the walkway between the two rows of huts, booths, and tents, all of which were shuttered and closed up tight for the night. Bowie paused every now and then to sniff at an interesting smell, but we otherwise made steady progress. When we were about halfway across the park, we slipped into the dark alley between two huts. I wanted to get a look at the trailers, to see if there was anyone about.

Grayson hung back a bit with Bowie while I peeked around the back corner of the hut that offered costume rentals during the day. There were lights on in several of the trailers lining the edge of the park, but others were dark. Between the row of trailers and the huts, a little farther down from where I stood, a dozen or so people had gathered around a campfire. I studied the shadowy forms but couldn't recognize anyone from my vantage point.

I crept back between the huts to rejoin Grayson.

"There's a campfire with a bunch of people around it," I reported in a whisper as Bowie sniffed around my feet, tickling my toes with his nose. "Maybe if we can get closer, we'll be able to hear what they're saying."

"Even if the killer is at the campfire, they're not too likely to confess their crime while toasting marshmallows," Grayson said as we resumed our trek down the faire's main walkway.

I couldn't deny that he had a good point. "But maybe we'll find others hanging around elsewhere in the park. Or maybe we can get around to the other side of the trailers and overhear something through an open window."

Grayson snaked an arm around my waist and pulled me to a stop. "I don't know about the second possibility, but it looks like you're right about the first," he whispered in my ear.

I followed his gaze through the darkness and noticed something moving in the shadows. A person, I realized a second later.

Grayson kept a firm grip on Bowie's leash as we quietly crept forward.

Whoever was up ahead was pacing back and forth outside the main tent. As we drew closer, I realized that it was a woman, and she was holding a phone to her ear. When she turned to start pacing back in our direction, we darted out of sight behind the hut that stood next to the tent. Fortunately, we could hear her voice from our hiding spot.

"I know I don't own the costumes, but I know how they work. We can re-create them and take our own show on the road."

I thought I recognized the woman's voice, but I couldn't quite place it. I knew only that it wasn't Rachael speaking.

"But we can *make* a name for ourselves," the woman said.

It sounded like she was trying to convince the person on the other end of the phone.

"We'll be costars," she continued. "And we can make our show unique. Instead of just a quick-change act, we can incorporate acrobatics. I bet I could do the costume changes on the trapeze. That would blow people's minds!"

At the mention of acrobatics, I finally matched the voice to a person. I was certain the woman on the phone was Collette, the acrobat who'd also worked as Ozzie's assistant. No wonder she was talking about costume changes. It sounded like she intended to continue on performing the quick-change act, only with someone else.

I didn't catch any more of her side of the conversation. Her voice faded away and then disappeared entirely into the warm night air. I peeked around the corner of the hut. Collette was no longer in sight.

"She's gone," I said to Grayson in a low voice as I stepped out from our hiding spot.

Grayson joined me out in the open. "Do you know who she was?" he asked.

"Ozzie's assistant. Her name's Collette."

"Sounds like she doesn't plan to let Ozzie's death hold her back."

"Quite the opposite." I thought over what she'd said. "She won't have to be in Ozzie's shadow anymore, a mere assistant. If she goes ahead with her plan, it sounds like she'd get an equal share of the spotlight with her new partner."

"I wonder who that is," Grayson mused.

"No idea," I said. "But I already had Collette on my suspect list because of the argument she had with Ozzie shortly before he died."

"About Minerva the Mysterious?"

"Exactly. Maybe she was mad about more than just Minerva. Maybe she was tired of Ozzie being the one in the limelight. It was always his name in the headlines. It was always his face on the posters. If not for the costume-change act, Collette probably would have gone pretty much unnoticed."

"So is she taking over Minerva's spot at the top of your suspect list?"

I didn't have a chance to respond. A faint glow of light up ahead startled me into silence. I grabbed Grayson's hand and pulled him behind the hut again. Bowie had other plans. He strained at the leash, trying to get out in the open.

"Bowie, come here," Grayson whispered.

Bowie did what he was told, but not before letting out a loud woof.

"Hello?" a woman's voice—a different one this time—called out.

My heart jumped into overdrive.

A beam of light cut through the darkness, lighting up the edge of our hiding spot.

Footsteps drew closer.

"Hello?" This time the voice sounded uneasy.

I knew we were about to get caught. I was about to step out into the open, to use our planned excuse about walking our dog and not knowing we shouldn't be in the park, when Grayson pulled me close and kissed me.

After a split second of surprise, I melted against him, almost forgetting our precarious situation. Then the beam of light found us, and Bowie gave another bark.

I pulled away from Grayson and shielded my eyes against the light shining right in my face.

"Who are you, and what are you doing here?" the woman behind the light asked.

She lowered the beam so it was no longer directed at my eyes. I saw then that the woman was using the flashlight app on her phone.

"We're locals," Grayson said, answering the woman's question. "We were walking our dog and . . ." He glanced at me with a smile. "I guess we got carried away by the romance of a moonlit walk."

As my eyes adjusted to the relative darkness, I realized that the tall, dark-haired woman looked a bit familiar.

"You're not supposed to be here," she said. "How did you get in?"

"Into the park?" Grayson hooked a thumb over his shoulder. "We came through the woods. Sorry. We didn't realize the place was off limits."

"Aren't you one of the mermaids?" I asked before the woman had a chance to speak again.

"Yes." The tension had gone out of her stance. She turned her attention to Bowie. "Aren't you a cutie?"

Bowie wagged his tail as she patted him on the head.

"I'm Sadie," I said. "I own the local pub, the Inkwell." I gave Grayson's hand a squeeze. "And this is my boyfriend, Grayson."

"I'm Jasmine," the woman said. "I was at your pub the other night for a drink. I had a really great cocktail, the Happily Ever After."

"I'm glad you liked it," I said with a smile, not failing to register her name. "I'm sorry for your loss, Jasmine."

"My loss?"

I pretended to be puzzled by her confusion. "Sorry. I thought you were involved with Ozzie Stone."

The bewilderment cleared from her face. "I guess you could say that. Wow. The faire gossip even spreads to the locals?"

"Like wildfire, apparently," Grayson said.

"Well, it's not like we were in a relationship, exactly," Jasmine said, "but thank you for the sentiment."

I hoped I could draw more information out of her. "I guess Ozzie wasn't the type for serious relationships."

Jasmine almost laughed. "He definitely wasn't. Although, some liked to think he was."

"You mean Minerva?" I asked.

She raised an eyebrow. "You really do know all the gossip."

"Like I said, I own the local pub. Most gossip runs through there."

She seemed to buy that explanation. "Minerva liked to think she owned Ozzie, but he was much more into casual relationships, if you know what I mean."

I was pretty sure that I did.

"Did Minerva know about you and Ozzie?" Grayson asked.

"She found out last week." Jasmine touched a hand to her cheek. "That crazy witch nearly scratched my eyes out."

"She attacked you?" I said.

"Like some lunatic. The other mermaids had to pull her off me. It's a good thing she didn't leave any marks. It's not exactly easy to hide stuff under makeup when you're swimming underwater all day." Jasmine's phone buzzed in her hand. She glanced at the screen. "I've got to go. You should leave too. The park's supposed to be closed at night."

"We'll head on out," Grayson assured her, but she was already walking off toward the glow of the campfire.

"So Minerva has a temper," I said once we were alone. "And to answer your earlier question, no. Collette isn't my top suspect. After what Jasmine just told us, Minerva the Mysterious still holds that honor."

Chapter 21

We decided not to hang around the park any longer. I was still tempted to sneak around the trailers in the hope of overhearing some snippets of conversation, but Grayson convinced me it wasn't a good idea. I'd noticed a security guard at the faire earlier in the day, and I figured there was a chance he was still around. If Jasmine mentioned our presence to him, and the guard found us still in the park, we could end up in trouble. I didn't want the local police getting called, so I went along with Grayson's suggestion that we give up on our investigation for the night.

I wasn't looking forward to another climb through the ravine in my flip-flops, so we made our way along the edge of the woods until we reached the temporary fence. To my relief, the fence ended at the tree line. All we had to do was venture a few feet into the woods and around the fence.

"Sorry," Grayson said once we stood at the edge of the road. "I guess we should have tried this route on our way in."

"It's no big deal," I assured him. "This way is riskier." I pointed at the streetlamp lighting up the area.

It was one thing to chance being seen on our way out of the park, but having someone spot us on our way into the fairgrounds could have put an end to our quest for clues before it even began.

"Still," Grayson said, "next time we'll go the easy route."

"Next time?"

He took my hand, smiling, as we headed down the road. "When it comes to you and sleuthing, there's always a next time."

I couldn't deny that.

"So, what's the next step, Detective Coleman?" Grayson asked as we crossed the Inkwell's footbridge a while later.

"I think I'll check the edge of the woods—in daylight—to see if there's any monkshood growing there. If there's not, that doesn't mean Minerva couldn't have found it somewhere else, but if there *is* some growing near the park . . ."

"It helps establish her opportunity to commit the crime," Grayson said, finishing for me, as we drew to a stop outside the gristmill's back door. "I'd help you with the search, but I've got a busy schedule tomorrow, and I'm betting you don't want to wait."

He was right about that.

"I won't be doing anything dangerous. If anyone asks what I'm doing, I'll say I'm looking for wildflowers. Plus, I have a pass to get into the faire, so I won't have to worry about getting kicked out of the park during daylight hours."

Grayson unhooked Bowie's leash so the dog could wander around on the lawn, sniffing and exploring. "Promise me you'll still be careful."

"I'm always careful," I said.

"Hmm." Grayson slid his arms around my waist and pulled me closer. "You and I might have different definitions of 'careful.'"

I looped my arms around his neck and decided to put an end

to our conversation with a kiss. It worked like a charm, distracting us both, until Bowie barked and bounded off toward the woods.

With a reluctance that matched my own, Grayson pulled away from me and called his dog. After a few more barks, Bowie came trotting back, and Grayson hooked the leash onto his collar again.

Grayson gave me another kiss, but only a brief one this time. "Hopefully, I'll see you soon," he said.

I smiled, even though I didn't really want him to leave yet. "Thanks for dinner. And for our . . . adventure."

Grayson bowed. "Thou art most welcome. Fare thee well, my lady."

I couldn't help but smile again.

I knew he was waiting to see me safely inside, so I slipped through the door and shut and locked it behind me. As I trudged up the stairs to my apartment, I had to admit to myself that I was officially crazy about Grayson Blake.

I woke up earlier than I would have liked the next morning, although Wimsey didn't mind at all. He never complained about getting his breakfast early. If I were so much as half a minute late, however, he always had something to say about it.

I knew I needed to be a responsible business owner and spend some time in my cubbyhole of an office before opening the pub at noon, but I decided that could wait for an hour or two. It would be best to search for the monkshood early in the day, before too many people attended the faire. That way I was less likely to be questioned about my actions. Or so I told myself, anyway.

After eating a quick breakfast, I set off for the park. As I passed by the Village Bean, an exiting customer opened the door, and the enticing aromas of coffee and baked goods wafted out on the morning breeze. I silently congratulated myself on my ability to resist the temptation to stop there instead of continuing on down the road.

I didn't make it much farther without stopping, however. A woman was walking along Creekside Road in my direction, with an adorable black toy poodle on a leash. I recognized the woman as one of the Inkwell's regular customers. Her name was Vanessa, and she worked at the Harvest Grill, the restaurant owned by Matt Yanders. It was that last fact that made me decide to strike up a conversation with her, rather than simply say good morning and continue on.

"Who's this cutie?" I crouched down to greet the dog after saying good morning to Vanessa.

"Her name's Mitzi." Vanessa smiled as I patted her dog.

Mitzi wagged her whole body and showed her pink tongue as I showered her with attention.

"Are you heading to the Renaissance faire?" Vanessa asked.

"For a short visit." I gave Mitzi a final pat and straightened up. "Have you been yet?"

"I went yesterday, my day off. It's a lot of fun."

"I've been a couple of times already," I said. "But the second time wasn't as much fun as the others. That was the night the illusionist died."

Vanessa's eyes widened. "Were you at the show when it happened?"

"Unfortunately."

"Yikes. I would have freaked out."

"It wasn't very pleasant." I wondered how well I could steer the conversation. "Have you met Matt's brother? He works at the faire."

Vanessa's expression transformed, bringing a sparkle to her eyes. "Flint? I've met him, all right. He's been to the restaurant a few times since the faire came to town. He's easy on the eyes, that's for sure."

"I can't argue with you there," I said. "I hope Matt's been able to spend time with Flint outside of the restaurant." I didn't mention that I knew he had, since they'd come to the Inkwell together.

"They've been spending a lot of time together," Vanessa said. "They've hung out around town, and Matt's gone to the faire a couple of times."

I pounced on the opportunity to ask one of the questions that had been hovering on the tip of my tongue since I'd greeted Vanessa. "Did Matt have a chance to check out Ozzie Stone's show?"

"I don't know."

I kept my disappointment to myself. "I guess he wasn't there the night I was. I didn't see him, anyway. He was probably at the restaurant."

"No, he wasn't at the restaurant that night."

I perked up at that. "Really?"

"He took the evening off."

"To go to the faire?"

Vanessa shrugged. "I don't know where he was. He didn't say. But I'm sure he would have mentioned it if he'd seen Ozzie die."

Unless he was the one who'd poisoned the illusionist.

Mitzi yipped at another woman and dog heading our way along Creekside Road.

"That's Mitzi's BFF, Roxy," Vanessa said.

Mitzi tried to take off down the road.

"Sorry!" Vanessa said to me, hurrying after Mitzi. "Nice talking to you, Sadie!"

Mitzi reached her best friend, and the two dogs had a joyful reunion. Under other circumstances, I would have smiled at the sight, but something weighed too heavily on my mind. I'd hoped to walk away from my conversation with Vanessa knowing that Matt had an alibi for the night Ozzie died. Maybe someone else could provide him with one, but Vanessa couldn't. I might be able to find a way to ask Matt where he'd been that night, but I didn't want to risk seeming too nosey. He was a regular patron of my pub, after all, and a member of one of the Inkwell's book clubs. I didn't want to end up on his bad side.

I decided to shove that problem to the back burner for the time being. Hopefully, Matt had a perfectly innocent explanation for why he'd spent the evening away from his restaurant. I wanted Damien's name cleared, but I hoped it wouldn't be at Matt's expense.

Trying not to dwell on that thought, I kept walking and reached the park about a quarter of an hour before the gates were scheduled to open. I strolled on past the gates and down the edge of the park to the woods. When I thought no one was looking my way, I darted into the trees so I could skirt around the end of the temporary fence.

Once inside the fairgrounds, I paused to check the photos I had on my phone, reminding myself of what I was looking for. I walked slowly along the tree line, studying the underbrush. Plenty of ferns grew between the trees, along with many other plants that I couldn't identify. I didn't, however, see any monkshood.

It would have been impossible to scour the whole patch of woodland for the poisonous plant, but I was determined to do a thorough job of checking the edge of the woods. I made my way along the tree line and went back and forth a couple of times, without any luck. I pushed aside ferns and vines, not ready to give up. I took a step into the woods and almost grabbed a plant to shove it aside. Jerking my hand back, I let out a sigh of relief.

I was pretty sure I'd almost grabbed a handful of stinging nettle. I'd done that once in the past, when I was about ten years old, and it was an experience I didn't wish to repeat.

Although I glanced around, I didn't spot any similar plants. Still, I didn't want to risk coming into contact with stinging nettles, and where there was one plant, there were likely others, even if I couldn't see them right at the moment.

I backed quickly out of the woods, nearly falling over in my haste.

I decided it was time to give up on my search for the monkshood and treat myself to a mocha latte from the Village Bean.

I didn't even have a chance to turn my back on the woods before a chilling scream tore through the summer morning.

Chapter 22

I reacted without thinking. By the time a second scream followed the first, I was already running in the direction of the noise. Flint and Hamish had the same reaction. They took off in a flash from where they'd been standing near the Mad Hatter, Hamish with his lute in hand. I followed hot on their heels as they veered off the main walkway to the grassy square that separated the main part of the faire from the jousting arena. On the right side of the square was a blacksmith's shop, and on the left was a weaving studio. The pillory that sat right in the middle of the grass seemed to be what was drawing everyone's attention.

At first, I couldn't see much, because Jasmine—in a regular Renaissance outfit rather than her mermaid costume—stood between me and the pillory. A group of three women in Renaissance garb had gathered nearby, and they were taking photos with their cell phones. Their phones and modern tote bags gave them away as fairgoers rather than actors.

"What's wrong, Jasmine?" Flint asked as he ran up to her.

She stepped aside, her hands covering her face as she sobbed.

I gasped as I skidded to a stop.

Someone had locked Minerva in the pillory, and her hands hung limply from the holes on either side of her drooping head. Her long hair was wet and tangled and hung down to the ground.

"She really looks dead!" one of the fairgoers said with delight as she snapped another photo.

Flint deftly stepped between the group of onlookers and the pillory, blocking their view. The women didn't seem to mind. They simply started snapping photos of Flint instead.

Meanwhile, he discreetly pressed two fingers to the side of Minerva's neck.

He straightened up, his expression grim.

"Go find Rachael," Flint said to Hamish in a low voice. "And tell her to call nine-one-one."

Hamish's eyes widened.

Flint grabbed his arm before he could move. "Take Jasmine with you."

Jasmine was still crying into her hands, her back to Minerva's body. Hamish put an arm around her and led her away.

I stared at Minerva, my numb brain trying to process everything.

"She's dead?" I whispered to Flint, even though on some level I'd known that as soon as I'd seen her.

Flint met my gaze with his somber one for a brief second. Then he smoothed out his expression and faced the growing number of fairgoers migrating in the direction of the pillory.

"I cry your mercy, my good lords and ladies," Flint said. "Prithee wend back. I fear we must close the village square for a spell."

There were a few mild protests, but Flint managed to herd everyone out of the square without too much trouble. I stayed behind and edged around the other side of the pillory. Minerva's clothes were soaked, her blouse and scarves plastered to her skin.

Sunlight glinted off something on the ground next to Minerva's body. I leaned in closer. It looked like an eyelet, probably from someone's costume. I studied Minerva's clothing. As far as I could tell, she wasn't wearing a corset or anything else with eyelets.

I swallowed against a wave of nausea. Poor Minerva. I wanted to unlock her from the pillory, to release her body. It seemed cruel to leave her there, but I stepped farther away without touching anything. There was no question in my mind that I was staring at a crime scene.

"Sadie," Flint said, returning to my side, "we need to clear the area."

I nodded and tore my eyes from Minerva's body, my mind still numb.

Flint accompanied me to the entrance to the square, where two faire workers were setting up a barricade to keep people away. When I reached the main part of the grounds, a scene of mild chaos greeted me. The early faire attendees were gathered in clusters, chatting and watching with wide eyes as workers dashed to and fro, speaking urgently with one another in hushed voices. A couple of people filmed the action with their phones.

I found a rustic bench and sank down onto it. Another murder. My mind was still trying to come to terms with that.

"Is it true?" a male voice said quietly.

I glanced up to see Toby standing with Collette at the end of the bench. Neither appeared to take any notice of me.

Toby held three green balls in one hand. He'd probably been getting ready to juggle for an audience when Jasmine screamed. Seeing him and Collette together like that made me realize that they shared a strong resemblance. They both had chestnut-brown hair and gray eyes, and their noses were similar. I wondered briefly if they were related, but that thought slid to the back of my mind as I focused on their conversation.

"I caught a glimpse of her body," Collette said in response to Toby's question. "She's locked in the pillory, and she sure looks dead to me."

"Locked in the pillory," Toby echoed. "She didn't do that on her own. Someone must have killed the witch."

Collette shrugged. "Well, you know what they say about karma."

Collette's words and her unconcerned demeanor shocked me. Toby didn't seem upset by Minerva's death either. I wasn't positive, but I thought I saw a hint of a satisfied smile on his face as he turned away and wandered off through the crowd.

I hadn't failed to noticed that the vest he wore as part of his costume was laced up with eyelets. There didn't appear to be any missing from the garment, though. Collette wore modern leggings and a tank top, with nary an eyelet to be seen.

I was about to say something to Collette when she too sauntered off. Instead of following her, I stayed put. I suddenly wasn't sure if my legs would support me. I'd come across dead bodies before, but that didn't make it any easier. Even though I hadn't really known Minerva, her death left me shaken. Not everyone liked her—and it seemed some people fiercely *dis*liked her—but surely she hadn't deserved to be killed. And leaving her body displayed like that in the middle of the faire's village square seemed like an extra stroke of cruelty.

I wanted to go home, but I'd been one of the first people on the scene. The police would probably want to speak with me, even though there wasn't much I could tell them.

Shontelle's boyfriend, Officer Eldon Howes, arrived first, and another officer, whose name I didn't know, showed up shortly thereafter. Detective Marquez wasn't far behind them. I remained on the bench while they checked out the scene.

As much as I would have liked for my mind to leave me in

peace, I couldn't shut it off. Minerva was the second person attached to the faire to be murdered in the past week. While it was possible that she and Ozzie had been killed by two separate people, for completely different reasons, I found that hard to believe. Another possibility was that some deranged person was picking off members of the faire one by one, simply because they were crazy. However, I thought the most likely scenario was that one person had targeted both Ozzie and Minerva, with no randomness involved in the choosing of those victims.

But who would want both Ozzie *and* Minerva dead?

Certainly not Damien.

Maybe this terrible turn of events would help him.

I didn't have a chance to ponder that thought any further. Flint pointed me out to Eldon as one of the first people to see Minerva's body. When Eldon asked me to accompany him to a quieter part of the fairgrounds, I did so willingly. I wanted to get my statement over with so I could return to the comforting familiarity of home.

When Eldon asked his first question, however, I was no longer quite so eager to answer.

"What were you doing here so early?" he asked. "I understand the faire opened to the public very shortly before the body was found, and I'm told you came from the opposite direction of the gates."

Maybe Flint had told him that. Or Hamish. It didn't matter, really.

"I was out for a walk," I replied. At least that was true.

"Inside the fairgrounds?"

I pointed toward the trees. "Along the edge of the woods."

To my relief, he didn't question me further on that point. If he knew I'd been looking for monkshood, I was sure he would have lectured me about staying out of the investigation. Eldon was a good guy, and genuinely nice, but he took his job seriously. That was a good thing, of course, but it meant he likely wouldn't approve of my amateur detective work.

All the rest of Eldon's questions were easy to answer. When he was done, I told him about the eyelet I'd seen on the ground, in case it had any significance.

"I noticed that too." He scanned the small crowd still gathered outside the barricade at the edge of the village square.

I wondered if he was thinking about all the costumes he'd have to check for a missing eyelet. If that was the case, he didn't tell me. He asked me if there was anything else I had to share, and I replied in the negative.

"Will you be all right to walk?" Genuine concern showed in his blue eyes. "Or do you want me to get someone to drive you home?"

"I'll be okay walking, but thank you." I was hoping the fresh air would help rid me of my lingering nausea.

After Eldon moved on to speak with someone else, I searched for familiar faces. Flint stood near the barricade, speaking with Detective Marquez. I hoped she wouldn't notice me before I left, but no doubt she'd soon know that I'd been on the scene. I'd managed to dodge a lecture from Eldon, but that didn't mean I wouldn't get one from the detective in the near future. She didn't like me getting mixed up in her investigations. I knew that from past experience.

I kept searching the faces around me. Hamish had taken over the bench I'd claimed earlier, his instrument lying across his lap and his mouth set in a firm line. I couldn't read his expression. I scrutinized his costume as best I could from my vantage point, but it didn't seem to have any eyelets incorporated into its design. Maybe the eyelet had been lying on the ground by the pillory for days, but there was a chance it had fallen from the killer's costume.

I didn't see Toby or Collette anywhere, so I decided that

speaking with them would have to wait. Once I'd made up my mind on that, I didn't hang around any longer.

After I'd passed through the gates, I strode away from the park at a brisk pace. The closer I got to home, the more my stomach settled. I considered making a stop at the Village Bean, but I ended up passing the coffee shop by. Although my nausea had dissipated, my stomach still wasn't quite ready for coffee or food.

I knew from a quick glance at my phone that I should head straight into the Inkwell and park myself in my office until it was time to open the pub. That knowledge didn't have enough power to make me stray from the path that led to the Inkwell's parking lot. I didn't think I could concentrate on work until I'd spoken with Damien, so I hopped in my car and drove across town to see him.

There was no one in sight when I arrived, but when I climbed out of my car, I heard the sound of hammering coming from somewhere inside the house. I waited for the noise to stop before I knocked. Footsteps approached, and the door opened a second later. A tall, slim woman with dark hair stood in the doorway.

"You must be Tracey," I said. "I'm Sadie Coleman. I own the pub where Damien works."

Tracey smiled. "Of course. Damien's mentioned you." She stepped back and opened the door wider. "Please, come in."

As I stepped into the foyer, Damien came down the stairs from the second floor. I noticed a sprinkling of sawdust on his white T-shirt and his faded blue jeans.

"Hey, Sadie," he greeted.

"Morning," I returned. "Do you have time to chat?"

He gave me a wry grin. "I've got nothing but time these days."

Tracey offered me a drink, but I declined. I needed to get back to the Inkwell before too long.

Tracey headed toward the back of the house, leaving me and Damien alone in the living room.

"Are you working on some home renovations?" I asked, not bothering to sit down.

Damien stood by the couch. "I figured I might as well. I had a couple of projects I'd been meaning to get to. I decided to make the best of my house arrest."

I noted how quiet the house was now that the hammering had stopped. "Are the girls home?"

"They went into town to hang out with friends." Damien regarded me with apprehension. "Do you have bad news?"

I didn't tiptoe around the reason for my visit any longer. "There's been another murder."

Damien's forehead creased, and his eyes darkened. "Who died?"

"The fortune-teller from the faire. She goes by the name Minerva the Mysterious." I quelled the anxious jittering in my stomach. "Please tell me you were here all night and this morning."

"I had to be."

"And you can prove it?"

He hitched up his pant leg to reveal an ankle bracelet. "This thing can."

A relieved breath whooshed out of me. "That's good."

"This still doesn't prove that I didn't kill Ozzie. Unless the police know the same person killed both victims?"

"I don't think they know much of anything about the second murder yet," I said. "Minerva's body was just found in the past couple of hours. But I think the most likely scenario is that there's one killer."

"But until there's proof of that, the charge against me will stand." He stopped me before I could speak. "And it's not your job to find the proof."

"Maybe not, but I can't stop thinking about it. I had a list of people with a motive for killing Ozzie, but now I need to figure out who would have wanted to kill both Ozzie *and* Minerva."

"Does the second murder eliminate anyone from your suspect list?"

"Not really. Not yet, anyway. Collette, the acrobat who worked as Ozzie's assistant, was mad at him and Minerva. I need to find out more about *why* she was mad. And then there's Toby, the juggler and magician, who's been angling for his own show. I don't know why he'd want Minerva dead, but that doesn't mean he didn't. There's a minstrel named Hamish, who used to date Minerva, until she dumped him for Ozzie. And then there's Matt Yanders."

"Matt?" Damien echoed with surprise. "What's he got to do with any of this?"

"He had a confrontation with Ozzie a few weeks ago, when he was visiting his brother, who works for the faire."

Damien scrubbed a hand down his face. "Matt's a good guy. I'm sure he had nothing to do with the murders."

"I tend to agree with you," I said. "I'm hoping I can find a way to clear his name before he comes under any official suspicion."

"Even if he had a supposed motive for killing Ozzie, surely he had no reason to kill the fortune-teller."

"I'm hoping that's the case. But we still need proof that there's only one killer."

"Back up a second," Damien requested. "Was Minerva poisoned?"

"I'm not sure how she was killed," I said. "She was soaking wet and locked in the pillory at the faire. I didn't notice any obvious injuries on her."

"You saw the body?"

"Unfortunately."

He looked more closely at me. "Are you okay?"

"Yes, but I'm more anxious than ever to figure out who the killer is. What if they strike again?"

"Leave it to the police, Sadie. Seriously. This is getting too dangerous."

A cell phone rang.

Damien fished the device out of the pocket of his jeans and checked the display. "It's my lawyer."

I took a step toward the foyer. "I'll let myself out. And I'll talk to you again soon."

He answered the call as I crossed the foyer to the front door. I headed out to my car, relieved that he hadn't asked me to promise to stop investigating. That was a promise I couldn't have made. Until Damien was a free man again, there was no way I could give up on my quest for the truth.

Chapter 23

The next morning I forced myself to sit at my desk in my office and catch up on all the tasks I'd neglected the day before. The pub had been quite busy for a Tuesday, and the writers' group had met in the Christie room. Even with Zoe helping out in the evening, I hadn't had a chance to spend any time on office tasks while the pub was open. I knew that might be the case again today, so I was determined to catch up on everything before noon.

I took care of all the business chores first and then moved on to getting ready for the pub's Shakespeare trivia night. Once I'd quadruple-checked all the questions and answers, I printed out a copy of my quizmaster sheet. I tucked it away in my desk drawer and then finally allowed myself to leave my tiny office.

I made a beeline for the pub's coffee maker and put on a pot to brew while I phoned my mom. I wanted to see if she'd thought any more about coming to Shady Creek for a visit. As it turned out, she had.

"I don't know when exactly I could come," she said, "but late October looks clear on my calendar."

"That would be perfect." I smiled. "I'm sure you'll love the food and drink festival."

"That does sound nice." She paused, causing me to worry that she was about to back out of our tentative plans. "I'll have to find out if Gilda is willing to have me stay at her place."

"Why?" I asked with surprise. "I've got a guest room here in my apartment."

"You live above a pub, though," she pointed out.

"My own pub. It's not exactly rowdy, Mom."

"Still, I go to bed early. I think it might be too noisy for me at night."

"All right," I said. "We'll see what Aunt Gilda has to say, but I'm sure she won't mind having you stay with her."

We left our plans there, then chatted a few more minutes about other subjects.

After wrapping up the call with my mom, I poured myself a cup of coffee and carried it with me as I made a circuit of the pub, making sure everything was ready for the day's customers. Things seemed to be in order, thanks to the time I'd put in tidying up after closing the night before. The only job left to do was to dust all the books I had on display. With my feather duster in hand, I worked my way along the shelves.

Yesterday the main topic of conversation among pub patrons was the latest murder. I'd caught bits and pieces of the gossip and speculation, but none of it had been particularly helpful. Either people had talked about what I already knew or they had shared wild and completely unfounded theories about both murders. The one bit of good news I'd gleaned from overhearing conversations was that the locals strongly believed in Damien's innocence. If anyone had been in doubt before, Minerva's murder had changed their minds. It seemed most of the town believed, as I did, that there was only one killer at large, not two.

As I cleaned my books, I recalled the night when Minerva

had been at the Inkwell. She and Collette had exchanged angry words, and Minerva had told the acrobat that she would regret something if she went through with it. I wished I knew what it was that Collette would supposedly regret. Tilly had told me that Collette called Minerva a fraud during her argument with Ozzie. Maybe that had something to do with Minerva's threat.

I really needed more information.

Once I'd finished dusting, I opened the pub's front door and found the latest edition of the *Shady Creek Tribune* on the doorstep. Since Minerva had died just the day before, Joey wouldn't have had much time to put together a story about the second murder before printing the paper, but I hoped he'd managed to gather some information that I didn't yet know about. A quick read of the front-page article dashed that hope.

Joey had clearly talked to someone who'd been on the scene, because he knew Minerva's body had been locked in the pillory, soaking wet, but it seemed he didn't have anything to add to what I already knew. He'd included a short quote from Rachael and a brief statement from the police, neither of which revealed any details or helpful clues.

I folded the paper with a sigh and set it on the bar. Maybe the only way to find out more about my suspects was to talk with them directly, or with those who knew them well. As much as I wanted to do that right away, I had to open the pub in an hour.

I propped open the front door to allow the gentle summer breeze to waft into the building. Booker arrived for his shift, and I hung out with him in the kitchen for a while, enjoying a cup of coffee as we chatted. Once I'd emptied my cup, I left Booker to his prep work. I got comfy on a stool at the bar and decided to read *Murder Makes Scents* by Christin Brecher for the half hour left until the Inkwell opened for the day.

I'd made it through one chapter when someone tapped softly on the open door.

"Did you open early today?"

I couldn't help but smile when I saw Grayson. After setting my book on the bar, I slid off my stool.

"The door, but not the business," I said. "It's too nice out not to let the air in."

"So I get you to myself for a few minutes?"

"Hopefully," I said.

I stepped into his embrace, and he kissed me in a way that made me forget about murders, suspects, and everything else. If only our kiss could have gone on forever.

Grayson kept hold of my hand as we sat on neighboring stools at the bar. "I just heard the news this morning."

"About Minerva's murder?" I guessed.

"I heard about that last night. I wanted to text you, but things were crazy at the brewery until late. What I meant was I heard from Juliana this morning that you were one of the people to find the body."

I wasn't all that surprised that the brewery's head of public relations knew about that fact. It hadn't taken long for half the town to find out that I'd been on the scene.

"Jasmine, the mermaid we talked to the other night, was the first one to find the body," I said. "I heard her screaming and went to see what was wrong."

Grayson's thumb traced soothing circles on the back of my hand. "Are you all right?"

"Yes. Mostly." I wished we were sitting closer, so I could rest my head on his shoulder. "It was awful to see her like that, but I managed to sleep without nightmares last night."

That had been a blessing. I had worried that I might not sleep at all, but I'd tossed and turned for less than an hour before falling into a deep slumber.

"Not to make light of Minerva's death," Grayson said, "but this could be good news for Damien, if he has an alibi."

I told him about my visit to Damien's house the day before and the fact that his ankle bracelet would confirm that he'd never left his house. I also told him about my goal of finding proof that only one killer was involved in both murders, so Damien could be exonerated.

We talked about my various suspects but didn't come up with anything new. When we'd exhausted the subject, Grayson picked up the paperback I'd left on the bar.

"Is it good?" he asked.

"Very good. It's the second book in the Nantucket Candle Maker Mystery series. I've been hooked since I read the first one last month."

He set the book down. "Have you ever been to Nantucket?"

"No," I said with a sigh. "I've always wanted to go, but it's never happened. How about you?"

"Same. Maybe one day."

Mel arrived, and I realized that the first customers of the day likely wouldn't be far behind her. I enjoyed Grayson's company too much to want to say goodbye, so I walked with him as far as the footbridge, delaying the inevitable as long as I could.

We paused on the bridge, and I leaned into him, listening to the creek babbling cheerfully below us.

"What if we don't manage to clear Damien's name?" I asked, my spirits doing a nosedive. "I feel like I'm going in circles."

"Hey." Grayson held me close and ran a hand down my hair. "Don't give up." I felt his grin as he pressed a kiss to the top of my head. "Not that you could, even if you wanted to."

My mood lightened slightly, and I rested my head against his chest, comforted by the sound of his heartbeat. "I'm definitely a lost cause."

"I wouldn't put it that way."

"Hopelessly nosey?"

Laughter rumbled in his chest. "I plead the Fifth."

I raised my head to scowl at him, but I couldn't keep the expression in place, especially once he kissed me.

I still didn't want to say goodbye, so I accompanied him to the edge of the road, then let go of his hand with reluctance. I watched as he walked away and disappeared up the driveway that led to the brewery. When I finally turned around, I noticed a silver car heading toward me. As it slowed down and came to a stop, the driver's side window lowered.

"Ms. Coleman."

"Shoot," I muttered when I saw Detective Marquez behind the wheel.

No other vehicles were on the road, so I moved closer to make it easier to speak with her.

"Detective," I greeted cautiously.

"I understand you were at the fairgrounds yesterday when the deceased was found," she said, her voice even but her eyes sharp.

"I gave my statement to Officer Howes."

"I'm aware." She regarded me more closely than I would have liked. "You were at the fairgrounds before the gates opened."

"Yes. Well, not exactly. I mean . . ." I realized I was babbling. "I was out for a walk in the woods at the edge of the park." That was sort of true. I had been a few feet inside the tree line for part of the time.

The suspicion in Marquez's eyes didn't disappear, but I didn't give her a chance to lecture me.

"Damien has an alibi for the latest murder, thanks to his ankle bracelet." I couldn't help but point that out.

"We have to confirm that with the electronic-monitoring company."

"And when you do?" I pressed. "Will you at least be open to the possibility that he didn't kill Ozzie Stone?"

"My mind is open to all possibilities, Ms. Coleman." She scrutinized me again. "Do you have anything you'd like to share with me?"

I realized she should probably know about Minerva's threat to Collette, and some of the other things I'd overheard.

"A few things," I admitted.

"Do you have time right now?"

I glanced over my shoulder. I hadn't noticed any customers arriving at the Inkwell yet. I returned my attention to the detective, holding back a sigh. "I'll pour you a cup of coffee."

Chapter 24

By the time I'd shared everything I could think of with Detective Marquez—without admitting to being on the fairgrounds when I didn't belong there—customers had claimed three of the pub's tables. Marquez didn't fail to tell me to leave the investigating to the professionals, but fortunately, that was pretty much the extent of her lecture.

I was relieved when she left the Inkwell. I could never completely relax around the detective. She was always watching me far too carefully, and somehow her scrutiny always made me feel guilty, whether I had reason to or not. I respected her, but I most definitely didn't want to end up on her bad side for any reason. Sometimes preventing that from happening was like balancing along a tightrope.

Mel had taken care of all the customers so far, but I jumped in to help her, and the familiar routine of working calmed me. I felt even better when Aunt Gilda arrived at the Inkwell.

"Are you sure you're all right?" she asked as she greeted me with a fierce hug.

I'd told her and Shontelle via text message about seeing Minerva's body.

I returned the hug. "I'm sure."

As I released my aunt, Shontelle came into the pub. When she spotted me and Gilda, she hurried over our way.

"I had to come and see for myself that you're okay," she said when she reached us.

Gilda set her purse on a nearby stool. "You had the same idea as me."

"I'm fine," I assured them. "It shook me up a bit, but I've recovered."

Shontelle gave me a quick hug. "You don't have very good luck with dead bodies. You're always coming across them."

"Hopefully, my luck will change in that regard. I've seen more than enough dead bodies to last me a lifetime."

I knew my tendency to end up where cadavers were wasn't entirely luck's fault. My never-ending curiosity and habit of sticking my nose in murder investigations had a hand in leading me to some of the bodies I'd seen. I didn't bother to admit that out loud.

Shontelle and Gilda settled on stools at the end of the bar.

"What can I get you?" I asked them.

"Just a cup of coffee for me," Gilda requested.

"Same here," Shontelle said. "I have to get back to the shop soon. I'm sorry I couldn't come by yesterday, after you texted me. The shop was busy all day, and then Kiandra and some of her friends had a sleepover at our place."

I grabbed the coffeepot. "I'm guessing that meant not much sleep for you or the kids."

"Not as much as I would have liked, but the girls were pretty good, so I shouldn't complain."

I filled two mugs and slid them across the bar.

Aunt Gilda stirred some cream into hers. "I hear the faire's been shut down, at least until the weekend."

"I guess that's not surprising," I said. "It might make things more difficult, though."

"What things?" Shontelle asked.

"I was hoping to talk to some of the people who work at the faire."

"I hope you're not getting mixed up in any trouble, honey," Aunt Gilda said. "I know you're curious by nature, but it's much safer to let the police do the investigating."

"You sound like Detective Marquez." I smiled to soften the words.

"She's a smart woman. You should listen to her. And to me."

I decided a quick change of subject was in order. "I think I've convinced Mom to come to Shady Creek."

"That's great!" Shontelle said. "I'd love to meet her."

"I definitely want her to meet you."

Shontelle took a sip of coffee. "And Grayson?"

I hesitated. "We'll see."

Aunt Gilda patted my hand. "Your mom will love Grayson."

"You think so?"

"Why wouldn't she?" Shontelle looked from Aunt Gilda to me.

I twisted one of the rings I wore on my right hand. "She just . . ."

Aunt Gilda finished the sentence for me. "Has a tendency to find fault with things?"

I nodded. "And I don't want that to happen."

"I really don't think you need to worry, sweetheart," Aunt Gilda said. "Grayson's a good man. Your mother would be hard pressed to find anything to complain about there."

I hoped she was right. The more my feelings for Grayson grew, the more important it was to me for my family to like him. Aunt Gilda already did, and so did my younger brother, Taylor. He'd met Grayson when he came to visit last Christmas, before I'd started dating Grayson. My mom and my older brother, Michael, hadn't even known of Grayson's existence until a couple of weeks earlier, when I'd mentioned to my mom on the phone that I was dating someone new. She'd seemed wary rather than happy for me, probably because my last relationship had ended in disaster.

"Is it okay if Mom stays with you when she's here?" I asked Aunt Gilda. "It'll likely be in late October."

"Of course. But don't you want her here with you?"

"Yes, but she's not keen on staying above the pub. She thinks it'll be too noisy."

"I'm happy to have her at my place," Aunt Gilda said. "I'll call her later today to let her know that."

"Thank you," I said, relieved to have that settled.

Aunt Gilda and Shontelle chatted together while I looked after some of the other customers. Gilda left a few minutes later, giving me another hug on her way out. When I returned to the bar, I asked Shontelle if she wanted me to top up her coffee.

"No, thanks. I have to run in a few minutes. But I wanted to talk to you without Gilda here."

"What about?" I asked, curious. "Eldon?"

Shontelle shook her head. "Your investigation. I'm guessing you're not going to quit."

"I don't think I can."

"That's what I figured. Maybe I can get you onto the fairgrounds, even though they're closed to the public. I'll ask Rachael if we can drop by to see her."

I smiled, liking that idea. "That would be great."

Shontelle set down her coffee cup and stood up. "But I don't want you getting into danger any more than Gilda does. You need to be careful."

"Always."

Shontelle raised an eyebrow at that but didn't argue. "I'll be in touch after I contact Rachael."

She tried to pay me for the coffee, but I wouldn't let her. As she threaded her way around the tables, heading for the door, I got back to serving customers.

A few hours later, Zoe showed up for her shift. Her sister had already arrived and was in the kitchen, working. I was getting better at telling the twins apart, but I still found it helpful that Teagan had a streak of red through her dark blond hair, while Zoe didn't.

I smacked a hand to my forehead when I saw her. "I totally forgot to tell you about Tilly."

"Who's Tilly?" Mel asked as she wiped up some spilled beer.

Zoe joined us behind the bar. "I don't know anyone by that name."

"She's the mystery muralist," I said.

They both caught on to my meaning right away.

"How did you figure that out?" Zoe asked.

I told them about the times I'd seen Tilly around town, and how she'd had blue paint on her clothes.

"She looks about eight or nine years old," I added. "She and her mom moved to town a few weeks ago. I was thinking the kids' mural program at the community center would be good for her."

"Definitely better than going around painting buildings without permission," Mel said. "It would be good to channel her creativity in a positive way."

"Absolutely," Zoe agreed. "The programmer at the community center is on board with the idea. We just need a bit more time to get things organized. Do you know how I can get in touch with her mom?"

"I know her mom's name is Tamara Wilburn, and they live on Larkspur Lane."

"It shouldn't be hard to find them. There aren't many houses on that road. I'll drop by and talk to her mom sometime soon," Zoe said before disappearing into the back so she could leave her purse in her locker.

"That's one mystery solved," Mel said before following Zoe.

If only the murder cases were as easy to wrap up.

Business picked up later in the evening, and it didn't begin to slow again until the kitchen closed for the night at nine o'clock. It was around that time when Joey showed up. I came back to the bar after delivering drinks to a table of four and found him sitting slumped on a stool, his face glum.

"What's the matter?" I asked him.

"I just had dinner with Sofie at the Harvest Grill."

Sofie owned the local bakery, Sofie's Treat. She and Joey had been dating since May, like me and Grayson.

"And that's a bad thing?" I wasn't sure I'd ever seen him looking so dejected.

"It wouldn't have been if Sofie hadn't broken up with me over our entrées."

"Ouch. I'm sorry, Joey." I thought I detected a shimmer of tears in his eyes before he blinked. "Let me get you something to drink, on the house."

"A whiskey sour?"

"Coming right up."

I mixed his drink, then added half a wheel of orange and a maraschino cherry before setting it on a coaster in front of him.

"Thanks, Sadie." He downed half the drink in one go.

We both winced.

"What happened?" I asked once he'd recovered. "I thought things were going well between the two of you."

"So did I, but she thinks we'd be better off as friends."

"Ouch," I said for a second time.

"Tell me about it." Joey stared into his drink. "Story of my life."

I wanted to cheer him up, but I wasn't sure that was possible.

He took another drink of his whiskey sour—a much smaller one this time—and then fixed his gaze on me. "I wanted to interview you yesterday, but I ran out of time. I was running around all day, getting the story together about the fortune-teller's murder."

"And you heard that I saw the body," I guessed.

"Word gets around."

I had to excuse myself for a moment while I mixed drinks for two other patrons. As soon as I was free again, I returned to Joey.

"I'll have a follow-up story in the next edition of the paper," he said. "Can I get that interview sometime this week?"

"Sure."

Joey finished off his drink. "Maybe Damien will be a free man soon. I hear he's most likely got an alibi."

"The police just need to confirm it," I said. "I sure hope the charge against him will be dropped."

"But another local might be about to end up in hot water."

"Who?" I asked.

Joey lowered his voice. "Matt Yanders."

I decided not to let on that I was already worried about that possibility. "Why do you say that?"

Joey nudged his empty glass toward me. "Because it turns out the fortune-teller jilted Matt at the altar."

Chapter 25

"Where did you hear that?" I asked with surprise and dismay.

"Brandon, one of the waiters at the Harvest Grill, is a real gossip." Joey pulled a couple of bills from his wallet and set them on the bar.

"Your drink's on the house," I reminded him.

He pushed the money toward me. "Then this is for the next one."

I mixed him another drink and then crossed the pub to clear and clean a recently vacated table. Two customers asked for refills of their beers, so I took care of those drinks before checking in with Joey again.

"When did all this happen?" I asked, going straight back to our conversation.

"I'm not sure. I'm guessing it was quite a while ago, though. Brandon said it happened in Boston, and Matt's been living here in Shady Creek for at least five years." Joey plucked the maraschino cherry out of his half-finished drink and chomped on it. "I haven't confirmed the rumor yet, but I intend to."

"I hope it's not true," I said.

"There's probably at least a grain of truth to it."

My expression was likely almost as glum as Joey's now. "But that means Matt had a motive for killing Ozzie *and* Minerva. I don't want him getting arrested."

"Even if he's the killer?"

"I can't believe that he is."

Joey narrowed his eyes. "Hey, wait a second. Matt had a motive for killing Ozzie Stone?"

I realized my mistake. "Did I say that?"

"We both know you did."

I pretended to zip my mouth shut.

"You're not going to share? Even though I just got dumped by Sofie?"

I set a bowl of pretzels in front of him. "Consolation prize."

"Gee, thanks," he mumbled.

I left him munching on the pretzels and got back to serving the pub's other customers.

I knew for certain that Damien hadn't killed anyone. I didn't know Matt as well as I did Damien, but I desperately wanted to believe he was innocent.

I had to keep digging, to figure out who was really behind the murders.

Hopefully, the answer to that question wasn't one I should be dreading.

Shontelle came through for me before the end of the day. We met up at the Village Bean the next morning so we could get drinks to take with us to the fairgrounds, where we'd arranged to meet up with Rachael. I bought myself a mocha latte, and Shontelle ordered a caramel one for herself and hazelnut for Rachael.

From the coffee shop, we walked over to the park. Instead of heading for the main gates, which were currently locked, we made our way along the edge of the park, near where the trailers were parked. Shontelle sent a text message to Rachael, letting her know we'd arrived. Within minutes, Rachael appeared at a smaller side gate, a security guard at her side. The guard unlocked the gate, and we hurried through it.

"How are you holding up?" Shontelle asked Rachael, giving her a hug after handing over the hazelnut latte.

"I've been better." Rachael had dark rings beneath her eyes.

"Do you think the faire will reopen?" I asked as the three of us walked slowly along the line of trailers.

"I sure hope so. But at the same time, I'm worried about everyone. Two people have already died on my watch. If we lose someone else . . ." Her voice broke.

Shontelle put an arm around her. "It's not your fault."

Rachael blinked away a sheen of tears and drew in a steadying breath. "Maybe not, but I don't want anyone else getting hurt."

"Keeping the faire shut down might not keep anyone any safer," I said. "After all, Minerva was killed after hours. I'm sure if the murderer wants someone else dead, they won't let a shutdown stop them."

Rachael shuddered.

"Not that anyone else is being targeted," Shontelle said quickly.

Rachael took a long drink of her latte. "The faire could get completely dissolved, though."

"Is that likely to happen?" Shontelle asked.

Rachael shrugged. "It seems more and more likely. I don't know if the faire can recover from this. I think there's a good chance that everyone here could be out of a job by the end of the summer, if not before then."

We passed between the ends of two trailers and headed for the campfire Grayson and I had seen the other night. A few lawn chairs had been set up around the fire. Only two were occupied at the moment, by Toby and a woman I didn't recognize. I did, however, recognize the woman coming out of a nearby trailer. Collette wore yoga pants and a tank top and was pulling her hair into a ponytail.

I hung back half a step so Rachael couldn't see me when I discreetly tipped my head in Collette's direction. Shontelle gave me the barest of nods. As she asked Rachael what she planned to do if she lost her job, I changed direction and followed Collette over to the campfire. Before I got there, the woman I didn't recognize exchanged a few words with Collette before walking off toward a nearby tent. I smelled the scent of cooking bacon coming from over that way.

When I was a stone's throw away from the campfire, Flint crossed my path. It took me a second to realize it was him. I'd never seen him in jeans and a T-shirt before. He had his leather arm bracers clutched in one hand, but there was no other sign of his usual costume.

"Morning, Flint," I called out.

He stopped and smiled when he saw me. "Hey, Sadie. I hear you're having a Shakespeare night at the pub."

"Tomorrow," I confirmed. "Will I see you there?"

"Hopefully. Sorry I can't stop and chat. I've got to get these arm bracers fixed. I'm determined to stay optimistic about the faire reopening, and I want to make sure my costume is ready to go when it does."

"No worries," I assured him. "See you around."

He strode off, and I continued on to the campfire.

Collette had settled on one of the chairs across the fire from Toby. I plopped down in one of the other free seats.

"Morning," I greeted brightly.

Collette looked at me with a hint of surprise, but Toby only glowered at me.

"You don't belong here," he grumbled.

"Toby!" Collette narrowed her eyes at him.

"It's all right," I said quickly. "But I'm here with permission.

My friend knows Rachael from college." I nodded toward where they stood, not far from the tent giving off the cooking smells. "I'm so sorry you suffered another loss."

Toby's glower didn't ease in the slightest. "Not much of a loss."

He got up from his chair and stomped off.

"Sorry," Collette said. "My brother can get moody."

So they were related, as I'd thought they might be.

Collette looked at me more carefully. "You work at the local pub."

I nodded. "I'm the owner."

She leaned back in her chair. "This is a nice town. I would have enjoyed being here under different circumstances."

"It can't be easy, first losing Ozzie and then Minerva."

"It's terrifying."

We watched as Toby entered one of the trailers and slammed the door behind him.

"I take it your brother didn't like Minerva much," I said.

"I can't say I did either." Collette frowned. "Toby isn't the easiest person to get along with, but he's still my little brother, and I don't like it when people are cruel to him."

"And Minerva was?" I guessed.

"Toby and I were raised by a single mother. She passed away six years ago, and it's been really hard on Toby. Minerva claimed she could communicate with the dead, and Toby wanted to believe that so badly. He handed over a bunch of money just for that witch to tell him that our mother's message for him was that it was time for him to grow up and get a real job."

I winced. "I can see how that would be upsetting."

"It crushed Toby. And it was completely false. My mother never would have said that to him. She worked at a Renaissance faire herself, and she was thrilled that Toby and I were doing the same. She always encouraged us to follow our dreams. She didn't care about us having traditional jobs. She just wanted us to be happy. After I heard what Minerva said to Toby, I could have wrung her neck." Bitterness practically dripped from her last words.

I tensed in my chair, not sure what to say.

Collette jumped to her feet. "Excuse me. I'm going to go get some breakfast before it's all gone."

She passed Shontelle and Rachael on her way into the tent. The other two women came over and joined me by the campfire.

"Any luck?" Shontelle asked me.

"I'm more certain than ever that Collette and Toby belong on my suspect list," I said. "They were both upset with Minerva. But I didn't find out why Minerva threatened Collette the other night."

"Minerva threatened her?" Rachael said with surprise.

I told her what I'd overheard at the Inkwell.

Rachael nodded with understanding. "I think I know what that was about. Collette told Minerva she was going to expose her as a fraud."

"Could she have done that?" Shontelle asked.

Rachael shrugged. "Minerva *was* a fraud, but I don't know if there was any way Collette could have proven it." She sighed. "My bosses want me to find another fortune-teller, and quickly. On top of finding a replacement for Ozzie."

"You're not going to give Toby his own show, after all?" I asked.

"I don't think it would work out. He doesn't have the flair and showmanship."

Toby's mood wasn't likely to improve anytime soon, then.

"If your bosses want you to find replacements, then isn't that an indication that the faire is going to stay open?" Shontelle asked.

"I'm not so sure." Rachael sounded dispirited. "If no one else dies, and if I can really wow my bosses with the replacements I bring in, maybe we'll be okay. But I'm not going to hold my breath. Things aren't looking good."

I spotted Hamish the minstrel exiting the nearby tent, two other men with him.

Shontelle noticed me watching them. "Who are they?"

"I know the guy in the middle," I said. "Hamish. He's on my suspect list."

"Hamish?" Rachael sounded surprise. "He wouldn't hurt anyone."

"He didn't like Ozzie." I told her and Shontelle about the comments I'd overheard Hamish making at the Inkwell.

Rachael shook her head as I finished up the short tale. "The night Ozzie died, Hamish was performing on the stage in the village square. He was there for a couple of hours, at least. I was there too, until I heard that something had gone wrong at the show tent."

"He couldn't have slipped away at all?" I asked.

"Nope." She clearly had no doubt about that. "He was up on the stage the whole time with some of the other musicians."

"That's some progress, at least," I said. "That's one name I can cross off the suspect list."

Unfortunately, many more still remained.

Chapter 26

We didn't stay at the fairgrounds much longer. Shontelle's mom was watching the gift shop, but Shontelle had promised to relieve her before too long. As Rachael accompanied us to the side gate, I told her about the Shakespeare trivia night at the Inkwell. She wasn't sure if she'd be able to attend, but she promised to let the other faire workers know about the event.

"What's Kiandra up to today?" I asked Shontelle as we walked back to the center of town.

"She's over at a friend's place."

Something occurred to me. "I know someone her age who could use a friend." I told her about Tilly.

"We should get her together with Kiandra sometime," Shontelle said, as I'd hoped she would. "And I'd love to meet Tilly's mother."

"So would I."

I stopped short on the sidewalk outside the Village Bean. Matt Yanders had just entered Aunt Gilda's hair salon.

"What is it?" Shontelle asked.

"I think I've got another opportunity to dig up some more information."

Shontelle smiled. "I'll leave you to it, then."

"Will I see you at the Shakespeare trivia night?" I called as we parted ways outside Sofie's Treat.

"If my mom can babysit Kiandra," she said over her shoulder. "I want to see you in your costume!"

I hoped my costume would look good. I knew it fit, because I'd tried it on, but I hadn't yet worn it with full makeup to gauge the complete effect.

I didn't want to enter the salon when Matt was at the hairwashing station. I figured it would be better to strike up a conversation once he was parked in front of the mirror, getting his hair cut. To delay my arrival by a few minutes, I popped into Sofie's Treat.

In recent weeks I'd often seen Joey in the bakery, working on his laptop at one of the tables while enjoying one of Sofie's delicious baked goods. I wasn't surprised to find that he wasn't there this morning. My heart ached for him. He'd really liked Sofie.

I purchased a box of assorted donuts to share with my employees. By the time I'd done that, I figured I'd wasted enough time. When I entered the salon, Gilda and Betty both had clients in their chairs. I was glad to see Matt sitting in front of Aunt Gilda. I wasn't so pleased to see that Betty was cutting Vera Anderson's hair.

I gritted my teeth, remembering how Vera had gossiped about seeing me walking home from Grayson's house after I'd fallen asleep on his couch. Despite my dislike for the woman, I greeted her as cheerily as I did the other three people in the salon.

"I hear your mom's coming to Shady Creek," Betty said.

"In October." I perched on an empty salon chair. "In time for the food and drink festival."

Betty smiled, her eyes sparkling. "So she'll finally get to meet Grayson."

Vera sniffed. "Will she approve?"

"Why wouldn't she?" Betty asked. "Grayson's a great catch."

"Are you all ready for the Shakespeare trivia night?" Gilda asked me, effectively cutting off any further remarks from Vera.

"Pretty much," I said, doing my best to forget about Vera. "Will you be there?"

"I plan to be," Betty said. "But I don't have a costume."

"That's fine," I assured her. "Not everyone will."

"I'll be there," Matt said as Aunt Gilda trimmed his hair. "Hopefully, Flint will be too. And I doubt he'd pass up an opportunity to wear his costume."

"That will make a lot of people happy," I said with a smile. "He's very popular."

Matt rolled his eyes. "And he knows it."

Betty picked up the hair dryer and switched it on. I was glad that prevented Vera from rejoining the conversation.

"It's terrible what happened to Minerva," I said to Matt. "Are you doing all right? I hear you were close to her once."

Matt's face fell. "Does everyone know about that?"

"I don't know about *everyone*, but you know what this town's like."

"You knew the fortune-teller?" Gilda asked with surprise. "I certainly didn't know that."

"We almost got married." Matt's voice held no anger or bitterness.

"What happened?" I asked.

"She decided she loved someone else more than me." He sounded matter of fact about it. "She didn't bother to tell me that until our wedding day."

"How awful!" Aunt Gilda said, shocked.

Matt shrugged. "At least I found out before I married her. It was for the best."

"Still," Aunt Gilda said, "I'm sorry you went through that."

"Thanks," Matt said. "I'll admit it took me a while to get over it, but I did."

"Have the police talked to you about her death?" I asked.

"Why would they?" He seemed genuinely puzzled by the question.

"It's just . . . since you had a history with her, they might think you had a motive to harm her."

To my surprise, Matt laughed. "I wouldn't have wasted the energy." He sobered. "Seriously, though, I feel terrible that she died. She hurt me back then, but she didn't deserve what happened."

"The police might want to talk to you," I warned him. "Once they find out about your connection to her."

"I'm not worried. I heard she was killed sometime in the early hours of Tuesday. I'm seeing someone new, and we were together all night."

"Who's the lucky lady?" Aunt Gilda asked as she traded her scissors for the hair dryer.

"Diana Donovan. She teaches fitness classes over at the community center."

"I cut her hair," Aunt Gilda said. "She's a lovely woman."

She switched on the hair dryer, and I took that as my cue to leave. I picked up my box of donuts and waved as I headed out the door.

Finally, I felt as though I was making some progress with my investigation. I didn't think I needed to confirm Matt's alibi. I believed he'd told the truth about being with Diana when Minerva was killed.

I scratched his name off my mental list of suspects, and a small weight lifted off my shoulders. I still needed to clear Damien's name, but at least I was getting somewhere now.

My good mood added a spring to my step. When I reached the Inkwell, I skirted around the building to get to the back door.

I stopped short, the smile falling from my face.

A piece of paper hung on the door.

I stepped closer so I could read the block letters written on the paper.

Mind your own business. Or else . . .

The words frightened me, but not nearly as much as the knife that held the note in place.

Chapter 27

Like a spooked mouse, I scurried around to the front of the building. I felt safer there, since I was now in view of anyone out on the village green, but my nerves remained frayed. My immediate reaction was to phone nine-one-one, but I stopped myself before placing the call. Maybe I was overreacting. What if it was a silly prank?

I decided that was unlikely. I couldn't think of any reason why someone would have left me that note—especially with the added emphasis of the knife—except that someone wanted me to stop investigating the murders.

I shoved aside my hesitation and put the call through. The emergency dispatcher advised me to go somewhere safe, so I entered the pub through the front door and locked myself inside. As soon as I hung up, I set the box of donuts on the nearest table and made another call, this time to Grayson. Maybe it was silly of me, but I really wanted to hear his voice. I knew it would help to calm me.

He picked up after the second ring, sounding happy to hear from me. As soon as I told him about the note, his tone of voice changed.

"Stay inside and don't open the door for anyone but me or the police," he said. "I'm on my way."

I paced up and down behind the bar as I waited. I considered pouring myself a drink, but then I jumped when someone knocked on the front door.

"Sadie, it's me!" Grayson's voice helped to steady my racing heartbeat.

I hurried to the door and unlocked it.

He pulled me into a hug as soon as I opened the door.

"Are you okay?" he asked, still holding me tightly.

I nodded, my arms wrapped securely around his waist. I rested my head against his chest, the sound of his heartbeat soothing my frayed nerves.

Grayson stepped back so he could look me in the eye. I immediately missed the warmth and security of his embrace.

"The police aren't here yet?" he asked.

"It's probably not a top-priority call," I said.

He frowned at that. "I'll go take a look at the note. It's on the back door?" After I nodded, he added, "Maybe you should sit down."

I grabbed onto his hand. "I'm staying with you."

Most likely whoever had left the note was long gone, but I couldn't help but worry that they might be still lurking around, watching. I felt much safer now that Grayson had arrived, and I wasn't keen to let him go, even if only for a minute or two.

I kept hold of Grayson's hand as we rounded the corner of the building. When we reached the back door, we stopped. I glanced at Grayson as he studied the note from a few feet back. His expression was stormy, and a muscle in his jaw twitched.

His grip on my hand tightened. "Maybe this means you're getting close to the truth. Too close for the killer's comfort."

"I don't know about that," I said. "I've still got plenty of suspects and no real evidence to speak of."

"Who knows you've been asking questions?"

"A lot of people. Most of the people on my suspect list, probably."

And any one of my suspects could have left the note.

By unspoken agreement, Grayson and I returned to the front of the building. A police cruiser pulled up to the curb as we rounded the corner. I was relieved to see Shontelle's boyfriend, Officer Eldon Howes, climb out of the vehicle. I felt more at ease around him than any of the other officers from the local police department.

I quickly brought him up to speed on what had happened, and Grayson and I led him around the building to show him the back door. Eldon took some photos and pulled on a pair of gloves before carefully removing the knife from the door. He placed it in one evidence bag and the note in another.

The knife had left a gouge in the old red door. At least it hadn't pierced all the way through the thick wood.

"I'm guessing this has to do with the recent murders," Eldon said once he had both pieces of evidence bagged.

"Most likely," I admitted.

Eldon watched me with sharp eyes. "Did you really just happen to be at the fairgrounds the other morning, when the second body was discovered?"

I struggled not to fidget in the face of his scrutiny. "I might have been out looking for monkshood. Even if Minerva didn't have any in her possession, I thought maybe she could have found it close by and used it to kill Ozzie. Of course, she's no longer my top suspect, since she's been murdered too. At least, I'm assuming she was murdered."

Two uncomfortable seconds of silence ticked by before Eldon spoke again. "Sadie, by involving yourself in murder investigations, you're putting yourself at risk." He tapped the evidence bags he held in one hand. "This should make that clear."

"It does," I said. "But with Damien still under suspicion for Ozzie's murder . . ." I trailed off when I saw the set of Eldon's jaw.

"She's trying to help her friend," Grayson spoke up in my defense.

"I get that," Eldon said. He addressed his next words to me alone. "But you need to stop getting involved. It's too dangerous. I promise you that we're well aware of the fact that there could be one killer, and that Damien might be innocent."

"But the murder charge hasn't been dropped," I said.

Eldon sighed, and I realized I was pushing his patience to its limit. And I knew him to be a patient guy.

"Sadie," he said, "let us do our jobs."

"Of course." I didn't add that he and his colleagues could keep doing their jobs perfectly well while I continued investigating on my own.

"And if you notice anything else suspicious, or if someone makes you feel unsafe, call nine-one-one immediately, okay?"

"Definitely."

He seemed appeased by my agreement.

He pulled out his notebook and asked who all might know that I'd been poking my nose where it didn't belong. He didn't quite put it that way, but I knew that was what he meant.

I rattled off every name I could think of. "There's Collette, the acrobat who was also Ozzie's assistant. Her brother, Toby, might know I've been asking questions. Then there's Rachael— she's the faire's manager—Jasmine the mermaid, and possibly Flint Yanders. I think that's it."

Eldon jotted down the names and snapped his notebook shut.

"I'll look into who could be behind this," he promised.

Grayson and I walked with him back to his cruiser, and he drove off soon after.

I leaned into Grayson, suddenly tired. He wrapped his arms around me and rested his chin on the top of my head.

I sighed into him. "Can we stay like this forever?" I hadn't really meant to say that out loud.

Grayson kissed the top of my head. "I wouldn't mind."

Although his answer pleased me, I knew I'd kept him from the brewery long enough already. I stepped out of his embrace, but I couldn't hide my reluctance.

He brushed a thumb over my cheek. "I can stay if you want me to."

I did want him to, but I knew that was selfish of me, and unnecessary. "It's okay. You can head back to the brewery. I shouldn't have called you away in the middle of the day."

He brushed my hair away from my cheek and tucked it behind my ear. "I'm glad you called. I'd have been upset if you didn't. And I'd like to wait until Booker's here."

"Maybe he already is."

The Inkwell's parking lot was empty aside from my car, but that didn't mean anything, since Booker often walked to work.

I led the way into the pub through the front door.

Sure enough, Booker's voice boomed out from the kitchen. He must have shown up when we were around the back with Eldon.

Booker was in the middle of the chorus of "Sweet Caroline." The sound of his enthusiastic and pleasant singing brought a smile to my face.

"He's definitely here," I said.

I expected Grayson to head off, but instead, he made his way farther into the pub.

"Where are you going?" I asked.

"To say hi to Booker." He disappeared into the kitchen, and Booker's singing cut off.

I could hear the low rumble of both men's voices. Suspicious of Grayson's motives, I decided to follow him, picking up the box of donuts on the way.

The men stopped talking as soon as I appeared in the kitchen.

I set the donuts down on the nearest surface. "What's going on?" I asked, although I already had a pretty good idea.

Booker was in the midst of preparing a vat of chilled avocado and grapefruit soup. He set down the avocado he was holding and wiped his hands on his apron. "Grayson told me what happened." He folded me into a hug. "Are you okay?"

"I'm fine," I assured him as he released me.

Standing so close to Booker always made me feel tiny. The former college football player was well over six feet tall and had maintained his muscular physique in the years since the end of his athletic career.

Booker looked at Grayson over the top my head. "Don't worry. I'll keep an eye out."

Grayson nodded his thanks as I turned toward him.

I was fairly certain my suspicions had been spot on. "You don't need to rally all the men in my life to watch out for me. I can look after myself." I wasn't angry, but I didn't want people thinking I was weak.

"He cares about you, Sadie," Booker said before Grayson had a chance to respond. "So do I. And it's never a bad thing to have someone watching your back."

Grayson rested his hands on my shoulders. "What he said."

"Besides," Booker added with a cheeky grin, "if something happened to you, I'd be out of a job."

I couldn't help but smile, and it felt good after my recent scare. "If you keep being so sweet, you might make me cry."

"I'll blame it on the onions."

Of which there were none in sight.

As Booker went back to his singing and his prep work, I walked Grayson through the pub and out the front door. We came to a stop out in the sunshine, my hand in his.

"I'll call you this evening to see how you're doing," he said.

"You don't have to."

"What if I want to?"

I smiled. "Then I'd love to hear from you."

Grayson's blue eyes seemed to darken as they grew more serious. "Maybe you shouldn't be alone tonight."

My heart tripped over itself as I tried to decipher the exact meaning of his words.

"You could stay at my place," he continued. "Or maybe with Gilda."

"I'll be fine." The words popped out of my mouth before I had a chance to think them over. "I don't want to get chased out of my home."

"I could sleep on your couch."

"You don't have to do that." I realized my response could be interpreted in more than one way. "I mean, that's not necessary. Staying at my place. On the couch or elsewhere. Because I'll be fine." I sounded as flustered as I felt, and I knew my cheeks had turned pink, if not bright red.

To my relief, Grayson let the uncomfortable moment slip by. Not that *he* seemed uncomfortable. That was just me, because I was afraid he might have thought I'd read too much into his offer. Or not enough.

He put a hand to my face and stroked his thumb along my cheekbone, distracting me from my worries. "Be careful, okay?"

I could only nod, because the intensity of his gaze had stolen my breath away.

When he kissed me, I allowed myself to melt into him and forget about everything else. I could have sworn I'd almost floated away when someone cleared their throat.

Startled, I pulled away from Grayson.

Vera Anderson and another woman I didn't know stood a few feet away. Vera had a disapproving frown on her face, while her companion was fighting a smile.

"Don't mind us," Vera said, her voice chilly. "It's not like you have a business to run or anything."

Heat rushed to my cheeks again. I tugged my phone out of my pocket and checked the time. Two minutes before noon. I didn't think it was worth pointing out to Vera that I wasn't late opening the pub.

Unlike me, Grayson was grinning. He kissed me on the cheek and whispered in my ear, "See you soon."

As he headed across the footbridge, I held open the front door for Vera and her friend.

"What can I get you, ladies?" I asked as they chose a table in the middle of the room.

"A glass of white wine to start, please," the dark-haired woman requested.

"I'll have the same." Vera didn't look at me when she spoke.

"Coming right up," I said, forcing a smile even if Vera wouldn't see it.

"Making out like that for the whole world to see," Vera said to her friend in a loud whisper. "Talk about a lack of decorum."

My cheeks burned yet again as I slipped behind the bar and fetched a bottle of white wine.

Vera's companion stifled a giggle. "I wouldn't be worried about decorum either if I had such a fine man kissing me."

The mixture of embarrassment and anger brought on by Vera's words evaporated in a flash, and I had to struggle to keep a smile off my face.

As I poured two glasses of wine, I realized that it didn't matter what Vera thought of me or my relationship with Grayson. He made me happy, and that wouldn't change, no matter how judgmental Vera wanted to be.

Those thoughts allowed me to deliver the drinks with a genuine smile on my face.

Since I was no longer worried about what Vera might be saying about me, my mind was free to circle back to the question of who had left the frightening note on my door.

If I could find the answer to that question, I had no doubt in my mind that I would also know who'd killed both Ozzie Stone and Minerva the Mysterious.

Chapter 28

When I cracked my eyes open on Friday morning, a heavy weight settled on my chest, one that had nothing to do with the fact that Wimsey was perched there, staring into my eyes with his blue ones. Memories came rushing back to my wakening mind. I recalled the knife stuck into my back door, holding the threatening note.

I sat up abruptly, dislodging a disgruntled Wimsey. He hopped off my bed and padded to the bedroom door, glancing back at me as if to tell me to hurry up. He had me trained well, so I threw back the blankets and followed him into the kitchen, where I dutifully fed him breakfast.

That done, I peeked out the kitchen window, which overlooked the back lawn and the forest beyond. I didn't see anything other than a few birds. I returned to my bedroom and opened the curtains so I could take a look out over the village green. A few people were out and about, but nobody appeared suspicious. I didn't know what I'd expected to see. If the author of the note was keeping an eye on me, they wouldn't be sitting out in the open with a pair of binoculars trained on my windows.

I checked my phone and smiled when I saw a text message from Grayson, asking how I was doing today.

After sending him a quick reply, assuring him that I was fine and that the night had passed peacefully, I plugged my phone in to charge and hopped in the shower. It was only once I had my hair well lathered with shampoo that I realized it was Friday. A patter of excitement chased away my residual worries about the threatening note. The Shakespeare trivia night would be hosted at the pub that evening. I'd been looking forward to the event ever since I'd started planning it several weeks ago.

Once out of the shower and wrapped in a robe, I went to my closet and fingered the dress that was the main part of my wood nymph costume. It was too early to wear it, so I grabbed a sundress from another hanger. Originally, I'd planned to dress up as Ophelia from *Hamlet*, but then I'd spotted some nymph costumes while surfing through online stores, and I'd decided to take my inspiration from *A Midsummer Night's Dream* instead. The Internet had a wide range of fairy and nymph costumes available. Some were far too risqué for my taste, so I was glad when I'd found one that was cute and not too revealing.

I styled my hair into a side braid and ate a quick breakfast before heading downstairs to the pub. After taking care of a few tasks in my office, I took a walk across the southeast corner of the village green to Aunt Gilda's salon. She'd texted me the previous afternoon, asking why the police had been at the Inkwell. Apparently, Betty had spotted Eldon's cruiser as she'd made the short trip from the salon to the Village Bean for a latte. I'd been so busy at the pub when I'd seen the text that I'd simply told her that it was nothing serious and I'd fill her in later. I didn't want to leave her hanging any longer than I already had.

It turned out that I'd timed my visit perfectly. Aunt Gilda's first client of the day was on his way out the door when I arrived, and it wasn't yet time for her next one to show up. Betty, too, was free. Even better, while I was in the midst of greeting Aunt Gilda with a hug, the bell above the door jingled, signaling the arrival of Shontelle. She had a take-out cup from the coffee shop in one hand.

"Morning!" she said cheerily. "I saw you through the window on my way back from the Village Bean and decided to pop in to say hi."

"I'm glad you did," I told her.

Betty rearranged bottles of hair products on a shelf. "You're just in time for Sadie to tell us why the police were at the Inkwell yesterday."

"The police?" Shontelle turned to me with surprise. "How did I not know about this before?"

"It wasn't a big deal," I said quickly, not sure that they'd agree with me once I finished explaining. "Someone left a note for me on the back door."

Shontelle arched an eyebrow in suspicion. "What kind of note?"

I hesitated before answering. "A threatening one."

Aunt Gilda drew in a sharp breath.

I hurried to tell the rest of the tale and assured them that I was fine. I didn't, however, mention the part about the knife. Aunt Gilda had already gone pale enough. If I added that detail, I was afraid she might faint. Or never let me out of her sight again.

"I thought you were going to leave the investigating to the police," Aunt Gilda said when I'd finished relating the brief story. She'd regained some of her color, but I knew she wasn't pleased with me.

"Damien's freedom is at stake," I reminded her. "I couldn't sit back and do nothing. Besides, all I did was ask a few questions. I even had Grayson with me once and Shontelle another time."

A woman entered the salon. Aunt Gilda flashed her a distracted smile. "Good morning, Gwyneth. I'll just be a moment." She refocused her attention on me and lowered her voice. "You should stay with me for a few nights."

"That's not necessary. I'll be all right. I promise." I gave her a quick hug and made a dash for the door before she could protest.

Shontelle followed me out onto the sidewalk. "Gilda's right, you know. It might be better for you to not be alone in your apartment for the next while." She raised an eyebrow again. "Unless you haven't been spending the nights alone since we last talked."

My cheeks burned. "I have, actually."

"Maybe you should rethink that plan," she said with a smile. "I've got to run. Be careful, Sadie."

"I will," I promised as she headed off down the sidewalk with a wave.

I strolled across the corner of the green on my way back to the pub. I darted my gaze left and right as I approached the old gristmill, checking to see if anything seemed amiss. I didn't see anyone other than a young man walking his dog along Creekside Road.

After I crossed the footbridge, I quietly made my way past the Inkwell's front door and peeked around the corner. Aside from the birds in the trees, all was quiet. An uneasy tension hummed through me as I crept farther around the building until I could see the back door. No note today, thank goodness.

Relieved, I retraced my steps to the front door and let myself into the pub. I busied myself with getting ready to open for the day, but that didn't keep my thoughts away from the murders. Now that Minerva had fallen victim to what I believed was the one killer at work, I no longer had a prime suspect. I needed to figure out which of my remaining suspects had the most evidence pointing their way. How exactly I'd do that, I wasn't sure, but I wanted to start by talking to Collette again. Ever since Grayson and I had overheard her phone call, I'd been wondering if her ambitions could have driven her to murder. I'd initially thought anger was her most likely motive, but if getting Ozzie out of the way cleared the path to having her own show, maybe that made her motive even stronger.

I couldn't talk to her right away, unfortunately. I didn't have time to pay a visit to the fairgrounds before opening the pub. Rachael had promised to tell the faire workers about the Shakespeare trivia night, though, so I was hoping Collette might show up on my turf later on. If not, I'd seek her out tomorrow morning, whether the faire had reopened by then or not.

I was glad when Booker arrived to start his shift. Despite the assurances that I'd made to Aunt Gilda, Shontelle, and Grayson, I felt more at ease when I wasn't alone in the old gristmill. I joined Booker in the kitchen for a cup of tea while he got busy with his prep work. Not long after I'd finished my tea, Mel showed up.

"I met Tilly and her mom this morning," Mel said before she even had the door shut behind her.

"That's great!" I second-guessed myself. "Right?"

I hoped the meeting had gone well.

Mel quickly put my worries to rest. "Definitely. Her mom, Tamara, seems really nice. I'm going to introduce her to some of the other local artists. She showed me some of her pottery, and it's amazing. She's got a lot of talent."

"I'm glad to hear it went well."

Mel took up her post behind the bar as I flipped the sign on the front door.

"That's not all," Mel said. "Zoe got the green light from the community center for the fence murals, and Tilly's the first child signed up for the program."

"That's fantastic news."

Mel grinned. "Hopefully, it'll put an end to her graffiti career."

"I hope so too." If it didn't, Tilly would likely end up in hot water, but I felt confident that she'd stick to more welcomed projects in the future.

"Tamara's also going to sign her up for art classes in the fall," Mel said.

Happiness welled up inside me. "That's awesome. Not only will she have an artistic outlet, but she'll also be able to meet other children her age."

"She seems like a nice kid," Mel said. "I think she'll make friends in no time."

The first customers of the day arrived, and Mel got busy mixing their drinks while I took their food orders to Booker in the kitchen.

"All ready for tonight?" Mel asked when I returned to the bar.

"I think so." I mentally went over my preparations, hoping I hadn't forgotten anything.

"Don't worry. It'll be great," Mel said, as if she could read my mind. "The last trivia event was a big hit, remember."

"It was." I hoped this one would be just as good.

Business picked up, and a steady stream of customers kept us busy for the next several hours. Shortly after Zoe and Teagan arrived for their evening shifts, I took a break so I could have some dinner and change into my costume before the Shakespeare trivia night got underway.

As I ate an omelet up in my apartment, I sent a text to Damien, checking in to see how he was doing. I missed having him at the Inkwell, and I hoped it wouldn't be long before he was back to work and living his life freely.

He sent a response as I was cleaning up my dishes, letting me know that he was doing fine, all things considered. I wished I had good news to share with him. Somehow, I really needed to crack the murder cases. Not tonight, though. I doubted I'd have much time to think during the pub's event, let alone solve two major crimes.

Once Wimsey was fed and had settled down for a nap on the

back of the couch, I turned my attention to my costume, carefully removing the dress from its hanger. The skirt of the dress reached my knees and was made of several layers of raggedly cut chiffon in various shades of green. The dark green bodice laced up at the front with gold ribbon and had leaves and vines embroidered on it.

After zipping myself into the dress, I moved on to my makeup. I applied emerald-green eyeshadow and an earthy-toned lipstick before lightly dusting my cheekbones with sparkly gold powder. Then I undid my braid, brushed out my hair, and clipped the costume's headpiece in place. The base of the headpiece was made from fake ivy and vines. Dark brown feathers angled up and back. It looked like a woodland crown.

When I stepped back from the full-length mirror in my bedroom so I could study the full effect, a forest nymph smiled back at me. I looked better than I'd hoped, and I was glad I'd changed my mind about which character I wanted to dress up as. Not only did I love my current look, but the short, sleeveless dress would also be far more comfortable in the heat of the summer evening than the long-sleeved medieval maiden dress I'd almost ordered.

Time was ticking away, so I checked my makeup one last time and then slipped my feet into some gold flip-flops before making my way downstairs. I decided to pop into the kitchen to see how things were going in there before I returned to the bar.

Zoe had just brought in a stack of dirty dishes when I arrived.

"Whoa!" She stopped in her tracks. "Sadie, you look—"

"Freaking amazing!" Teagan said.

They often finished each other's sentences.

"Thank you," I said, unable to contain an excited smile. "Everything okay here?"

Zoe set down the dishes, and Teagan handed her a platter of nachos.

"Everything's perfect," they said in unison.

"It's getting crowded out there," Zoe added as she swept through the swinging door with the nachos.

A sudden attack of nerves froze me in place. "Are you sure I don't look ridiculous?"

"Are you kidding?" Teagan plated a burger with a side of fries and another with a salad. She handed both plates to me. "You could win your own costume contest."

"I'm pretty sure I'd have to disqualify myself since I'm one of the judges." My smile made a reappearance as I did my best to steady my nerves. "Thanks, Teagan."

"Go have a blast." She shooed me out of the kitchen.

As soon as I passed through the door, I saw that Zoe was right. The main room of the pub was nearly full now, and a few people had migrated into the two smaller overflow rooms. I'd left the front door standing open, but it was still getting quite warm inside. It wasn't to the point of needing the air-conditioning, though.

Zoe told me which table had ordered the burgers, and I wound my way around the other patrons to deliver them. I opened a couple of windows on my way back, letting the gentle evening breeze find its way inside.

I received several compliments on my costume as I worked my way across the room, including from Betty and Aunt Gilda, and that helped my confidence. I noticed Joey sitting at the bar, a half-finished pint of beer and some nachos in front of him.

He did a double take when he saw me. "Wow. Sadie, you look incredible." He produced his phone. "Can I take a picture for the paper? I'm doing an article on the trivia night."

"Sure?" I suddenly didn't know quite what to do with myself. Now I understood Cordelia's hesitation about having her photo taken at the faire.

Fortunately, another customer at the bar requested a pint of beer. I got distracted as I fetched the drink, and realized with relief afterward that Joey had snapped the picture while I was too busy to be awkward.

I was glad to see that several other people had shown up in costume. I spotted a few customers in general Renaissance-era garb, as well as a young couple I was pretty sure were meant to be Romeo and Juliet. There were also three women dressed as witches, presumably the ones from *Macbeth*. I suspected one man was meant to be Shakespeare himself, although I didn't know for certain yet. Another woman had dressed as the soothsayer from *Julius Caesar*. I knew without a doubt that was the character she was portraying when I overheard her telling her friends to "beware the Ides of March."

My study of the costumes came to an abrupt halt as Grayson walked into the Inkwell. He wore jeans and a T-shirt, but he looked better than anyone else in the pub. In my opinion, anyway.

"You look incredible," he said when he reached the bar.

"Thanks," I managed to say.

The heat of his appreciative gaze made my knees weak. Part of me wished the pub were empty aside from the two of us, even though I was grateful for the roaring business. I wanted nothing more than to kiss Grayson right then and there. I could tell from the look in his eyes that he wanted that kiss as much as I did.

A bell dinged in the kitchen.

"Sorry," I said with reluctance, still unable to take my eyes off of Grayson. "I have to go."

"It's fine. I'm not going anywhere." He settled on one of the two barstools not already occupied.

Realizing that I was still staring at him, I gave myself a mental shake and dashed into the kitchen. The next time I had a moment to breathe, it was time to get the trivia competition underway. I'd left all my papers in my office, so I hurried down the hall and collected everything I needed. When I turned away from my desk, Grayson was standing in the doorway.

"Can I steal half a minute?" he asked.

I took his hand. "Maybe even a whole one."

The kiss that followed probably took up most of that time.

"I'm sorry," he said afterward.

"For what?"

"Not wearing a costume. I didn't want to let you down, but I'm not really comfortable in costumes."

I started shaking my head before he'd finished speaking. "You didn't let me down. Not even close." It was sweet that he'd worried about it, though. "The costume thing is just for people who enjoy dressing up. All I care about is that you're here." I kissed him again to emphasize my words. "I wish I could spend more of the evening with you, but it's getting kind of crazy out there."

"Don't worry. The crowd's a good thing, and I'm hanging around until you lock up later."

"You don't have to go back to the brewery?"

Sometimes he had to check on whatever beer he had brewing.

"Not tonight." He rested his forehead against mine. "Let Rome in Tiber melt, and the wide arch of the ranged empire fall! Here is my space."

My heart did a fluttering dance in my chest. Quoting Shakespeare. Could he be more wonderful? I didn't think it was possible.

"I . . ." My voice died in my throat. I couldn't believe I'd almost blurted out that I loved him. But I did love him.

In that moment, I knew it without a shred of doubt.

Chapter 29

I couldn't say it out loud, though. What if he wasn't there yet?

My emotions swirled inside me like a whirlpool. "I'm really glad you're here."

I hoped he didn't notice the unsteadiness of my voice.

I gave him a quick hug so he couldn't get a good look at my face. Then I took his hand and led him back into the pub. Someone had claimed his stool in his absence, so he joined Joey and three other locals at a table with an extra chair.

Several people from the faire had arrived over the past half hour. Rachael sat at a table with Jasmine, Flint, Matt, Toby, and Hamish. Matt and Rachael wore modern clothing, but the others had come in costume. Flint caught my eye and winked. He raised his pint glass in a salute before taking a long drink.

While I was glad some of the faire workers had turned up, I was even more pleased to see how many locals had come out for the event. I smiled and waved at Cordelia and a few other familiar faces before calling for everyone's attention. I explained how the trivia contest would work and then asked people to gather with their teams. There was some shuffling of chairs as I passed out the answer sheets and made sure everyone had something to write with.

"Where's Collette?" I heard Jasmine ask the others at her table as I passed Matt an answer sheet and a pencil. "She was supposed to meet us here."

"She's probably just running late," Flint said, unconcerned.

Jasmine checked her phone with a frown before setting it on the table. "She was really looking forward to this."

If they said anything more about Collette, I didn't hear it. I hoped she'd show up before the night was over so I could have a chance to talk to her.

I finished making my rounds and returned to my post by the bar. It took another minute to get everyone settled down and quiet, and then I began.

"First question," I said to the room. "What was Shakespeare's longest play?"

I heard someone at the table closest to me whisper, "*Hamlet*," to their teammates. I couldn't tell how many other groups knew the correct answer.

I continued through my list of questions while Zoe kept everyone supplied with food and drinks. I was glad to see Joey smiling as he chatted with Grayson. Sofie hadn't shown up for the trivia night, and perhaps that was for the best. Her presence might have put a damper on the evening for Joey.

Eventually, I reached the final question on my list.

"What did Shakespeare leave to his wife in his will?"

I noticed a few puzzled expressions around the room. Grayson, however, leaned closer to his teammates and spoke quietly. Joey immediately jotted something down on their answer sheet.

Across the pub, Cordelia's face had brightened at the question. She, too, whispered to the others at her table, and one of her teammates wrote down their answer.

After another minute or two, I declared the contest over and collected all the answer sheets. It seemed the competition had stirred up everyone's appetites. Suddenly, everyone wanted a fresh drink or something to eat. For an overwhelming moment, I wasn't sure how I was going to be able to score the answers. There was far too much demand to leave Zoe working on her own.

I might have looked slightly frazzled when Grayson appeared at my side.

"I'll give Zoe a hand while you figure out who won," he said.

I threw my arms around him and gave him a quick kiss. "Thank you!"

A few people whistled and cheered, and I remembered we had an audience. Hopefully, my makeup covered up my blush.

Grayson joined Zoe behind the bar, while I made another trip to my office. I scored each team's answers as quickly as I could. Only three teams had answered the final question correctly, writing that Shakespeare had left his "second-best bed" to his wife in his will.

It didn't surprise me that Flint's team ended up as the winning one. I knew many of the people who worked at the faire were actors who also participated in theater productions at other times of the year. No doubt they were well acquainted with William Shakespeare's life and writings.

"Congratulations to the Trueheart Trivia Troupe," I announced once I'd returned to the pub. "You've won Inkwell gift certificates!"

Enthusiastic cheers rose up from Matt and Flint's table.

I handed out the prizes, hoping that their new owners would have a chance to use them. Every one of them except Matt would be leaving town within the week.

It turned out I didn't need to worry about that. They all put their certificates to use right away, ordering food and another round of drinks. Collette still hadn't shown up, but Jasmine no longer seemed worried. Maybe the two cocktails she'd already consumed had something to do with that.

Next, I handed out the prizes for the best costumes, after quickly conferring with Zoe, my fellow judge. We easily came to a unanimous decision. The three women dressed as the witches from *Macbeth* were declared the winners, much to their delight, and I gave them each an Inkwell certificate as well. Although I didn't know the women, they all lived locally.

"That was so much fun," Cordelia said to me as I passed by her table a short while later. "And we're twins!"

"We are!" I agreed. "I see you didn't go with your medieval maiden dress, after all."

Instead, Cordelia had dressed up like a forest nymph, complete with a garland of fake leaves and flowers in her hair. Our costumes weren't identical, but there was no mistaking the fact that we were both nymphs.

"I decided to save the other dress for Halloween, when the weather's cooler," she said.

"Good choice."

Joey appeared beside me. "Hey, did you two plan to be twins?"

"Nope," I said. "But great minds think alike." And the fact that we were both redheads made us match even more.

Joey held up his phone. "I need a photo."

I was more relaxed about this picture since I wasn't the only subject. It was easy to put an arm around Cordelia and smile as Joey snapped the photo.

That was my last chance to chat until the kitchen shut down for the night. After that, the crowd slowly thinned out.

Over at the faire workers' table, Toby stood up and began juggling. Soon he had the attention of almost everyone in the pub. He finished juggling to a round of applause and cheers. Then he made his way around the room, performing magic tricks.

When I returned to the bar from delivering a tray full of drinks to a table across the room, Grayson claimed one of the stools. We both watched Toby as he held a coin in the palm of his hand. He tapped the coin with a pen, and it disappeared. He then took the cap off the pen, and the coin seemed to fall out of the cap and into his hand.

"How does he do that?" I asked with amazement.

Grayson leaned one arm on the bar. "Magic's all about misdirection and quick movements." He grinned at me. "The entertainment type, anyway."

His grin stirred up a surge of elation and nerves, reminding me of the fact that I was in love with him. Not that I needed reminding. It had been on my mind ever since my revelation earlier.

Not wanting Grayson to figure out my thoughts, I busied myself behind the bar.

Toby spent a few more minutes amusing the patrons before returning to his friends. The group left the Inkwell soon after. Collette had never made an appearance. Maybe she'd simply been too tired for a night out. I was disappointed that she hadn't shown up, but then I reminded myself that I wouldn't have had time to question her, anyway. Hopefully, I would the next day.

Only a dozen or so customers remained at last call. Joey was one of them. He and Grayson were sitting at the bar now.

"How are you doing, Joey?" I asked.

He took a drink of the beer I'd poured for him a few minutes earlier. "All right, I guess." The smile I'd seen before had disappeared.

"Why so glum?" Grayson asked him.

Joey's shoulders slumped.

"He and Sofie broke up," I answered for him.

"That's the nice way of putting it," Joey said morosely. "She dumped me."

Grayson clapped him on the back. "Sorry to hear that."

"I'm glad you showed up tonight," I said. "Did you get your mind off things for a while?"

"Thanks, Sadie. I did, yeah. And now I can print a story about the trivia night."

"I appreciate that."

"I'm definitely including that picture of you and Cordelia."

"Better that than the one of me on my own." The thought of having my picture in the newspaper made me feel a bit shy. Sharing the spotlight helped to ease that feeling.

I left Grayson and Joey alone for a minute while I cleaned up a table and carried all the dirty dishes into the kitchen.

"Have you got anything new to print about the murders?" I asked Joey when I returned to the bar.

"I've got the cause of death for the second victim."

"How did you manage that?" I was a tad envious of his ability to get that information.

"Detective Marquez."

"She shared that with you?" Now I was really envious. "There's no way she'd do that with me."

Grayson and Joey both laughed.

I glared at them before saying to Joey, "Spill your secret."

"What can I say? I'm the local press."

"Shouldn't that be even more reason not to tell you things? Whatever she shares with you is guaranteed to get printed in the paper and posted online."

"Maybe she just likes me more than you." He gave me a cheeky grin.

"Not possible," Grayson said in my defense, although he sounded amused.

"Thank you," I said to him.

"Then maybe it's my charm and devastating good looks," Joey said.

Grayson nearly choked on his laughter.

It was Joey's turned to glare. "Thanks, man."

"You are good looking," I assured Joey, figuring he deserved the compliment after what he'd been through with Sofie. "But somehow I doubt that would sway Detective Marquez."

"Okay, you're right. She's releasing an official statement tomorrow morning. The victim's family has been updated, so she gave me the information a bit early."

"Did Minerva have much in the way of family?" I asked. "And what about Ozzie?"

"Minerva, aka Mina Young, has a sister and some cousins. Her father is still alive, but they were estranged, by all accounts. As for Ozzie, he has two brothers, and his mother's around, but she lives in a nursing home. Sounds like she's got dementia."

I wondered if she understood that her son had been murdered. It might be best if she didn't.

"I can't believe you haven't asked me *the* question," Joey said, amusement in his eyes.

"I was getting there," I assured him. "So? What was the cause of death?"

"Drowning."

"I guess that explains why Minerva was soaking wet."

"Marquez thinks she was drowned in the mermaid tank, and then the killer moved her body to the pillory."

Despite the fact that it was still warm in the pub, I shivered. The picture of what Joey had described was far too vivid in my head.

"I guess that's not great news for Damien," Grayson said.

I frowned. He was right.

"Probably not," Joey agreed. "If the MO had been the same as with Ozzie's murder, that would have made a stronger case for there being a single killer."

That was the exact same thought that had run through my head.

I checked the clock and decided it was time to close up for the night.

Joey and the last few stragglers eventually made it out the door. Grayson helped me cart all the dirty dishes to the kitchen and load them in the dishwasher. I decided to leave the rest of the cleanup for morning. I needed to get some sleep, so my mind would be sharp the next day, because I still needed to clear Damien's name.

Chapter 30

Grayson was true to his word and hung around until I'd locked up. He didn't linger much longer, thanks to a giant yawn that escaped me, giving away how tired I was now that the trivia event was over. Although I was always reluctant to say goodbye to him, time apart would give me a chance to at least attempt to get my muddled thoughts and feelings sorted out.

Not that there was all that much to sort out.

I was in love with Grayson, and I was no less certain of that when I woke up the next day. Really the only issue was whether I should tell him how I felt. The thought of doing so both scared and excited me. I wanted to say the words to him, but I couldn't get past the fear that he might not feel the same way. I knew he liked me, and liked me a lot, but I didn't want to run the risk of scaring him off if I shared the extent of my feelings too soon.

Maybe I needed to talk to Shontelle. Or maybe I just needed to see how things played out between me and Grayson over the next while. Or do both of those things.

I let myself obsess about my relationship with Grayson until

I'd finished all the cleanup in the pub that I hadn't taken care of the night before. After that, I firmly shoved all such thoughts aside. I still had a couple of hours before I needed to open the Inkwell for the day. My plan was to make good use of that time.

Armed with a mocha latte from the Village Bean, I walked over to the park, hoping for a chance to speak with Collette. I wasn't entirely sure how to strike up a conversation with her and get the information I wanted, but maybe winging it would work out. Not that I expected her to confess to the murders simply because I asked her a few questions, but maybe she'd let something slip that would help me in my investigation. Or maybe I'd have better luck talking to her brother, Toby. He might know about his sister's aspirations to have her own acrobatic magic show, and how far she was willing to go to make it happen.

I stopped in my tracks halfway to the park. If Collette wanted her future show to get picked up by the faire, wouldn't that quash her brother's chances of having his own magic show? I doubted Rachael would want both on the program. Maybe Collette and Toby were planning to have a show together? Or maybe Collette was imagining a show independent of the Renaissance faire.

After taking a sip of my latte, I resumed walking. The questions in my head seemed to keep multiplying, while answers were in short supply. Hopefully, I could change that.

My first challenge would be to gain access to the fairgrounds. Before leaving the Inkwell the night before, Joey had mentioned that the earliest the faire would reopen was Sunday, which was now one day away. I hoped I could get in on the pretense of visiting Rachael. Otherwise, I might have to get in through the woods. I'd worn sneakers in case that happened, but it was a last resort.

When the park was within view, my pace suddenly slowed. A police cruiser was parked by the main gates.

It took only a second to recover from my surprise. I hurried forward, worried that the killer had struck again. Maybe it was a good thing that there was only one cruiser present, unless no other officers had yet had a chance to arrive on the scene.

I spotted Eldon leaving the fairgrounds through the main gates, heading for his cruiser. I intercepted him before he could reach the vehicle.

"What's going on?" I asked. "Has someone else been killed?"

"Morning, Sadie." Eldon eyed my latte with what I thought was a hint of longing. "There hasn't been another death, as far as we know."

I pounced on his last words. "As far as you know?"

Eldon removed his hat and ran his hand through his blond hair. "The faire's manager called to report one of the workers missing."

"Not Collette?"

He set his hat on the roof of his cruiser. "Maybe I shouldn't be surprised you've already heard."

"I hadn't heard," I said, "but she was supposed to meet some of her friends at the Inkwell last night, and she never showed up. I put two and two together. Do you think she's in danger?"

"Most people seem to think she got scared by the murders and decided to take off."

"Without telling anyone?"

Eldon leaned against his cruiser and crossed his arms over his chest. "That's why the manager decided to report it. She thought it was a bit strange, especially since Collette left her clothes and other belongings behind."

"What about Collette's brother? He works for the faire too."

"I had a word with him. He doesn't think his sister would have taken off without telling him."

"So you're going to look into it?" I pressed.

"If she doesn't show up soon."

"But not yet?"

"It's only been twelve hours since she was last seen."

"But there's been two murders here recently," I pointed out unnecessarily.

"Which is cause for heightened concern."

"But you're not going to do anything for another twelve hours?" I couldn't mask my disapproval.

"I'm going to start looking into it right away," Eldon said. "We're just not going to raise the full alarm yet." He uncrossed his arms and straightened up. "There's always a chance she met someone in town and spent the night with them."

"I hope that's all that happened. What if she took off because she's the killer? Is she on your suspect list?"

"Most people connected to the faire are," he said. "Don't worry, Sadie. We're looking at this thing from all angles."

"I know." And I did know that, but I wished things would move along faster so Damien could get back to living his life and the real killer could get locked away.

Eldon opened the driver's door of his cruiser but didn't climb in right away. "About that note that was left for you."

My ears perked up. "Yes?"

"We were able to trace the knife back to a set used by the faire's cook."

"The cook threatened me?" I hadn't even met the person who cooked for the workers, as far as I knew.

"That's not looking likely, but pretty much any of the faire workers could have had access to the knife."

"So someone from the faire probably left the note," I concluded.

"Most likely, especially since everyone else's access to the fairgrounds has been limited over the past few days."

That was good information to have, but unfortunately it didn't narrow down my list of potential culprits. The only person ever on my list who didn't work for the faire was Matt, and I'd already eliminated him from the suspect pool.

Eldon placed his hat on his head. "What brings you over here this morning, Sadie?"

I'd hoped he wouldn't ask me that, but I wasn't the least bit surprised that he had. "I was hoping to talk to a few people."

Leaving my response vague didn't help me.

"I figured as much. How about I give you a ride back to the Inkwell instead?" When I hesitated, he added, "They're not letting anyone through the gates this morning aside from the workers and the police."

That meant my presence would likely get noticed quickly, even if I did manage to get in through the woods.

Eldon stood waiting. He wasn't about to take his eyes off me.

Reluctantly, I gave in.

"Could you drop me at the Spirit Hill Brewery instead?" I requested.

"Hop in."

It took only a minute or so to reach the brewery's driveway.

"Here's good," I said, and Eldon pulled over to the side of the road. "Thanks for the ride."

"Don't go looking for trouble, Sadie," Eldon warned as I climbed out of the cruiser.

I ducked my head back into the vehicle and smiled. "Of course not."

I shut the door before he could respond, and I waved over my shoulder as I made a start up the driveway. He—and others—might disagree with me, but I didn't think I ever went looking for trouble. It did, however, have a habit of finding me, anyway.

I bypassed Grayson's house and continued on to the brewery, knowing that was the most likely place to find him. I stopped in at the offices and asked Annalisa if Grayson was in.

"He's been holed up in his office for over an hour," she said. "Head on back."

I did so, noticing that Grayson's door stood half open. I peeked inside his office. He sat at his desk, frowning in concentration as he typed away on his laptop. He was so focused on what he was doing that he didn't notice me in the doorway.

"Knock, knock," I said as I stepped into the office.

He glanced up, startled. "Sadie." He stood up and shut his laptop in one quick movement.

I thought I saw a flash of fear in his eyes as he stepped away from his desk.

He quickly composed himself. "This is a nice surprise."

I forced a smile, wondering if that was the truth. Whatever he'd been working on, I was certain he didn't want me to see it.

He kissed me, but I kept it short.

"I was passing and thought I'd stop by and fill you in on the latest news. Unless you've already heard?"

"Not another murder, I hope."

"I'm really hoping not, but Collette's gone missing. She told her friends she'd be at the Inkwell last night, but she never showed up. No one's seen her since yesterday evening."

"She's the acrobat, the one we overheard on the phone when we were at the fairgrounds after dark?"

I nodded. "I don't know if she took off because she's the killer or if something terrible has happened to her. There's another possibility. Some people think she got scared by the murders and left without a word."

"Doesn't she have a brother at the faire?"

"She does. I'm hoping to get a chance to talk to him."

My gaze strayed to Grayson's closed laptop for a split second. Uncertainty thrummed through me. Why would Grayson hide something from me?

All my old anxieties and insecurities bubbled to the surface.

When my ex had started hiding things from me, it was because he had a gambling addiction. One that had ended up destroying our relationship. I'd been so wary to trust another man after that, but I'd become so certain that Grayson was different, that I didn't need to worry about such things with him. Was I wrong?

The mere thought made me feel slightly ill.

I'd meant to tell Grayson the news about the knife that had been left with the threatening note, but now all I wanted to do was get out of there. I glanced at my phone, pretending to check the time, though the numbers on the screen didn't even register in my mind.

"I'd better get going," I said, taking a step backward.

Grayson captured my hand in his. "Sadie, is everything all right?"

"Of course!" My answer and my smile were probably a bit too cheerful. "But I really need to get going." I pulled my hand from his. "See you later!"

I dashed out the door and didn't slow my pace until I was halfway down the long driveway. As I walked, I took the last sip of my mocha latte. I regretted it immediately. The liquid sat heavily in my stomach. I tried to convince myself that I had nothing to worry about, but it was too late. My worries had already taken off at a gallop, and there was no way I could rein them in now.

My phone rang, and I welcomed the distraction.

I checked the display and answered the call. "Hi, Mom!"

Once again, I probably sounded too cheerful. I wouldn't have made a good actress.

Fortunately, my mom didn't seem to notice.

"Good morning," she said. "I'm glad you're up. I thought you might still be lounging around in bed."

My mom had never understood how I could be anything other than a morning person like her.

"Nope. I've been up for a while." Not that I'd achieved what I'd hoped. My morning certainly wasn't going as planned.

"Good," my mom said. "I wanted to set a firm date for my visit. I was thinking the third week of October."

"You mean you really are coming to Shady Creek?"

"Why do you sound so surprised?"

"Oh . . . I guess I thought you might be too busy in the end." Really, I'd worried she'd simply change her mind and decide to stay home in Knoxville, but I was pleased that didn't seem to be the case.

"I'll mark in the trip right now if you still want me to come."

"Of course I want you to come," I said with complete sincerity. "I'm looking forward to it. Mark it down and make it official."

"Done. I've got to run now. I'm meeting Mary-Lou Wentworth and Tina Avalos for brunch."

"That sounds nice," I said. "Have a great time."

"I will. Thank you. And, Sadie?"

"Yes?"

"I hope I'll have a chance to meet that boyfriend of yours when I visit."

I gulped, suddenly a bundle of nerves. "Of course."

We said our goodbyes and ended the call.

Tears prickled at my eyes. I blinked them away, determined not to let myself get upset, and yet I couldn't help but wonder if I'd still have a boyfriend when my mom arrived in Shady Creek.

Chapter 31

I hoped I was overreacting about Grayson. I wanted someone to tell me that was the case, because then it might be easier to believe. When I reached the end of Grayson's driveway, I crossed Creekside Road instead of heading for the Inkwell. I dropped my cup into a recycling bin next to a bench on the village green and carried on across the grass. The sun shone brightly again, and many people were out and about, enjoying the weather or visiting the shops. Even though the faire was currently shut down, it still looked as though there were quite a few tourists in town. That was good news for the Inkwell and all the other local businesses.

Shontelle's shop, the Treasure Chest, was my intended destination, but I stopped halfway across the green. Kiandra was out playing with Tilly, the two girls running around, laughing.

Kiandra waved when she spotted me.

"Hi, Sadie!" She ran over my way, her new friend right behind her. "Do you know Tilly?"

"We've met," I said with a smile. "Hi, Tilly."

Tilly grinned at me. "We're playing vampires!"

"Oh?"

"Do you think there are any more vampires in Shady Creek?" Kiandra asked me.

"More vampires?" I echoed. "I don't think there's ever been any vampires here."

Kiandra's eyes were wide and serious. "That lady who died was one."

"She was a fortune-teller," I said, wondering how that information had become so twisted. I was surprised Kiandra even knew about Minerva's death, but then, maybe Tilly had told her.

Kiandra shook her head in response to my words. "No, she really was a vampire. Tilly heard someone say so."

"A grief vampire," Tilly chimed in, completely serious.

Kiandra grabbed Tilly's hand and pointed across the green. "Look at that puppy!"

The girls squealed and ran off.

"Bye, Sadie!" Kiandra called over her shoulder.

I watched them go, puzzled by our conversation.

I heard someone else call my name.

Shontelle stood outside the Treasure Chest, waving at me. I crossed Hillview Road to reach her.

"It's been a busy morning," Shontelle said, "but I finally got a moment's peace. I had to step outside to enjoy the weather, even if only for a minute."

"It's a beautiful day." I looked back out over the green, where Tilly and Kiandra were on their knees, playing with a labradoodle puppy while its owner watched with a smile. "I see Kiandra met Tilly."

"They hit it off right away," Shontelle said.

"That's great news."

I wondered if I should bring up the whole vampire thing, but Shontelle spoke again before I'd made up my mind.

"I'm sorry I didn't make it to the trivia night. My mom wasn't available to babysit."

"No worries," I assured her. "I understand."

"Did it go well?"

"Yes." The word came out on a sigh.

"You don't sound so sure."

"The trivia night was great," I said. "It's what happened a few minutes ago that's got me down."

She took my arm as a group of women passed us on the sidewalk. "Let's go in the shop."

Once inside, I told her about my visit to Grayson's office.

"Are you sure he was hiding something?" Shontelle asked when I'd finished. "Maybe he just shut his laptop because he was done working."

I shook my head. "He was definitely hiding something. I know the signs. It took me long enough to pick up on them when I was with Eric, but I'm not that naïve anymore."

Tears welled in my eyes. I was glad there weren't any customers in the shop to see me break down.

"Oh, hon." Shontelle gave me a hug. "Grayson is a good guy, and he's crazy about you. I'm sure of that. I bet there's a completely innocent explanation for his behavior."

I wiped at a tear that had managed to escape my eye. "But what if there's not? Shontelle . . . I'm in love with him. I just realized that last night. What if he's about to break my heart?"

She hugged me again. "If he does, you know I'll be here for you. But I really don't think that's going to happen. You need to talk to him."

"Maybe you're right." Although, I dreaded the thought of bringing up the subject with him. What if he told me something I didn't want to hear?

"I am right," Shontelle said.

"You think I'm overreacting?"

"Understandably so, with your history, but yes. I truly believe everything will be fine if you talk to him and tell him what's got you worried."

The bell over the door jingled, and three women in their fifties bustled into the store. Tourists, I suspected, judging by the way they were already laden down with purchases from other shops and exclaimed at the goods on display near the door.

I quickly wiped my cheeks again, in case I still had tear trails on them.

"Thanks, Shontelle. I'd better go."

"Think about what I said."

I promised I would and hurried out of the shop while Shontelle greeted her customers.

My stomach grumbled, and I had a sudden craving for one of Sofie's donuts. One with pink icing and sprinkles. Or perhaps a Boston cream donut.

Maybe emotional eating wasn't the best practice, but in that moment I didn't care. I waved to Aunt Gilda through the window of the salon as I passed by, but I didn't slow down. She and Betty were both busy with clients.

When I entered Sofie's Treat, I drew in a deep breath of the deliciously scented air. As I got in line behind an elderly woman, I glanced at all the people sitting at the small tables in the bakery. Maybe Eldon had saved me time by bringing me back to the center of town instead of letting me linger at the fairgrounds. Toby sat at one of the tables, on his own, a cup of coffee and an apple fritter in front of him. The fritter was half gone, but at the moment he didn't seem to be eating. He simply sat there, staring out the window, his gaze distant.

I ended up choosing a Boston cream donut. Instead of getting it to go, I decided to stay at the bakery. After I had paid and had my donut on a plate, I plunked myself down in the chair across from Toby.

"Hi," I said brightly. "You're Toby, right?"

He scowled at me. "You keep showing up everywhere."

"I live in Shady Creek," I pointed out.

His scowl didn't ease up. "But you were at the fairgrounds when we were closed."

"My friend went to college with Rachael. We stopped by to visit her."

I wasn't sure if he'd even heard me. He stared down at his apple fritter and then picked it up and took a big bite. I couldn't resist my donut any longer, so I had a taste, savoring the scrumptious blend of donut, chocolate, and custard. Exactly what I needed.

"I'm sorry about Collette," I said after I'd enjoyed a second bite. "I hear she's gone missing."

Toby kept eating and ignored me.

"Do you think she got spooked by the murders and took off?" I asked.

He glared at me. "No way. Not without me."

"Are you sure?" I pressed. "Or maybe she met someone local last night and simply hasn't returned to the fairgrounds yet?"

"She would have texted me." He chomped down on his apple fritter.

I took the opportunity to eat some more of my own treat.

"So you think something bad happened to her?" I asked a moment later.

"Why do you care?"

"Why wouldn't I care?" I countered. "She seems like a nice person." I didn't bother to mention that she, along with him, was one of my murder suspects. "I don't want her coming to any harm."

To my surprise, Toby's scowl faded away and tears filled his eyes. He blinked them away but sniffed loudly. "Something bad has happened. Two murders, and now Collette's missing. That doesn't add up to anything good. She's always looked out for me, especially since our mom died. She wouldn't take off without telling me. She never would have left me to worry."

I resisted the impulse to give his hand a squeeze. I didn't think he'd appreciate such familiarity from me, a near stranger.

"When was the last time anyone saw her?" I asked.

Toby eyed me with suspicion. "Are you a reporter?"

"No, but my friend was charged with Ozzie's murder. I know he's innocent, and even the police know he didn't kill Minerva. He's got one of those ankle bracelets that keeps track of him. I'm sure that'll prove he had nothing to do with your sister's disappearance too."

Toby finished his fritter and took a big gulp of his coffee. "I saw her about an hour before the rest of us left for the pub. Maybe just before six? She said she was going to work out in the main tent and would meet us at the pub later on."

"Did anyone else see her after that?"

"If they did, they're not admitting to it."

As he took another drink of coffee, I studied him closely. Collette might have taken off without telling Toby if she was guilty of murdering Ozzie and Minerva. But if she hadn't left town of her own accord, then was her disappearance related to the murders? I doubted Toby would have hurt his own sister, considering how close they seemed to be, so if Collette had fallen victim to foul play, he likely wasn't the killer. Of course, I didn't yet know for sure that Collette wasn't responsible for her own disappearance, but my conversation with Toby had me leaning so far in that direction that I was in danger of toppling over.

"No one's been out looking for her yet?" I asked.

"A bunch of us checked every inch of the fairgrounds," Toby said. "There's no sign of her. Rachael called the cops, but I doubt they'll do much."

"They're looking into it," I told him. "And I'm sure they'll step up their investigation if she doesn't turn up soon."

"What if it's already too late?"

The despair in his eyes sent an ache through my heart. I couldn't bring myself to answer his question.

"Does she know anyone in Shady Creek? Is there anywhere she might have gone to hide if she felt she was in danger?"

Toby shook his head. "We've never been here before. We don't know anyone outside of the faire."

He drained the last of his coffee and stood up. "I'd better get going. I need to go see if anyone's found anything."

He left without another word.

I checked my phone and realized I needed to get back to the Inkwell.

As much as I wanted to go out searching for Collette, I'd have to leave that to the police and her friends.

For the moment, at least.

Chapter 32

As much as I tried, I couldn't get Collette's mysterious disappearance off my mind. I wasn't even sure I wanted to. Thinking about Collette kept me from replaying my last visit with Grayson over and over in my head, and from worrying about the future of our relationship. I needed to talk to him—Shontelle really was right about that—but I hadn't yet worked up the nerve. So, for the time being, I focused on someone else's problem.

The pub had filled up quickly after I opened, but the crowd of customers had died down after the lunch rush. If I wanted to get away for a while, this was the time to do it, when Mel could easily handle everything on her own.

"Do you mind if I take off for an hour?" I asked Mel.

"Of course not," she said as she filled a glass with stout. "Go ahead."

"Thanks, Mel. Text me if you need anything."

She didn't ask where I was going, and I was grateful for that. Not that she would have tried to stop me. But if Aunt Gilda happened to show up and ask where I was, Mel wouldn't be able to tell her, and Aunt Gilda wouldn't have to worry. My aunt had a good reason for not liking my tendency to investigate murders. I'd tangled with killers in the past, and I'd suffered a concussion on one such occasion, something I didn't wish to repeat. I didn't think I was in any danger carrying out my current plan, though. All I wanted to do was ask a question or two of someone I doubted had anything to do with the murders.

Walking at a brisk pace got me to the fairgrounds in a matter of minutes. The gates were locked tight, which I'd expected. I peered through the chain-link fencing.

"Hello?" I called out.

A burly man dressed in black jeans, a black T-shirt, and sunglasses appeared from behind the ticket booth. He was the same security guard who'd let me and Shontelle through the other gate when we'd come to visit Rachael.

"Sorry, ma'am," he said. "The faire's closed."

"I know. I was hoping for some news about my friend Collette. I know she's missing, and I'm worried about her."

The security guard removed his sunglasses and regarded me with a touch of suspicion. "Your friend?"

"We went to college together," I fibbed, borrowing from Shontelle's connection to Rachael.

I wasn't sure if the man believed me, but after staring at me for another few seconds, he finally spoke again. "There's no news."

"I know she left her clothes behind, but did she take her phone with her?" I asked before he could turn away.

"Apparently, since it's nowhere to be found. But she's not answering it." He slid his sunglasses back on. "Which I guess you'd know, since you're her friend."

His tone of voice told me he wasn't completely buying that story. I pressed on, anyway.

"Did you see her leave last night?"

"Nope." He crossed his arms over his wide chest.

He had an intimidating air about him, but that didn't put me off.

"Could she have left by the gates without you seeing her?" I asked.

"Not before six o'clock or after seven that night," he said. "I left these gates unlocked for an hour because a bunch of the faire workers were planning to head into town for the evening. After seven, anyone wanting in or out needed this key." He held it up for me to see. "It was on me the whole time."

"What about the other gate?"

"It stayed locked the whole evening."

I tried another question, hoping he wouldn't clam up on me. "Are you the only security guard working here?"

Even though I couldn't see his eyes through his dark sunglasses, I could feel his gaze boring into me.

"Nope." His voice had taken on a hard edge.

Maybe he was worried that I was up to no good. I didn't want to fuel that belief.

I stepped back from the gates. "Thank you for your time."

I walked back to the Inkwell at a more leisurely pace, mulling over the new information I'd gathered from the security guard. My thoughts scattered when I reached the foot of the brewery's driveway. I knew I shouldn't put off my talk with Grayson, no matter how worried I was about what he might say. Most likely everything was fine between us, and I'd simply read too much into his actions the day before. If that was the case, I needed to find out, so I could quit worrying. And if something wasn't right, it was better to know now than later.

Not giving myself a chance to change my mind, I marched up the driveway to the brewery. Nervous butterflies flitted about in my stomach as I entered the main office, but I didn't let them deter me. Annalisa was typing on her computer at the reception desk. She stopped working and smiled as the door drifted shut behind me.

"Hey, Sadie. Sorry, but Grayson's not in at the moment."

Disappointment replaced my nervousness.

"That's all right." I backtracked to the door.

"Do you want to leave a message?"

"No, thank you," I said quickly. "I was just dropping in to say hi."

The phone rang on her desk, and she grabbed it.

I waved and pushed open the door.

So much for getting my chat with Grayson over with.

I returned to the Inkwell and immediately got back to work by clearing a table that a group of four had vacated as I came in the door. I carried the armload of dishes into the kitchen, where Booker was preparing a platter of Paradise Lox, one of the pub's appetizers.

"I hear you went out for a while," he said as I loaded the dishwasher.

I realized he'd paused in his work to watch me closely. "And you think I went looking for trouble?" I smiled so he'd know I wasn't offended.

"A safe bet, I figured." He got back to adding lox and salmon cream cheese to crostini.

"All I did was talk to the security guard at the fairgrounds. No trouble at all."

He eyed me. "I hope the security guard's not the killer."

"I don't think he is." Although, I didn't know that for sure.

"Did you find out anything useful?"

I shared the information I'd managed to get out of the security guard.

"So," Booker said once I'd finished, "the acrobat either left through the main exit between six and seven yesterday evening or . . . she never left at all?"

"According to her brother, they searched every inch of the fairgrounds and didn't find her."

"So if she didn't leave through the main gates, she disappeared into thin air? The illusionist is dead, so I'm guessing that's not likely."

"Her brother's a magician too," I said, "but no, I doubt that's what happened. She either left through the gates during that one-hour window or she left through the woods."

"There's no temporary fencing at that end of the park?" Booker asked.

"Nope. Grayson and I got into the fairgrounds that way a few nights ago."

He raised an eyebrow. "Sleuthing after dark or romantic shenanigans?"

"Sleuthing, of course." I added soap to the dishwasher.

"Not necessarily a given, considering the sparks between you two."

Thinking about Grayson was dampening my mood, so I quickly moved the conversation back to Collette's disappearance.

"I think I should check the woods." I shut the dishwasher and turned it on.

"Wouldn't the police have done that already?"

"I'm not sure. Maybe they're holding off until she's been missing for a while longer."

"Do me a favor?" Booker requested.

"What's that?"

"Don't go searching the woods by yourself. Take Grayson with you."

"I won't go alone," I promised. I couldn't make the same guarantee about who my companion would be.

I carried the food Booker had prepared out to waiting customers. The next time I had a moment to myself, I sent a text message to Shontelle, asking if she knew if the police had searched the woods for Collette.

She replied right away, saying she didn't know, but she'd ask Eldon for me.

When I checked my phone an hour later, I had another response.

The police are heading out to search the woods this afternoon, but the acrobat's brother said she's terrified of creepy-crawlies and never would have gone into the forest.

Collette was terrified of bugs but enjoyed flying through the air on a trapeze. Fears didn't always make sense, and I thought that was a perfect example.

I thanked Shontelle for the information and tucked my phone beneath the bar.

Collette had most likely left through the main gates between six and seven, when they had been unlocked. I couldn't, however, completely rule out the possibility that she'd gone into the woods. Even if she was scared stiff of trekking through the trees and undergrowth, she might have gone that way if she was fleeing for her life.

Had she figured out who had killed Ozzie and Minerva, and had the murderer realized she knew their identity?

It was a possibility. Another one to add to the list.

At this point, I wasn't sure if I'd ever get any of Shady Creek's mysteries solved.

Hopefully, the police would succeed where I'd so far failed.

Chapter 33

The dinner rush wasn't yet underway when Grayson showed up at the Inkwell. An attack of nerves hit me when I saw him heading toward the bar. At the same time, I knew more than ever that I was in love with him. I needed to put my insecurities and anxieties to rest for good.

"Go ahead and take a break," Zoe said to me when she saw Grayson. "I'm fine here on my own."

"Thanks, Zoe."

I summoned all the courage I could find as I stepped out from behind the bar and took Grayson's hand.

"Hey," he said in greeting.

I smiled but didn't wait for a kiss, instead leading him through the door to the back hallway.

"Mind if we go up to my apartment for a minute?" I asked once we were alone.

He gestured toward the stairs. "After you."

Wimsey greeted me as soon as I opened the door at the top of the stairway. I gave him a quick cuddle before setting him on the couch.

Grayson shut the door, his gaze on me. "Is something wrong?"

My nervousness threatened to overwhelm me.

Grayson took my hand. His thumb moved in soothing circles. "What's going on, Sadie? Are you okay?"

The concern in his blue eyes was sincere, of that I was sure. It gave me the courage to speak.

"At your office yesterday, I got the sense you were hiding something from me."

"Ah." He didn't let go of my hand, but he dropped his gaze from mine.

A surge of fear and anxiety brought tears to my eyes. "So I was right? The last time someone tried to hide things from me . . ." I couldn't finish, but I didn't need to. Grayson knew enough about my past to fill in the blanks.

He squeezed my hand and met my gaze again. "It's nothing like that. I promise. I didn't want you to see what I was working on, because it wasn't finished. And even once it was finished, I didn't know if I'd have the courage to actually give it to you."

My worries still had a chokehold on me, making it hard to get my next words out. "Give what to me?"

Grayson reached into the back pocket of his jeans and pulled out a folded piece of paper. He hesitated for half a second before handing it to me.

My hands trembled as I unfolded the paper, not knowing what to expect. Despite Grayson's reassurances, I couldn't help but wonder if he'd written me a breakup letter.

I stared at the paper and noticed right away that the words weren't set out like a letter.

More like a poem.

I glanced up at Grayson. I'd never seen him look so uncertain, but his eyes held no regret. That steadied my nerves enough that I could read what he'd written.

I could say you are the sun of my soul
But your light it shines much brighter by far
The sun, while bold, does not make me feel whole
I will always want to be where you are

The sun above can scorch and it can burn
It can leave a mark without being seen
It can hide as if it wishes to spurn
And wither plants of the most ardent green

But you are warmth without the scalding bite
Beauty fair without the blinding peril
You illuminate through both day and night
Sweeter than an angel's dulcet carol

The sun it does not always make me smile
But your light comforts me through every mile

By the time I finished reading, I had tears running down my face.

"You wrote me a sonnet?" I could hardly believe it.

Grayson took the paper from me and set it on the coffee table. Then he grasped both of my hands.

"I was trying to find a way to let you know how I feel about you."

"It's beautiful. And it's the most romantic thing anyone has ever done for me." I let go of one of his hands just long enough to wipe away my tears. "I can't believe you took the time to write that. It's amazing."

"You like it?"

I wrapped my arms around him. "I love it. So much." I pulled back so I could look him in the eye. I no longer had any doubts about saying my next words. "And I love *you*, Grayson."

I could have sworn the shade of his eyes darkened.

"I love you too, Sadie." He kissed me in a way that no words could ever describe. Then he wrapped his arms around me and rested his forehead against mine. "I know we haven't been dating for long, and I didn't want to scare you off by telling you too soon, but I've known for a while."

I had to wipe away more tears. "Really?"

"Since before we even started dating."

I leaned against him, resting my head on his chest, and listened to the beat of his heart. I didn't think I'd ever felt so happy before. It was almost overwhelming.

"I'm sorry I worried you," he said.

"I jumped to conclusions because of the things that happened to me in the past. I'll try not to do that again."

"So I'm forgiven?"

I smiled, my eyes still watery. "There's nothing to forgive."

He kissed me again.

"There's only one problem," I said with a sigh.

"What's that?"

"Now I don't want to go back to work."

Grayson smiled. "How about I stay and keep you company?"

I took his hand and gave it a squeeze. "I'd like that very much."

I floated on a cloud of happiness for the rest of the evening. Grayson sat at the bar while I worked with Zoe. Sometimes he chatted with me, and other times with the locals who showed up for drinks or a bite to eat. After the last customer had left, Zoe and Teagan set off for home. I locked the door behind them and checked my phone. Shontelle had sent me an update on the search for Collette.

"Everything okay?" Grayson asked as he filled a tub with dirty dishes.

I realized I was frowning at the screen. "There was a bad accident on the highway. The police sent most of their officers to the scene, so they didn't have a chance to search much of the woods before dark."

"They'll probably get back to searching in the morning."

"What if that's too late?" Worry gnawed at me. "If something bad happened to Collette . . ."

Grayson left the dirty dishes and came over to put an arm around me. "There's not much else anyone can do. You remember how hard it was to see in the woods even before it was completely dark. It would be pointless, and probably not even safe, to keep searching at night."

"You're right." I stacked some dirty plates.

"Besides," Grayson added, "if Collette ran off for whatever reason, there most likely won't be anything to find in the woods."

"That's true." I grabbed cleaning supplies from beneath the bar and started wiping down tables. "I just have this nagging feeling that she could be in danger."

"We could volunteer to help with the search first thing in the morning," Grayson said as he collected more dirty dishes.

"I like that idea."

We agreed to meet up bright and early. Then, after a prolonged goodnight kiss, Grayson headed home to take Bowie for a late-night walk and I collapsed into bed. A strange mixture of elation and worry swirled around inside me until sleep caught me in its grasp.

Chapter 34

I was so eager to get on with the day that I didn't have any trouble getting out of bed the next morning, even though I'd set my alarm for earlier than normal. Wimsey approved of getting his breakfast before the usual time, and he purred away happily as he ate. I didn't have much of an appetite, so I settled for a piece of toast and a cup of coffee.

After a quick shower, I dressed for a trek through the woods, in jeans, a T-shirt, and sneakers. I braided my hair to keep it away from my face and then jogged downstairs and out the door. Grayson and I had arranged to meet at the foot of his driveway, so I made my way there, noting that I was one of the first people out and about in this part of town. Two women were doing yoga in the middle of the village green, and a couple of other townsfolk were out walking their dogs, but otherwise all was quiet.

When I reached Grayson's driveway, he hadn't yet appeared, so I pulled out my phone and sent him a quick text, letting him know I'd arrived. He responded right away, saying he was just getting back from walking Bowie and would meet up with me in a minute or two. I took the time to text my younger brother, Taylor, telling him that our mom would be coming to visit Shady Creek in October.

You should come too, I added to the original message.

Taylor must have been up early as well, because his response came a minute later.

Ha ha! Sorry, sis. You're on your own!

I sent back an emoji with its tongue sticking out.

I hoped my mom wouldn't spend her entire visit criticizing everything about my life. She meant no harm, but she had trouble understanding me and Taylor. My older brother, Michael, had inherited our dad's flaming red hair, but personality-wise he was much more like our mother, practical, and not entirely understanding of people who didn't see things exactly his way. Taylor and I, on the other hand, shared more similarities with our late father. It hurt that our mother often said she wished Taylor and I were more like Michael, but Taylor seemed to let that roll off his back. I was trying to get better at that myself. It was a work in progress.

I tucked my phone in the pocket of my jeans when I heard footsteps coming down the driveway. A huge smile appeared on my face when I saw Grayson. I met him with a hug and a kiss, and we held hands as we walked down Creekside Road in the direction of the park. I was so glad I'd brought up my concerns with him. Not only had he put my worries to rest, but now our relationship was stronger than ever too. Part of me had been holding back before, but now I knew I didn't need to do that. I trusted Grayson, with my heart and everything else.

As we got closer to our destination, I hoped our early morning excursion wouldn't be pointless. Although, even if the police hadn't shown up to resume the search of the woods yet, I figured we could always hunt for signs of Collette on our own. I wasn't sure what Detective Marquez would think about that, but if there wasn't any police tape or anything else to keep us out of the woods, then I figured there was no reason why we couldn't go for a woodland walk, even if it wasn't intended as a simple stroll.

We made our way along the edge of the park, outside the temporary fencing. When the patch of woods came into view up ahead, I noticed a lack of a police presence immediately. Fortunately, there was no barricade of any sort to keep us out of the woods.

"Do you want to wait and see if the police show up?" Grayson asked.

"No way," I said. I was itching to get into the woods.

Grayson grinned. "I figured that would be your answer."

We entered the woods, taking the same trail we'd followed previously. I was glad of the fact that we were here in daylight this time. Sunlight filtered down through the canopy, and the gentle morning breeze carried pleasant outdoorsy scents with it. Birds twittered and sang in the branches over our heads, and a chipmunk chattered in a nearby tree.

Under other circumstances, it would have been an enjoyable summer morning's walk, but a sense of uneasiness followed me with every step. I had to let go of Grayson's hand after a while, because the path became too narrow to walk side by side, but I was glad for his presence close behind me. Chances were that we wouldn't find anything during our search, but with a killer on the loose and Collette missing, I couldn't help but worry that danger might lurk behind a tree or in the shadows.

Despite my anxieties, we didn't see or hear any sign of other people in the woods. After close to twenty minutes of walking, Grayson's footsteps slowed behind me. I stopped on the path and faced him.

"We've gone beyond the width of the park now," he said. "That doesn't mean Collette didn't go this way, but maybe we should focus our search closer to the park."

I agreed with him. This patch of woodland wasn't particularly wide, but it did stretch on between farms on the outskirts of town.

"Maybe we should walk through the ravine," I suggested. "Collette would have had to cross it or walk the length of it if she wanted to get away from the park."

Grayson was on board with that plan, so we left the narrow path. Our progress was slow as we climbed over fallen trees and pushed aside branches, all the while trying not to trample too many plants. I kept an eye out for monkshood along the way, but I didn't spot the poisonous plant anywhere. Fortunately, I didn't see any stinging nettles either.

I had to focus on each step I took to make sure I didn't go tumbling down the steep embankment. When we finally reached the bottom of the ravine and started walking along it, the trek wasn't quite as difficult.

"How come I didn't know you're a writer?" I asked Grayson as I glanced around for any clues as to Collette's whereabouts.

"I'm not."

I could hear his footsteps behind me, cracking twigs and crunching on dry leaves now and then.

I stopped and turned around. "But you wrote an entire sonnet. And it's amazing!"

Grayson grinned and put his hands to my cheeks. "I'm glad you think so, but I don't even know if I got my iambic pentameter right."

"Even if you didn't, I still love it."

"That's all that matters to me."

He gave me a quick kiss before we got back to trekking along the ravine.

"Iambic pentameter or not, I think you've got talent," I said. "Maybe you should join the Inkwell's writing group."

Behind me, Grayson laughed. "I don't think I'm quite there."

I stopped so abruptly that he almost bumped into me.

"What's wrong?" he asked.

"Nothing." I turned and smiled at him. "I just wanted to say that I love you."

He pulled me into another kiss. "I love you too, and I don't think I'll ever get tired of saying it."

"I'll never get tired of saying it or hearing it." I tore my gaze away from his, reminding myself that we were in the woods for a reason.

Before I had a chance to take another step, a voice shouted in the distance. It was too far away to make out the words.

"What do you think that was about?" I asked.

Another voice called out. Again, I couldn't distinguish any words.

"Maybe it's the police search getting underway," Grayson said.

"Or it was already underway and they found something?" I hesitated with indecision. "Should we keep going?"

"How about we finish walking the length of the ravine and then head back to the trail? If the police are still searching, we can join them, if they agree to it."

We kept walking. As we made our way farther along, the sides of the ravine slowly got lower. It looked as though a stream probably ran through the ravine at other times of the year, but now, in the middle of summer, it was completely dry.

I stepped over a fallen tree branch. My right foot slipped off a small rock, and pain shot through my ankle. I saved myself from falling by hopping on my uninjured foot.

"What happened?" Grayson grabbed my arm to help steady me.

I tried to put weight on my right foot. Another stab of pain made me wince. "I hurt my ankle."

"Is it broken?"

"I don't think so. Probably not even sprained. Just twisted, I think."

"Here, sit down for a minute." Grayson helped me settle on the thick branch I'd climbed over.

"I'll be fine." I moved my foot in a slow circle, rotating my ankle. Already, the pain was dissipating.

"Are you sure?"

"Positive." I stood up again, Grayson taking my hand to assist me.

I lost my balance and fell into him, but not because of my ankle.

I pointed at a spot a few feet ahead of us. "Grayson . . ."

His gaze followed my finger until he saw what had startled me.

Collette lay beneath a scraggly bush, partially buried beneath loose dirt and half-rotted leaves.

Chapter 35

I rushed forward, my sore ankle forgotten. After dropping to my knees beside Collette, I reached toward her and then jerked my hand back.

"Do you think she's . . . ?" I didn't want to say the word, and I was scared to touch her, in case she was too cold to still be alive.

Grayson crouched down next to me and brushed the leaves away from Collette's face. He checked for a pulse in her neck.

I held my breath, worried he might not feel anything.

"Her pulse isn't strong, but she's alive and breathing," Grayson said.

The breath I was holding whooshed out of me with relief. I brushed more dirt and leaves away from her face.

"She probably didn't bury herself," I said. "Unless she was trying to hide."

Grayson leaned in closer to Collette. "There's some blood on her shoulder."

He was right. A few dark red specks marred her pink hoodie.

Grayson carefully put a hand to Colette's head. He ran his

fingers over her scalp without moving her. When he pulled his hand away, there was blood on his fingers.

"A head wound." I shivered, despite the warmth of the summer morning.

The voices we'd heard moments before had quieted, and even the birds had stopped singing.

The silence around us felt eerie and almost oppressive. I glanced around, twisting so I could see behind us.

"Do you think she was attacked by the murderer?" I whispered.

"It's possible." Grayson stood up.

I didn't fail to notice that he glanced around too, as if checking for danger.

"She's probably been here since Friday night." I touched a hand to her arm. Even though she was still alive, her skin was cold.

"At any other time of the year, she probably wouldn't have survived this long."

Grayson's words nearly made me shiver again.

He had his phone out now. "I'll call nine-one-one, but maybe we can get the attention of the other searchers. If that's who's out here."

My eyes widened. "What if it's not the police?"

"Just in case, we'll stick together and stay with Collette."

I nodded my agreement. There was no way I wanted to head off through the woods alone or to stay with Collette while Grayson went for help. If we had no other choice, I'd have to do one of those things, but I hoped that wouldn't prove necessary.

While Grayson talked to the emergency dispatcher, I stayed at Collette's side and held her cold hand. She didn't stir. I brushed more leaves and dirt away from her but then forced myself to stop. Although I didn't like leaving her partially buried, I wasn't sure if the police would want me disturbing the scene.

Grayson held his phone away from his ear while he spoke to me. "The dispatcher's going to try to get in touch with the searchers." He returned the phone to his ear and responded to a question I couldn't hear.

I stayed focused on Collette, trying to will her to regain consciousness.

Had the murderer tried to kill her and then left her here, thinking she was dead?

If so, could Collette identify her attacker?

If I had the scenario right, then whoever had harmed Collette and left her for dead was most likely the same person who'd killed Ozzie and Minerva.

"Collette?" I said quietly. "Can you open your eyes? You're safe now."

I hoped that was true. Either way, she didn't respond to my voice.

"Grayson Blake?" a voice called out from somewhere in the distance.

Grayson ended his phone call, put two fingers in his mouth, and let out a loud whistle. "Down in the ravine!" he yelled.

Bushes rustled and twigs snapped, the sounds growing louder.

Grayson called out again.

At the top of the embankment, a short way back along the ravine, a figure emerged from the trees.

"Detective Marquez!" I waved an arm in the air.

She spotted us and carefully made her way down the embankment, Officer Rogers behind her. Eldon was there too, but he said something to Marquez and then disappeared into the trees again.

The detective slid the last few feet down the embankment and made quick progress in our direction.

I let go of Collette's hand and backed away from her so Marquez and Rogers could move in closer.

"She's alive, but her pulse is weak," Grayson said as Rogers crouched down next to Collette.

Marquez surveyed the area around us. I wondered if she was looking for signs of danger.

Rogers spoke into her radio, reporting Collette's condition to someone.

"The paramedics are on their way," Marquez said to us. "Tell me everything."

It didn't take long to explain how we'd found Collette. By the time we'd finished, two paramedics were clambering down the side of the ravine, carrying a stretcher with them. Eldon followed close behind.

Grayson and I backed farther away from Collette to give the professionals room to work. He put an arm around me, and I leaned into his side, hoping and praying that Collette wouldn't end up being another murder victim.

Chapter 36

At least half an hour had passed by the time the paramedics checked Collette over, gently placed her on the stretcher, and made the careful trek out of the woods. As the ambulance sped off, its siren wailing, I stood with Grayson at the side of the road, a short distance away from Detective Marquez and her fellow officers.

The sun shone brightly from a brilliant blue sky, and the day was already getting too warm for the jeans I wore, and yet on the inside I felt chilled. Collette hadn't regained consciousness, and I feared for her well-being. Even if she pulled through, she might suffer long-term consequences from her head injury. I didn't even like to think about that possibility.

The detective joined us, and Grayson and I answered more questions, as well as some of the same ones again. I knew Marquez wanted to be especially thorough, not only because Collette was likely the victim of an attack, but also because this could all be related to the recent murders.

When Detective Marquez finally seemed satisfied with everything we'd told her, she walked several paces away and made a phone call.

"Things keep getting worse instead of better," I said to Grayson.

He rubbed my back. "Whoever's behind all this is going to make a mistake sooner or later, and that mistake will get them caught."

"But how many more people have to get hurt before that happens?" I tried to push aside my growing despair, without much success.

Grayson's phone chimed. He pulled it out of his pocket and checked the screen.

"Everything okay?" I asked as he read a new text message.

"I'm needed at the brewery."

I glanced over at Marquez and her colleagues. They weren't paying us any attention.

"I think we're free to go," I said.

"How about I walk you back to the Inkwell?" Grayson offered.

"Actually, I think I'll hang around a little longer. Until Detective Marquez tells Toby what happened to his sister."

"Do you want me to stay with you?"

"No, you go ahead," I said. "I won't hang around here much longer."

He kissed me on the cheek. "I'll see you later."

He headed off down the road. Marquez was still talking on the phone, and Eldon and Rogers were speaking to each other over by one of the police cruisers. I walked away from the woods, until I reached the chain-link fence set up along the edge of the park. I peered through the metal loops, but Toby wasn't in sight.

The poor guy. My heart ached for him. No doubt the news about Collette would hit him hard.

I was about to turn away from the fence when I saw a flash of blond hair. Tilly had darted out of sight between two of the trailers. An unpleasant, jittery feeling worked its way up my spine. The killer could be on the fairgrounds. It was the worst place for Tilly to be hanging out.

I considered telling Marquez about Tilly so the detective could go fetch the girl and take her home. Then I remembered how much trouble I'd had getting Tilly to talk to me instead of running away. If she saw Marquez heading her way, she might go into hiding.

Maybe I'd have better luck on my own.

After backtracking a few steps, I slipped into the woods again, unnoticed by the police. I ventured only far enough into the trees to get around the end of the fence. This time, I wasn't concerned about where I entered the fairgrounds. If someone spotted me and told me I shouldn't be there, I'd tell them the truth about why I was there, and hopefully, that would put an end to the problem.

Once inside the fence, I jogged toward the trailers. I slowed to a walk when I reached the closest one. Smoke drifted up from the firepit, but I couldn't see any flames, and the lawn chairs set up around it were all empty. Three women exited one of the trailers and walked off across the fairgrounds, but otherwise all was still.

I followed the same path as the three women, passing between the nearest tents to the faire's main walkway. From there I could see a few more people off in the distance. I thought I recognized Toby as one of them. I hesitated, wondering if I should tell him that he needed to speak with Detective Marquez.

Movement off to my left caught my eye, tearing my attention away from Toby. Tilly had just slipped inside the Mad Hatter.

I jogged over to the hut and opened the door.

"Tilly?" I called from the threshold. There were no lights on inside, and I had to wait a moment for my eyes to adjust to the darkness. "It's Sadie."

Tilly peeked out from behind a stand holding a variety of flamboyant hats.

"I want to try on some of the costumes." She snagged a feathered hat and plopped it onto her head. She spun around and checked out her reflection in a full-length mirror, giggling at the sight.

"I'm sorry, sweetie." I took the hat off her head and returned it to the stand. "You really shouldn't be here."

"But it's so much fun."

"I know, but you can have fun elsewhere. Why don't we go see if Kiandra's free to play?" I took her hand and led her to the door.

She didn't resist. "Okay."

We left the fairgrounds the same way I'd entered. The police and their vehicles were no longer parked at the side of the road when we broke free of the woods. Hopefully, one of the officers would get in touch with Toby soon. I was sure he'd want to go to the hospital to be with his sister.

Just as I was thinking of him, I saw Toby through the gap between two trailers. He stood by the firepit now, on his own. I stopped and called out his name. When he glanced my way, I waved. I knew he saw me, but he didn't make a move to come over to the fence. Maybe he didn't recognize me.

Tilly fidgeted beside me. "Is it okay if I go see Kiandra now?"

I glanced at Toby and then back at her. "Will you go straight there?"

She drew an *X* over her heart. "I promise! Bye!"

She took off.

"Tilly, wait!" I called before she could get far. When she stopped and turned back to me, I said, "There's something I want to ask you."

Chapter 37

As soon as Tilly told me what I wanted to know, she ran off. I watched her go, wanting to make sure she didn't go back onto the fairgrounds. To my relief, she ran the length of the park and then kept going toward the center of town.

I turned back to the fence, only to find that Toby had disappeared.

I weighed my options. I could head for the police station and report to Marquez what Tilly had told me, or I could go in search of Toby. Now that I had new—and possibly vital—information, I wanted to ask him some questions.

After another moment of indecision, I settled on a compromise. I scrolled through my contacts until I found Detective Marquez's direct line. When I put a call through to her number, she didn't answer, so I left a voicemail, and shared my new theory as succinctly as possible. In a rush at the end, I added that I was going looking for Toby on the fairgrounds. I texted the same information to Grayson for good measure.

After tucking my phone away, I returned to the woods yet again so I could skirt around the fence. I'd reached the nearest trailer when I stopped and questioned my plan. Maybe I should go home and wait until Marquez got back to me. I'd almost decided to do that when Toby emerged from the tent that I thought was the workers' canteen.

I jogged over his way. I'd ask him a few questions and then get out of there, hopefully taking him with me. Once he knew what I did, he might be in as much danger as Collette.

I'd almost reached Toby, who was back by the firepit, when I heard someone say my name.

I stopped short. Flint waved and strode over my way. It was only the second time I'd seen him wearing regular clothes instead of his costume.

"Morning, Sadie," he greeted. "What brings you here?"

"Um . . ." I wasn't sure what to say. "I need to have a word with . . ."

"Rachael?" he guessed.

I didn't try to correct him, and he didn't give me a chance to.

He hooked a thumb over his shoulder. "Last I saw her, she was near the tavern." His gaze strayed toward the canteen. "I'm off to grab some breakfast. See you around."

I waited until he had disappeared into the canteen before I approached Toby by the firepit. I didn't consider him a suspect any longer. He might not have liked Ozzie or Minerva, but he never would have hurt his sister. I believed that without a doubt.

"Hey, Toby," I said as I sauntered up beside him.

He was staring into the smoking embers. When he glanced my way, his forehead furrowed with surprise. "Oh . . . you again." He didn't sound as unfriendly as when I'd met him at the bakery, but he went right back to staring at the firepit.

"Have the police been in touch with you this morning?" I asked.

His head jerked up. "Should they have?" He patted his pockets and swore. "I left my phone in the trailer."

He shot off and ran full tilt for one of the trailers. He disappeared inside and then came out at a slower pace, staring at his phone. He put the device to his ear as he walked back my way.

As he got closer, I saw all the color drain from his face.

He dropped into one of the lawn chairs and lowered his phone. He stared at the device with a glazed expression.

"Did you have a message from the police?" I asked.

He nodded. "A detective. She said Collette's in the hospital." His gaze snapped back into focus as he looked at me. "Is that why you were asking me if I'd heard from the cops?"

"Yes." I hesitated. "What did she say, exactly?"

"That Collette was found in the woods this morning. That she's unconscious but alive." His voice hitched on his last word.

"My boyfriend and I found her."

"What happened? How did she get hurt?" His distress almost brought tears to my eyes.

"I wish I knew."

He jumped to his feet. "I have to get to the hospital." He looked around as if he were lost.

"Do you have a way of getting there?" I asked. "The hospital is in the next town. We don't have one here in Shady Creek."

He ran a hand through his hair, agitated. "I don't have a car, but I'll get someone to drive me."

Without another word, he ran into the canteen tent.

I hoped he wouldn't have any trouble finding someone to drive him to the hospital.

I wasn't eager to hang around the fairgrounds, but I was hoping to gather more information before returning to the Inkwell. I wandered away from the firepit, keeping a sharp lookout for familiar faces.

Luck was with me that morning. As I strolled along the faire's main walkway, I spotted Hamish sitting on a rough-hewn wooden bench outside the tavern. He was on his own, strumming his lute.

"It's Hamish, right?" I said when I reached him, even though I had no doubts about his name.

He stopped strumming. "That's right. Who are you?"

I sat down on the bench beside him. "I own the local pub."

Recognition showed in his eyes. "I thought you looked familiar." He resumed playing his lute again, but he stopped after a few notes. "How'd you get in here? The fairgrounds are closed today."

I ignored his question. "There's something I wanted to ask you about the evening Ozzie died."

He stiffened, suddenly wary. "Why? Are you a cop as well as a pub owner?"

"Definitely not a cop. I'm just . . . an interested party."

"I don't know why you think I can help you. I was playing a concert that evening. I didn't hear about what happened until Ozzie was already dead."

"There's still a chance you can help me." I checked to make sure no one else was within earshot. Confident that we were alone, I lowered my voice and asked the questions that were burning holes in my mind.

When I had my answers and had thanked Hamish, I walked off, an uneasy energy humming through me. I ducked into the main tent as I pulled out my phone, hoping for privacy while I tried calling Detective Marquez again. As I listened to the ringing at the other end of the line, I remembered what Grayson had said about magic. It was all about misdirection. I now thought that was true with regard to the murders as well.

When the call went to voicemail, I lowered my phone from my ear.

And that was when someone knocked it out of my hand.

Chapter 38

The dagger aimed at my heart had a wickedly sharp point.

I took an automatic step backward, but the dagger followed. All I could hear was the pounding of my pulse in my ears. When I forced myself to look away from the sharp point of the dagger and at Rachael's face, I couldn't miss the hard glint in her eyes. It scared me almost more than the weapon.

"Rachael?" Her name came out as little more than a squeak. I cleared my throat, trying to steady myself. "What's going on?"

"Don't play innocent with me." Her voice had a dangerous edge to it, one I'd never heard from her before. "I was in the tavern when you were talking to Hamish. I heard every word of your conversation."

My mind raced as fast as my pulse as I tried to figure out what to do and say next. "All I asked him about was his concert."

She glared at me. "You asked him if I was by the stage for the entire concert or if I could have slipped away for a while without anyone noticing."

She really had heard every word.

"I was just trying to establish everyone's whereabouts for the night Ozzie died," I said.

"You've been sticking your nose where it doesn't belong," she countered. "Clearly, you didn't heed the advice in the note I left for you."

My gaze slid back down to the dagger. She still held it steady, directed at my chest.

"I want to clear my friend's name," I said.

"And in trying to do that, you figured out too much."

"I don't know what you're talking about." The lie was a long shot, but I was desperate.

"You asked Hamish if he'd ever heard me call Minerva a grief vampire."

"And he said he hadn't."

"But you know I used that term for her. Somehow, you know, and you've put two and two together. I can tell."

I took another step back. Again, Rachael advanced with me. Barely two inches of space separated me from the dagger's sharp point.

I wasn't about to explain how I'd found out that Rachael had called Minerva a grief vampire. I didn't want Tilly on a killer's radar. The girl had overheard Rachael mumbling the words under her breath while glaring at the fortune-teller. Once I'd had that bit of information, I'd realized what a mistake it was for me to overlook Rachael as a suspect.

"Now I have to figure out what to do with you," Rachael grumbled, as if I'd greatly inconvenienced her, which I probably had.

"You don't need to do anything with me." I edged back another step.

For once, Rachael didn't move with me.

"You think I want to go to jail? If I don't get rid of you, that's where I'll end up. You know too much."

"Like Collette?"

Rachael smirked. "No one knows what happened to her. Maybe she just ran off."

I almost blurted out that Grayson and I had found Collette alive, but I stopped myself. If I couldn't get out of this situation, I didn't want Rachael speeding off to the hospital to make another attempt at silencing the acrobat forever.

Instead, I hoped I could distract her and keep her from killing me immediately.

"Ozzie was a decoy, wasn't he?" I said. "Minerva was the intended victim, but you decided to complicate matters by killing Ozzie too."

"You're smart, but not that smart. I had another reason for killing Ozzie."

"What's that?" I edged back another few inches.

Something soft brushed against my shoulder. A gasp died in my throat when I realized it was one of the suspended silks touching my arm.

"I wanted Minerva to suffer." Tears filled her eyes, but her voice was laced with bitterness. "I wanted her to know what it feels like to lose a loved one. I wanted her to suffer the way *I* suffered."

"When you lost your mom." I'd taken a guess, but the flash in Rachael's eyes told me I was on the right track.

"Even before I lost her." Tears escaped and slid down her cheeks. "That woman preyed on my mom's grief and hope, draining her until she was broken and penniless. Minerva pretended to communicate with my sister and father, to pass messages to and from my mom. All for a price, of course. And I didn't realize what was happening until it was too late. By then my mom had nothing left—no money, no hope. She died within weeks."

"I'm sorry, Rachael." And I was, even though her mom's suffering didn't justify the murders or the attack on Collette.

I wasn't sure she heard me.

"I don't want blood on my hands," she said through her angry tears.

"Good." I didn't bring up the fact that she already had plenty of blood on her hands, figuratively speaking.

She wasn't listening to me, anyway. "So we're going to arrange an accident."

Her gaze darted to the side. When I looked that way, I realized what she had in mind. She wanted me to climb the ladder up to the high wire.

I shuddered, and my heart raced faster. Numbness worked its way into my fingers and toes.

Rachael had her focus back on me again. She jerked the point of the dagger toward the ladder. "Go on. Climb." When I hesitated, her eyes hardened. "Don't worry. I'll be right behind you."

I definitely didn't want to go up that ladder. Maybe I could kick Rachael in the face as she followed me up, but then I'd still have to get past her to escape the tent. That wouldn't be easy if my kick didn't render her unconscious.

I shot a glance over Rachael's left shoulder.

As I'd hoped, she automatically looked that way.

The point of the dagger drifted away from me.

I grabbed onto the aerial silk and jumped up and back. I swung forward and kicked my legs out in front of me. My feet slammed into Rachael's midsection.

She flew back with a grunt and hit the ground, sprawled on her back. The dagger clattered out of her grasp.

As the silk swung me backward, I let go and dropped to the ground.

Rachael rolled up onto her knees and made a grab for the dagger.

Detective Marquez burst into the tent. "Police! Hands where we can see them!"

Rachael froze, the dagger inches from her fingers.

I raised my hands in the air.

Marquez, Eldon, and Officer Rogers rushed over with their guns drawn. Within seconds, Eldon had Rachael's hands behind her back, cuffs securing her wrists.

Marquez lowered her weapon.

"Are you okay, Sadie?" she asked me.

"Yes," I said, the word coming out as faint as I felt.

I thought I saw a corner of the detective's mouth twitch.

"You can lower your hands now," she said.

I'd forgotten they were in the air.

I dropped my arms and grabbed onto the silk for support as relief rushed through me, leaving my legs weak.

Chapter 39

The evening sun warmed my skin and brought a smile to my face. It was the perfect weather for a barbecue. Damien had his grill fired up on his back porch and was cooking burgers, hot dogs, and shrimp skewers. Grayson passed around bottles of cold beer from his brewery, brought over to Damien's place in a large cooler.

Across the yard, Damien's daughters played badminton with Kiandra and Tilly, the game punctuated by bursts of laughter. The happy sound washed over me, raising my spirits higher. I'd needed this get-together more than I'd realized.

The events of a couple of weeks ago had dampened my spirits. Although the police had arrested Rachael for the murders of Ozzie and Minerva, and for the attempted murder of Collette, I'd been slow to shake off the melancholy that had settled over me after the showdown at the fairgrounds.

The charges against Damien had been dropped, and he was once again a free man, back to work at the Inkwell, with a cloud of suspicion no longer hanging over his head. Yet every time I thought about Rachael and the murders—which was often—

sadness weighed heavily upon my shoulders. Rachael had suffered so much, but her thirst for revenge had gone way too far. The memory of my confrontation with her had followed me like a dark shadow for days.

That had improved, but it wasn't until this evening, while hanging out with my friends, that I finally felt as though I was close to banishing that shadow for good.

I took a sip of cold beer and got up from the Adirondack chair where I'd been relaxing and watching the badminton game. Tilly's mom, Tamara, stood near the steps to the back porch, chatting with Mel, the twins, and Booker and his girlfriend.

Shontelle, with a glass of wine in hand, wandered over to my side. "You've been awfully quiet so far this evening. Everything okay?"

"Just relaxing," I said. "Maybe for the first time in a while."

Shontelle rested a hand on my shoulder. "This barbecue was a good idea."

I smiled. "I'm glad Eldon was able to make it."

A smile touched Shontelle's lips as well as she looked over at Eldon, who stood on the porch, talking with Damien and Grayson. "Me too."

Noise from the badminton game diverted our attention momentarily. Bryony, in an attempt to hit the birdie, had ended up sitting on the ground. She seemed unharmed, but a fit of giggles had overtaken her. That got the other kids laughing too.

"Any word on how Collette's doing?" Shontelle asked after taking a sip of wine.

I'd visited Collette in the hospital the week before, and she'd promised to keep me updated on her condition by text message. I'd last heard from her two days earlier.

"She suffered a bad concussion," I said, "but she's out of the hospital now. It'll be a while before she's back on a trapeze, but her chances of a full recovery are good. She was planning to start an acrobatic magic show with her magician boyfriend, who lives in New York City, but she broke up with him after her run-in with Rachael. Now she and her brother, Toby, are hoping to have a future show together."

She was certain that Toby would do well onstage, once he had built up his confidence. Apparently, Ozzie had made a practice of putting him down on a regular basis. That had amplified Toby's insecurities and had driven him to sending the illusionist hate mail, something he'd confessed to his sister. Now he and Collette just wanted to put the past behind them and move forward.

"I hope things work out well for her," Shontelle said. "She's lucky to be alive."

There was no denying that. I'd heard from Detective Marquez that Rachael had thought she'd killed Collette out in the woods, after chasing her across the fairgrounds at dusk. Like Tilly, Collette had overheard Rachael muttering disparaging remarks about Minerva, only Rachael had realized that Collette heard her. Worried that Collette had suspicions about her—which she did—Rachael had tried to silence her in a permanent fashion, striking her in the head with a rock.

"Food's ready!" Damien called out from the back porch.

Kiandra and Tilly let out squeals of happiness. They dropped their rackets and ran for the porch. Bryony and Charlotte followed close behind.

Shontelle and I stayed put for the moment, letting the kids get their food first.

Eldon wandered over, a bottle of beer in hand. "How have you been doing since everything went down, Sadie?"

"All right." I gazed around at all my friends. Teagan and Zoe were laughing with Booker and his girlfriend, and Mel and Tilly's mom were heading for the grill to get some food. Everyone looked happy and at ease. "And better every day."

"I'm glad to hear it," Eldon said.

"Can you fill in some gaps for Sadie?" Shontelle asked. "Some of the details have been bugging her."

I'd admitted that to Shontelle days earlier.

"I can share some things," Eldon said. "Fortunately, we know quite a bit about how events unfolded. Rachael's planning to plead guilty to all charges. She was pretty open about things when we questioned her."

"How did she poison Ozzie?" I asked. "I know she used monkshood, but how did she administer the poison?"

Eldon took a sip of beer. "The bullet."

"What bullet?" Shontelle asked. "He was shot?"

I shook my head. "He did a trick where Collette shot a gun at him and he caught the bullet in his teeth. At least he made it look like he did. He collapsed a few minutes later."

"Rachael used a concentrate or paste of juice from the roots of a monkshood plant," Eldon explained. "Her mom was a botanist, so she knows a good deal about plants. She found the monkshood growing at the back of someone's garden at the edge of town when she was out for a walk. Once she prepared the poison, she laced Ozzie's bullet with it right before the show. He had the bullet tucked inside his cheek before and during the trick, so he could put it between his teeth once the gun was fired. It didn't take long after he put it in his mouth for the poison to start to work."

Shontelle shuddered. "It must have been a terrible way to die."

I tried to push away the memory of Ozzie collapsing, struggling to breathe in his last moments.

"And that was all to get revenge on Minerva?" Shontelle said.

"Apparently," Eldon confirmed. "She wanted Minerva dead, but not before she suffered the loss of Ozzie, the man she loved. Then Rachael asked Minerva to help her with something over at the mermaid tank one night. Once they were up at the top of the tank, she pushed Minerva in and held her under until she drowned."

"And then dragged her all the way to the pillory?" I asked.

"It took some strength, but she did it," Eldon said. "Rachael thought it was fitting to lock her body in the pillory. I guess it sent a message that Minerva deserved to be punished." He paused to drain the last of his beer. "You'll be interested to know, Sadie, that Rachael's Renaissance costume was missing an eyelet from the bodice."

So the eyelet by the pillory really had been a clue as to the killer's identity.

"I had no idea Rachael was suffering so much," Shontelle said sadly.

Eldon put a hand to her back. "You hadn't seen her in years."

"And she hid it well," I added.

"She's not the same person I remember from college." Shontelle swirled the wine in her glass. "I feel bad that she went through so much, but resorting to murder . . . She must have been unhinged to do that."

Damien hailed us from the porch. "Better come grab some food before it's all gone!"

As much as I appreciated Eldon filling in the gaps of the story, the distraction of food came as a relief. My mood had started growing darker again, and I didn't want to slide back in that direction.

The conversation turned to happier, lighter topics as we all grabbed food and dug into our meals. After I'd eaten my fill, I set down my plate on a picnic table and joined Grayson on the lawn, where he stood talking with Booker.

"I'm going to grab another burger," Booker said a few minutes later.

It didn't surprise me that he could eat more than one.

As Booker jogged off toward the grill, Grayson put an arm around my shoulders. I leaned into him.

"You doing okay?" he asked.

I knew he'd worried about me over the past couple of weeks.

"I am." I nodded at the scene in front of us, with so many of our friends gathered together. "This is helping."

He kissed the top of my head. "Good."

I tipped my head back to look up at him. "How about you?"

"If you're doing better, then so am I," he said.

Grayson regretted heading back to the brewery without me after the ambulance had whisked Collette away from the woods. I'd reminded him many times that it was my own decision to return to the fairgrounds, but that didn't stop him from wishing he'd gone with me.

He'd raced over to the park after reading my text message, but by then the police had already had Rachael in custody. Lucky for me, Rachael hadn't disconnected my call to Detective Marquez when she knocked my phone out of my hand. The detective's voicemail had picked up some of my conversation with her.

Marquez hadn't gone far after leaving the woods. She'd driven around to the faire's front gates, looking for Toby. She'd heard the voicemail shortly after it was recorded, and Hamish had pointed her and her officers in the direction I'd gone. I didn't like to think about what would have happened to me if things had played out differently.

"There's something I've been wanting to ask you," Grayson said.

I gave him my full attention. "What's that?"

"Now that you've got Damien back at the Inkwell, and with Zoe working for you part-time, I thought maybe we could manage some time for just the two of us."

I liked the sound of that. "What were you thinking?"

"Would you like to go to Nantucket with me at the end of the summer?"

"Nantucket?" A big smile stretched across my face. "You remembered that I want to go?"

"Of course I remembered." His smile almost outshone my own. "So is that a yes?"

I threw my arms around him and gave him a kiss.

"It's most definitely a yes."

Recipes

THE SECRET LIFE OF DAIQUIRIS

½ cup frozen mango chunks
½ cup ice
4 oz cream of coconut (see recipe below)
2 oz mango juice
1 oz coconut rum*
1 oz freshly squeezed lime juice

Add all the ingredients to a blender and blend until smooth. Pour the mixture into a cocktail glass and serve at once.

Makes 1 cocktail

*For the mocktail version, simply leave out the rum.

A MIDSUMMER NIGHT'S CREAM (MOCKTAIL)

6 oz cream of coconut (see recipe below)
½ cup frozen strawberries
½ cup water
½ cup ice
1 oz lime juice
Whipped cream, to taste

Pour half the cream of coconut into one cocktail glass and the other half into a second glass. In a blender, combine the strawberries, water, ice, and lime juice. Blend until smooth. Slowly pour half of the strawberry mixture over the back of a spoon into one of the cocktail glasses. It should form a layer over the cream of coconut. Top with whipped cream. Repeat with the second glass and serve at once.

Makes 2 mocktails

CREAM OF COCONUT

13.5 oz coconut milk
¾ cup granulated sugar

Combine the ingredients in a small saucepan and heat gently over low heat, stirring frequently, until the sugar has completely dissolved. Allow the mixture to cool before using.

(You can store any leftovers in a sealed container in the freezer for future use.)

SOFIE'S APPLE FRITTERS

Dough:

¾ cup warm milk
3 tbsp granulated sugar
2 tsp dry active yeast
2 tbsp butter, melted
⅓ cup dry apple cider
2 large eggs, lightly beaten
½ tsp vanilla extract
2 tsp ground cinnamon
¼ tsp salt
2½ cups pastry flour (plus more if needed)
Vegetable or canola oil for frying

Apple Filling:

3 medium Granny Smith apples (or preferred variety),
  peeled, cored, and cut into ½-inch dice (about 2 cups)
1 tbsp freshly squeezed lemon juice
1 tsp salted butter
¼ cup granulated sugar
¼ cup brown sugar
½ tsp ground cinnamon
2 tbsp dry apple cider
1 tbsp all-purpose flour

Glaze:

1½ cups powdered sugar, sifted
2 tbsp milk (or more if needed)
¼ tsp vanilla extract

Prepare the dough. Add the milk to a small saucepan and warm it to 110°F (43°C) over low heat. In the bowl of a stand mixer, combine the warm milk and 1 tablespoon of the sugar. Sprinkle the yeast over the top, give it a stir, and let stand until it is nice and foamy, approximately 5 to 10 minutes.

Add the remaining 2 tablespoons sugar, the melted butter, apple cider, eggs, vanilla, cinnamon, salt, and 1¼ cups of the pastry flour. Beat with a paddle attachment until combined. Switch to a dough hook and add the remaining flour. Knead for approximately 5 minutes, or until the dough is smooth and sticky. While the dough should be quite sticky, it should not be liquid. If necessary, add additional flour, 1 or 2 tablespoons at a time, until you have a sticky dough.

Brush the sides of a large bowl with vegetable oil, add the dough, cover with plastic wrap, and set in a warm place until the dough has doubled in size, approximately 1 hour.

Meanwhile, prepare the apple filling. Toss the apples with lemon juice in a medium bowl and set aside. In a large pot, melt the butter over medium-low heat. Add the reserved apples, sugar, brown sugar, and cinnamon. Cook, stirring frequently, for about 5 minutes, or until the apples are soft. Remove from the heat and stir in the apple cider and flour. Set the filling aside and allow it to cool completely.

Once the dough has doubled in size, scrape it out of the bowl onto a generously floured surface. Flour or oil your hands and then press the dough into a rough rectangle. Spread the cooled apple filling over the dough.

Take hold of one of the shorter sides and fold one third of the dough toward the middle of the rectangle. Then fold the opposite end over top, like you're folding a pamphlet. Next, coax the dough into a ball and place it back in the bowl. Cover with plastic wrap and set in a warm place until the dough has doubled in size again, approximately 1 hour.

Place the dough on a generously floured surface and roll it out until it's approximately one inch thick. Use a round 4-inch cookie or biscuit cutter to cut out circles of dough. Gather the scraps into a ball and roll out and cut again, until you've used up all the dough. Gently stretch each dough circle into a rough oval.

Heat the oil in a deep fryer to 375°F. Working in batches, slide pieces of dough into the hot oil and fry until deep golden brown, 1½ to 2 minutes per side. Remove the fritters from the oil and set on a plate covered with paper towels. After a couple of minutes, transfer the fritters to a wire cooling rack placed over a baking sheet.

Once the fritters are all fried, prepare the glaze. Combine the powdered sugar, milk, and vanilla in a small bowl and stir until smooth. If needed, add more milk, a little at a time, until you achieve a good drizzling consistency.

Dip each fritter in the glaze, place on the wire rack, and

allow the glaze to harden. If desired, dip again for double-glazed fritters.

These fritters are best eaten on the day they are made, but they can be stored overnight in an airtight container. If you want to save some for a later date, freeze them before glazing and then glaze once thawed.

Makes approximately 10 fritters

ACKNOWLEDGMENTS

I'm sincerely grateful to my agent, Jessica Faust, for helping me bring this series to life and to my editor, Elizabeth May, for helping me to shape and polish this manuscript. The entire Kensington team has been fabulous, and all the covers for this series have been gorgeous. I'm also grateful to Larissa Ackerman and the rest of the publicity department for all their hard work. Thanks also to Jody Holford, Sarah Blair, my review crew, my wonderful friends in the writing community, and to all the readers who have come along on Sadie's adventures in Shady Creek.

Keep reading for a special excerpt!

Murder is on the menu in the latest Pancake House Mystery, as a treasure trove of old letters spurs a killer to take some unsavory action. . . .

A WRINKLE IN THYME

By Sarah Fox

This summer, Wildwood Cove is hosting a special event, Wild West Days, to celebrate the town's storied past. Wildwood Cove's museum is also getting a new lease on life thanks to a longtime resident's generous bequest. Several locals, including Marley McKinney-Collins, owner of The Flip Side pancake house, offer to transfer artifacts to the beautiful restored Victorian that will become the museum's home. But there's an unappetizing development when a volunteer, Jane Fassbinder, is found dead—bludgeoned with an antique clothes iron.

Marley can never resist a piping hot mystery, and this one seems especially intriguing. Jane had recently unearthed some love letters from the Jack of Diamonds, a notorious thief who plagued Wildwood Cove over a century ago. As more locals meet with dangerous "accidents," it seems that someone is determined to keep that correspondence buried deep in the past. And unless Marley can sift through the likely suspects, she too could end up being nothing but history. . . .

Look for A WRINKLE IN THYME, on sale now where ebooks are sold.

Chapter 1

The new home of the Wildwood Cove Museum bustled with activity. As I entered through the back door, I heard voices murmuring off in the distance, muffled by the drone of the floor sander in use up on the second story. A hammer thudded out on the back porch, and something clattered to the floor down the hall. I took a quick step to the right when a teenage volunteer ran past me, her blond ponytail swinging.

Readjusting my grip on the heavy box in my arms, I entered a room to my left, nearly colliding with an empty dolly pushed by a man with dark hair. Like me, Frankie Zhou was volunteering his time to help move all the museum's artifacts, archives, and furniture from the small bungalow where they had been housed for years to their new location in this beautiful Victorian.

Frankie mumbled his apologies as he scooted past me with the dolly. With the way ahead of me now clear, I crossed the room without further problems and set the box down next to several others lined up against the wall. I dusted off my hands and stretched my back as I surveyed the room. The dark color of the refinished wood floors contrasted nicely with the new coat of white paint on the walls. Deep shelving units had been installed the day before and were waiting to hold the many boxes of archives currently sitting piled on the floor.

A pleasant breeze drifted in through the open window, helping to dispel the smell of fresh paint that lingered in the house. A longtime resident of Wildwood Cove, Gwyneth McIvor, had bequeathed her home to the museum. Located in the heart of town, the house was a white, two-story Victorian with front and back porches and lots of character. A crew of volunteers, which included my husband, had spent many hours fixing up the place to ready it for its new life as a museum. Those volunteers were still adding some of the final touches, but the bulk of the work on the main floor had already been done. The second story, which would serve as meeting and storage space, was still a work in progress.

This building was older than the bungalow that previously housed the museum, but the Victorian offered more space and more charm. The bungalow was cute, but the McIvor house practically oozed elegance and character from every nook and cranny. It had needed some TLC after Mrs. McIvor's death, but the volunteers had restored its stately beauty.

I paused for a moment by the window and drew in a deep breath of fresh air. My stomach rumbled with hunger, reminding me that I shouldn't dawdle if I wanted to get home and have dinner anytime soon. I headed for the door, then stopped just in the nick of time as the dolly reappeared, its wheels missing my toes by mere inches. Frankie appeared next, pushing the dolly, which now had four file boxes stacked on it. Jane Fassbender followed right on his heels. She had a clipboard tucked under one arm, and her long light brown hair was tied back in a loose braid. I didn't know her exact age, but I guessed she was probably in her midthirties, like me.

Jane was currently in charge of the Wildwood Cove Museum while its curator, Nancy Welch, was on an extended vacation, traveling for a year. It was a volunteer position for Jane, but she took it very seriously and had spent hours upon hours over the past weeks preparing for the move and coordinating the teams of volunteers.

"Just stack those boxes next to the others," she said to Frankie as he unloaded the dolly. "That's the last of them."

My back and arms could have sighed with relief. I'd lost count of how many boxes I'd hauled from Frankie's truck into the Victorian over the past couple of hours.

Jane smiled at me. "Thanks so much for your help, Marley. You too, Frankie."

"My pleasure." Frankie pushed his dark hair off his forehead and flashed a shy smile at Jane before heading out of the room with the dolly.

"I'm glad I was able to help," I said as Jane and I trailed after Frankie.

He turned right and headed out the open back door, while we made our way toward the front of the old house, where two large rooms would soon display the museum's artifacts. At the moment, everything was still boxed up.

We paused in the foyer when a woman's voice called out from behind us.

"Hello? Jane?"

We both turned at the sound.

An elderly woman with perfectly coiffed silver hair stood framed in the back doorway. She wore a navy-blue dress and held a silver-handled cane in one hand, though she didn't appear to be leaning much weight on it.

"Winnifred," Jane greeted. "Come on in."

The woman entered the hallway and stopped to peek into the room where Frankie and I had stacked the last of the boxes.

"I don't want to get in the way," Winnifred said after she'd turned her attention back to us, "but I couldn't help myself. I had to come by to get a look at the transformation."

"You're not in the way," Jane assured her. "As you can see, it's still a work in progress, but things are going well so far."

"I'll say." Winnifred came farther along the hall to join us in the spacious foyer. "The floors are beautiful."

"Dean's done a good job."

Dean Vaccarino was the man Jane had hired to refinish the floors. He was working upstairs as we spoke. He wasn't my favorite person, but he really had done a good job with the floors.

"Marley," Jane said to me, "have you met Mrs. Winnifred Woodcombe?"

"I haven't." I offered my hand to the elderly woman. "Marley Collins. It's nice to meet you, Mrs. Woodcombe."

Keeping a loose grip on her cane, Winnifred reached out with her free hand to clasp mine. "Likewise, my dear. Please, call me Winnifred. No need to stand on formality." She eyed me more closely. "You're the young woman who moved here from Seattle after you inherited the pancake house from Jimmy Coulson."

I smiled. "That's right."

"Winnifred has lived here in Wildwood Cove her entire life," Jane said. "She knows everyone and everything about this place."

Winnifred chuckled. "I've certainly had enough years to learn it all."

"I suppose sixty-five years is quite a long time," Jane said with a smile.

With another laugh, Winnifred patted Jane's arm. "That's so kind of you, dear. We both know my eightieth birthday isn't all that far off."

"Still two years to go," Jane said. She glanced around us. "Hopefully, the museum will be in order long before then."

Winnifred patted her arm again. "I'm sure it will be. Do you mind if I wander around?"

"Please, be my guest. Just watch your step. We've got boxes piled everywhere."

"I'll be careful," Winnifred assured her before venturing into the room to the left of the front entrance.

Jane picked up a stack of files from the top of a pile of boxes. "I'd better put these in my office before I forget."

She started back down the hall, and I fell into step with her.

"Winnifred donated money to cover the cost of the move," Jane told me in a low voice.

"That was good of her."

"She's a good woman. Wild West Days was her idea. She's a real champion of our local history, and she wants to find ways to get more people interested in it."

"I'm looking forward to the event, and I know lots of other people are too," I said.

Wild West Days would take place in four weeks. It was the first time Wildwood Cove was having the four-day festival, and it sounded like it would be a lot of fun. I'd heard there would be activities like gold panning, mechanical bull riding, and line dancing, as well as country music concerts and a stagecoach robbery reenactment. The hope was that Wild West Days would kick off the summer season and draw in some early tourists. Judging by the buzz already around town, the event would have a good turnout.

"Of course," Jane said, a hint of annoyance creeping into her voice, "not everyone involved in planning Wild West Days understands the importance of historical accuracy, but my hope is that Winnifred will have a good influence on the committee."

I wasn't sure what to say to that. Fortunately, Jane didn't seem to expect a response.

As for Winnifred having an influence on the committee, I didn't think that was far-fetched. Although I hadn't met Winnifred before, I'd heard of her. The Woodcombe family had lived in Wildwood Cove since the town was founded. Winnifred was currently the oldest Woodcombe in the area, and I knew she was highly respected. She was involved in several local organizations and regularly donated to charities and other worthy causes.

Jane dropped the files off in her office, and then we stepped out onto the back porch, where bright sunshine greeted us, along with the scent of freshly cut grass and the hum of a motor. I smiled at the sight of my husband, Brett, guiding a lawn mower around the yard, which was enclosed by a freshly painted white picket fence. When he spotted me, he sent a grin my way. After eight months of marriage, the sight of him could still take my breath away. I hoped that would never change.

"Winnifred's from one of the richest and oldest local families, but she never flaunts her wealth," Jane continued, tugging my attention away from my husband. Her eyes narrowed. "Unlike some people."

I followed her unwelcoming gaze and spotted a man in an expensive suit climbing out of a red Ferrari convertible parked in the back lane. He hurried around the car and opened the back gate, then held it for a woman in a red dress and matching stilettos, with what looked like a designer handbag in the crook of her arm. As she headed our way, she pushed oversized sunglasses up to sit on top of her bleached blond hair. Sunlight glinted off her gold jewelry.

I recognized the couple. I'd seen them around town once or twice, but I didn't know much about them other than the fact that they owned Oldershaw Confections, a candy company that had made millions for the Oldershaw family. The company had started out locally over a hundred years ago and had since become a nationwide success.

"Jane, darling," the woman trilled as she approached the back steps. "I've come to talk to you about the party."

"Heaven help me," Jane said under her breath, the words barely loud enough for me to hear. Then she pasted on a smile that bore some resemblance to a pained grimace. "Evangeline, you don't need to worry about the party. I've got everything under control."

Evangeline carefully navigated the steps and joined us on the porch. Her husband stayed down on the concrete walkway, his hands in his pockets as he casually surveyed the yard.

"Nonsense." Evangeline's red-painted lips stretched into a smile no more sincere than Jane's. "Of course I'm going to worry about the party. It's my money that's paying for it, after all." She crossed the porch to a wrought-iron patio set, then ran a finger along the arm of one chair to check for cleanliness. "Come," she said, pulling the chair out from beneath the table. "Let's get down to business."

With her face angled away from Evangeline, Jane rolled her eyes, but she obeyed the command and joined her at the table. Evangeline hadn't even acknowledged my existence, and I didn't expect that to change, so I gave Jane a discreet wave and descended the porch steps.

Brett shut off the lawn mower, the grass all trimmed now. With the motor no longer rumbling, the yard would have been peaceful if not for Evangeline's constant stream of chatter up on the porch.

Her husband gave me a half-hearted smile when I reached the bottom of the steps.

"Marley Collins." I offered him my hand, determined to be more polite than his wife. "Are you Mr. Oldershaw?"

He gave my hand a weak shake. "Hobbs, actually. Richard Hobbs. My wife is an Oldershaw. Well, Oldershaw-Hobbs now."

We both glanced up at the porch, where his wife sat with Jane. While Evangeline talked nonstop, Jane sat stiffly, her mouth in a firm line as she nodded every so often.

"You should see the dress I got for the party," Evangeline was saying. "I bought it last week in New York. A Valentino, of course. My sister was with me at the fitting. She said I looked just like Grace Kelly."

"I thought you were here to organize the party, Ev," Richard called, interrupting her chatter.

"Yes, Richard," his wife said with more than a hint of annoyance. "That's exactly what we're doing."

She resumed her chatter.

Richard gave a barely perceptible shake of his head. "We'll be here all day," he muttered.

"There's coffee in the kitchen," I told him. I hadn't particularly warmed to him, but I figured he was probably right—he was going to be waiting a long time for his wife. "Just inside, to the right."

Richard made a sound of acknowledgment and took the porch steps two at a time.

Brett had already loaded the lawn mower into the back of the cube truck he used for his lawn and garden business. Now he came along the path toward me, removing his work gloves and running a hand through his curly blond hair.

"I'm all done here for the day," he said. "Are you ready to get going?"

I kissed him and tucked my arm through his, then led him toward the back gate. "Very, very much so." I gave a subtle nod over my shoulder. "Do you know Evangeline and Richard?"

"I know *of* them, but I've never officially met them." Brett held the gate open for me. "They don't spend a lot of their time here in Wildwood Cove, and they don't much like rubbing elbows with anyone with a net worth of fewer than seven digits."

"But they grew up here?" I asked as we squeezed past the red Ferrari to get to Brett's truck.

"Not exactly." He unlocked the passenger door. "Evangeline's family is from here originally, but my understanding is that she was raised mostly in New York and just came here for holidays."

I climbed into the truck, and Brett shut the door before jogging around to the driver's side.

"Her family has always kept a house here, one of those big Victorians on Orchard Lane," he continued as he buckled up his seat belt. "She and her husband spend a few weeks in town each year. They've got a small office on Main Street, but the general consensus is that they like to keep one toe in Wildwood Cove not so much because they have any affection for the town, but because they like to feel like big fish in this small pond of ours."

"Let me guess," I said, thinking back over my brief encounter with Evangeline. "They like to throw their money around and act like they rule the roost."

"Exactly." Brett guided the truck out of the alley and turned onto the street.

"I've seen them driving that Ferrari around town. Way too fast."

"They make sure they're hard to miss. I think they'd like to believe we all envy them."

"Does anyone?" I asked, finding it hard to believe that anybody would. I hadn't found the couple the least bit enviable.

"I sure don't," Brett said. "I'll take pizza over caviar any day."

"Same here." My stomach grumbled. "Speaking of pizza . . ."

Brett grinned at me. "I already called in a take-out order. One vegetarian, one pepperoni. We'll pick them up on our way home."

"Forget Ferraris and Valentino gowns," I said. "You, Brett Collins, are priceless."

Chapter 2

I'd never seen Richard and Evangeline at my seaside pancake house, and that didn't surprise me. I had a sneaking suspicion that the restaurant wouldn't live up to Evangeline's standards, despite the scrumptious food whipped up by The Flip Side's chef, Ivan Kaminski, and his assistant, Tommy Park.

Even if the couple had dropped by the morning after I'd met them at the museum, there wouldn't have been room for them. We were in the middle of the breakfast rush, which was even busier than usual. I figured that was thanks to the beautiful spring weather, which was already hinting at the summer to come. It had drawn people out of their houses to stroll, jog, cycle, and seek out a tasty breakfast. The morning sunshine was so bright and warm that I'd put four small tables out front of the restaurant. It was early May, and I hadn't expected to put tables outside for another couple of weeks or so, but the beautiful morning had inspired me to do it today.

It had turned out to be a good idea. Every table, inside and out, was currently occupied. The large number of early diners kept me and my staff on our toes. Ivan and Tommy kept the pancakes, crêpes, and waffles coming, while I helped to serve customers, along with Leigh Hunter, The Flip Side's full-time waitress, and Sienna Murray, a high school senior who worked at the pancake house on weekends.

Leigh paused by the front door, which I'd propped open to let in the gentle sea breeze. "I smell summer in the air." She drew in a deep, appreciative breath before continuing on her way to the kitchen with a stack of dirty plates.

"It can't be summer yet!" Sienna said, sounding mildly alarmed.

Her reaction took me by surprise. She usually couldn't wait for summer to arrive. Before I had a chance to ask her about it, she made a beeline for the pass-through window, where Tommy had just set three plates, two laden with stacks of pancakes and one with a generous slice of Thyme for Breakfast Frittata—a tasty new addition to the menu—and a side of fruit salad.

I spent the next several minutes rushing to and fro, taking orders, delivering meals, and cleaning tables as soon as they were vacated. No table stayed empty for more than a couple of minutes before new customers swooped in to claim it.

I loved how busy we were, especially since it wasn't even the height of tourist season yet. The Flip Side was thriving and was one of the most popular restaurants in town. That thrilled me to pieces, but it also had me thinking about the future. If we were this run off our feet in May, we might have trouble keeping up when vacationers flocked to our charming seaside town in a few weeks' time. If any one of my employees were to get sick, we'd be in a bind.

Plus, Sienna would be heading off to college at the end of August. I didn't like to think about her leaving Wildwood Cove—she was a good friend as well as an employee—but I knew I'd have to find someone to replace her. Judging by our current booming business, I might have to hire more help even before her departure.

All thoughts about staffing would have to wait, though. At the moment, I had my hands full—literally and figuratively—and had to stay focused if I wanted to keep my customers happy.

"Are you looking forward to Wild West Days, Marley?" Gary Thornbrook asked as I set plates of blueberry pancakes in front of him and his friend Ed.

Despite the full house, the two men had managed to snag their favorite table. They showed up at the pancake house at least twice a week and always ordered the same meals. They'd been doing so for years, starting long before I'd inherited the business from my grandmother's cousin.

"I'm definitely excited," I said. "It sounds like it's going to be a fun event. I hear the two of you will be taking turns playing the part of the sheriff."

"You heard right." Ed grinned. "You should see our costumes. We went all out."

"We've got the clothes and pistols," Gary said. "Just props, of course, but they look good."

"What about the shiny badge?" I asked.

Ed poured syrup over his pancakes. "Of course. Can't forget that."

"Sounds like you're all ready to go," I remarked.

"We're hopin' to have us a hog-killin' time," Gary said with a phony drawl.

I couldn't help but laugh.

Ed cut into his stack of pancakes. "Hopefully, we'll do the real sheriff proud."

"I'm sure you will." I checked their mugs and noticed that they could do with a refill. "Let me grab the coffeepot."

On my way back to their table, I made a couple of stops to refill a few other diners' mugs. I loved how many familiar faces I saw at the pancake house each day. Working there had allowed me to connect with the community when I'd first moved to town, and my roots were now firmly planted.

"How are things going at the museum?" Gary asked when I returned.

"Everything's been moved to the new location," I said as I topped up their coffee mugs. "Now it's just a matter of getting everything organized and set up."

"Squatters!"

I nearly jumped out of my skin when a man at the table behind me practically spat out the word. If the coffeepot hadn't been nearly empty by then, I would have spilled the hot liquid all over myself. When I took in the sight of the man's angry scowl, I edged away from him, not sure if he was in his right mind or not. I was pretty sure I'd seen him at The Flip Side before, but I didn't know his name. He was short and stout, with thinning dark hair and beady eyes.

"Hardly," Ed said to the man, unfazed by his ire. "You know the court held that the house belongs to the museum fair and square, Angus."

The man stood up like a shot, his chair skittering across the floor. "There's nothing fair about it! That house should be mine!"

"But it isn't," Gary said calmly.

"Thanks to that woman's funny business," Angus grumbled. "She's a crook, and she's going to wish she'd never crossed me."

He stormed off toward the cash register, where Sienna was counting change for an elderly couple.

"Which woman?" I whispered, keeping an eye on Angus as he handed money to Sienna.

Fortunately, he didn't give her any trouble. He paid quickly and stomped out of the restaurant.

"Jane Fassbender," Gary replied, his voice as low as my own.

Several diners were waiting for their meals, so I couldn't

linger, but I desperately wanted to talk more about what had just transpired.

I got my chance to do so about ten minutes later, when I stopped by Ed and Gary's table to refill their coffee mugs again.

"What was all that about earlier?" I asked as I topped up Ed's coffee.

"You mean with Angus?" he asked.

Joan Crenshaw, another senior citizen who was also a frequent customer, spoke up from a nearby table. "Sour grapes."

Her breakfast companion, Eleanor Crosby, nodded in agreement, as did Ed and Gary.

"Gwyneth McIvor, the woman who bequeathed the house to the museum, was Angus's aunt," Eleanor explained.

"Angus thought he should inherit the house," Joan added.

"An unjustified sense of entitlement, if you ask me." Eleanor shook her head before cutting into her breakfast frittata.

"You're not wrong." Gary nudged his mug closer to me so I could refill it.

"He wasn't close to his aunt?" I guessed.

"He barely had anything to do with her," Joan said. "Even when her health took a sharp downward turn in the last couple months of her life. I think it was more than generous of Gwyneth to leave him the ten thousand dollars that she did."

The others all nodded in agreement again.

Ed took a sip of coffee and set down his mug with a thud. "If Angus Achenbach wants a house and more money, he should work for it."

I glanced around the pancake house, noting that I wasn't needed elsewhere at the moment. "He doesn't have a job?"

"Can't seem to keep one for more than a few weeks at a time," Gary said. "It's always been that way. It got so no one would hire him here in town."

Ed speared a piece of pancake with his fork. "Probably because he's so lazy."

That statement elicited sounds of agreement from the others.

"He'll get over the situation with Gwyneth's house," Joan said. She paused with her coffee mug halfway to her mouth. "Eventually."

I left them to finish their meals and attended to the other diners in the restaurant. The rush tapered off not long after, but we didn't have much of a lull before things picked up again around lunchtime. When two o'clock rolled around, I shut and locked the front door with a small sigh of relief. As much as I loved running the pancake house, I'd been on my feet since six in the morning, and they were letting me know that they wanted a rest.

Leigh and Sienna were still cleaning up the tables, so I ignored the aching in my feet and gave them a hand. Leigh headed out soon after, wanting to get home so she could keep her promise to her three daughters to take them to the beach that afternoon. I wished I could spend some time on the beach too, preferably with a good book, but I knew I likely wouldn't have a chance to do that today. I'd get my beach time another day, though. That was one of the many perks of living right next to the ocean. All I had to do was step out my back door to hit the sand and surf.

I loaded the last of the dirty dishes into the dishwasher and turned the machine on, then pulled a stool up to the island in the middle of the kitchen and sat down, finally giving my feet a rest.

"What a day," I said as I watched Ivan and Tommy do the last of their cleanup.

Tommy shut a cupboard door. "I think we fed an entire army."

I tugged the elastic out of my hair, releasing my ponytail. My curls were probably all frizzy, but I didn't care. "It sure feels like it."

"You work too hard," Ivan grumbled, his characteristic scowl firmly in place.

"The rest of you work just as hard as I do," I said. "Maybe even harder."

Ivan pinned me with his dark stare.

"But you're right," I added before he could lecture me. "I need to hire more staff. I think it would be good to have someone part-time to help you guys in the kitchen, someone who can step in if either of you gets sick. What do you think?"

I directed the question to Ivan. The kitchen was his domain. Even though I was his boss, I didn't want to step on his toes, and I respected his opinion.

"It's a good idea," he said as he hung a pot on a hook above the island.

I shifted my gaze to Tommy.

He turned on the faucet at the large sink so he could wash his hands. "I wouldn't say no to extra help."

"We need another server too," Ivan reminded me in his gruff voice.

"Sooner rather than later," I agreed.

Sometime in the next few days, I needed to get busy and draft help-wanted ads to put in the local newspaper. Not today, though. I had to swing by the grocery store on the way home. Brett was having a rare poker night at our place, and I'd promised to pick up some snacks to feed our guests.

After saying goodbye to Ivan and Tommy, I made my way down the hall toward the office, where I'd left my tote bag. Before I got there, I spotted Sienna hovering inside the small break room.

"Hey," I said. "I thought you'd already gone." I realized that she seemed anxious, her teeth worrying her lower lip. "Is everything okay?"

She hesitated for half a second before smiling, although the expression didn't reach her eyes. "Everything's fine. See you soon!"

She zipped past me and out the back door, barely giving me a chance to say goodbye.

I remained standing in the middle of the hallway, puzzled and a bit worried.

Sienna might have claimed that everything was fine, but she wasn't quite herself.